Shades *of* Persuasion

CHARNA AINSWORTH

The Letter's

SHADES OF
Persuasion

ISBN: 978-0-9855505-5-4

Song Title: *The First Time Ever I Saw Your Face*
Written By: Ewan MacColl
Sang By: Roberta Flack

Song Title: *In Your Eyes*
Written By: Peter Gabriel
Sang By: Peter Gabriel

Acknowledgements

To the following people I dedicate this novel:

My daughter, Maria, for all the joy she brings and for being my biggest fan.

Charlotte Henley, my sister, a wonderful friend and great editor.

Greg Smith, for his unending compassion and love during this process.

Barbara Burkhalter, my mom, who is a great proofreader and a shining star in everyone's life.

Charles Burkhalter, my dad, who believes in me and gave me a deep love for poetry and writing.

And to my beloved muse... who continues to inspire the poet... eternally.

Chapter 1

The roughness of his voice eased the tension between us. Steven was right, the same way he had been right so many times before. His reply had been simple and with the simplicity came the ease. So we started with a kiss. A long awaited release of missed opportunities floated away into nothingness as his lips touched mine. We were living in the here and now, heading precariously toward the moments to come. Beneath the big beautiful oak tree, memories flooded every part of my being as his lips lingered on my mouth. The moment we met, when we were both still so young and the look in his eyes when he said my name for the first time. Steven had made me feel like I was the only girl in the world from that very moment, until this very day.

One kiss and I was completely his again. With the sunshine pushing past the puffy white clouds, I handed him the rose. He lifted it to his face, smelling its sweet fragrance while looking into my eyes. All of my senses were on fire from being in his presence and feeling his gentle touch. Sweet melodies from birds singing were accompanied with the distant rustling of leaves blown by the breeze. This old oak tree had never failed to enchant us with its beauty. And now I could not think of a more perfect place to be to reconnect our lives and rekindle our love affair.

As his arms held me close, the memory of finding out about Amber, his childhood sweetheart, the girl he had dated throughout high school, made its way into my mind. When we first met I thought I had misread his feelings, that his apparent attraction had only been a fleeting moment but, I was wrong. Because regardless of their long relationship, by the glow of firelight and with that first kiss, I was Steven's girl from that moment on. Even with the disapproval from his family and nearly everyone in that small town, we stayed together. We were the epitome of young lovers, taking every chance, savoring every tidbit of time that we could steal to be with one another.

Between kisses, the exciting months we spent together as teenagers raced through my mind. The days shared just between us, growing and learning about life and happiness, enjoying all the moments of a young couple in love. He was my hero, saving the new kid in town from the loneliness and pressure of finding new friends. And I was his fantasy come true, not like any of the girls he had grown up with. Being born and raised in California, I spoke, looked, and certainly acted differently than all the girls he knew from Natchez, Mississippi.

Then I recalled standing in the driveway watching him drive away, leaving me alone. The pain caused me to pull away from Steven's embrace and stare out across the beautiful green grass. It was that memory that had us standing here today. That one moment, that one decision, had changed the course of both of our lives. Once we were set on our paths, neither one of us could change it. Again, he had done what he thought was right, leaving for college. It was only my reaction that had been perverse. But looking back onto the past with the wisdom of an adult does not change the way things turned out. The long and winding road had been littered with chances for each of us to rewrite our life story. Sure, we had our share of regrets; the should-have-beens, could-have-beens, but if we had made different choices, it's doubtful I would be standing underneath this tree today.

He pulled me back into his arms, leaning me gently back against the tree. Then with my mind blank, with a clean slate, I closed my eyes and awaited his kiss. Over and over our lips met as tears of joy washed away all of my apprehensions. He turned his attention to my tears, carefully kissing each one of them away as they fell. When I opened my eyes, I took his face in my hands and kissed him for the first time without fear. This was a kiss of completion, a coming together of long overdue passion that flowed from the deepest parts of our souls. There had been no passage of time, no lost moments or regrets that weighed us down. We were young and free and in each other's arms at last.

It was at that moment when I forgave him for leaving me, a young girl, standing in the driveway watching his taillights disappear in the distance. He had done what was right. He had done what was expected of him and left for college. It was me. I had done what girls do when their boyfriends leave. I had been sad, extremely sad. However, for some reason when Steven left, it cut me a bit deeper. Maybe it was because my Mom had left me, my dad and Cheryl, to go to New York too. Or perhaps it was because he was my best friend and I didn't want to wake up in that little hick town without him. But as we stood on these huge oak tree roots and he held me close in his strong arms, the pain of that memory melted away.

One long kiss led to another and another as my back pressed harder against the roughness of the oak trees' bark. As each moment passed our hands touched and caressed each other with growing vigor. I felt like a prisoner who had just been set free. All the chains that had me bound with doubt and insecurity, fell away from my mind and spirit as though they had never been there in the first place. No one else existed in this perfect moment Steven and I had created. We were alone, only standing before God, in His beautiful gifts of nature and the gift of our love for one another.

All of the words that I had rehearsed over and over in my mind were gone. The ones that explained every bad decision I had made, the ones that had kept us apart, had suddenly vanished as soon as his lips touched mine. Only the truth of this very moment remained. He was here and I was lost in the passion we shared. It was so familiar and yet totally brand new. We had known each other for a lifetime but it had been so long since we had given ourselves completely to each other.

The years of phone calls, chance meetings, messages, and poetic love letters poured through my mind. So many times, our paths crossed, sometimes for seconds, sometimes for hours and occasionally for days. Now, I began to wonder if I had taken a chance on us during any point in our history, would our lives be different. Would we be married? Would we have children? Or would we be strangers, instead of long lost lovers, holding on to each other like we never want to let go?

Slowly, Steven pulled me forward by the hips and wrapped his arms tightly around my back. Our bodies were pressed firmly against each other as he strove to get closer, hugging me tighter with each passing moment. It became increasingly harder to breath but I did not resist. Never in my life had I been hugged this way or held so tightly. I could feel his longing for me, years of longing bottled up deep inside. And at the same time, I sensed relief. Steven had finally reached the end of that longing, because today we were starting a new chapter together.

It was time to put the past to rest. We needed to let go of bad decisions, failed marriages and wasted opportunities. Something inside of me knew this was our last chance to get it right. Whatever happened was up to me and him. There was nothing and nobody standing in our way. Every choice we made from here on out was totally ours to make. It wasn't too late for us to begin our lives together, if that is what we both wanted.

The words of his last letter made me wonder why he would even come here. If there was any moment in my life that I knew Steven Cross was finished with me, it was when I read his farewell letter. But as tightly as he is embracing me, as if he will never let me go, I guess the letter changed his feelings. Because now, only a few weeks later we are to-gether again, just a couple of teenage love-birds turned into fully-grown lovers. Both hoping, we still might have a chance to get this thing right before we go our separate ways forever.

Slowly, he released me from his embrace and stepped back. Intoxi-cated with desire, I stared into his hazel eyes, eyes that were telling me without words I want you. He began studying my face, then my body as his eyes undressed me meticulously, working their way down to my feet. My temperature rose with each passing second and I could feel my cheeks turn rosy red. Time felt as though it was hesitant to pass while I watched his gaze drifting up towards my thighs. Small beads of sweat began to develop at the edge of my hair line when his eyes reached my waistline. My whole body trembled as I fought the urge to reach out for him. But instead, I stood perfectly still, knowing that he must be trying to make sure this was real, it was really happening.

His eyes lingered on my chest before his eyes, full of admiration, settled upon my eyes…full of fire. The wind blew, seemingly out of nowhere, lifting my hair and diverting his stare. He still did not speak. I felt at that moment, I could read his mind. A smile grew from his tiny grin until there was nothing I could do but smile back at him. When his smile melted, it was replaced with pain. Or perhaps it was fear. I knew in an instance that an old memory had filled his mind. It could have been one of the many times I had left the comfort of the surety of his true love for me. There was no way I could take this fear away from Steven except with love, passionate love. So I leaned forward, pressing my lips against his mouth and closed my eyes.

If there had ever been a kiss that could stop the world from spinning it was the kiss we shared at that moment. It was as though it was our first kiss yet it was full of mourning; the loss of wasted time. A kiss full of longing for a future we had begun to build from the moment his hand touched mine under this old oak tree. It was a kiss that answered so many questions without a single word being spoken. It apologized for making him miserable and breaking his heart. It spoke volumes of poetic phrases and played a melody that only his ears could hear. Each of which released his inhabitations and fear of loving me or losing me again.

As our lips parted, his eyes met mine and we stared, spellbound by our desires. His hand trembled as he brushed the hair away from my face. When I reached out to touch my palm to his cheek, he rested it gently in my hand. For a moment I caught a glimpse of the boy I had known. He was somewhere within the man that stood in front of me. This boy was my best friend. He was the only one I could trust with my deepest secrets. He was the only one who would never tell. But as I looked again, the boy was gone and a man stood in front of me.

This man standing before me had pursued me like no other. He had been relentless with his love and passion for me with a drive that would rival the love Romeo had for Juliet. Hours, days, months and years had been spent, secretly yearning for another chance to give our relationship a valiant effort. A chance to see if our apparent lust for each other was anything more than desire. Whatever had driven Steven to follow me all of these years had him here today, exactly where I wanted him, exactly where he said he would never be again.

As each kiss and caress grew with passion and intensity my mind raced with thoughts of feeling his body against mine. There was no doubt, no questions to ask, and no begging for forgiveness. We had traveled down different roads in life, both of them broken. Our paths had continually crossed which gave us the memories that stitched our lives together even until this day. And through all of this, through all of the ups and downs, the ins and outs, here we stood. Face to face, toe to toe, under this tree, planted and rooted in this park where we had spent many hours together in our youth.

If there was anyone else here, I could not have seen their face. Steven was the only one in my world. It did not matter to me if anyone was watching us. In fact, nothing except his kiss and touch concerned me. I readily returned his every advance, holding him tighter and kissing him harder. As his hands slid down the curves of my waist I moaned softly, arching my back. My chest thrust against his as our breathing became heavier with each passionate kiss.

"I want you," he whispered.

"I want you."

"Come on." He took my hand, led me to his truck and opened the door.

"Where are you taking me, Mr. Cross?"

"You'll see," he said, sitting the yellow rose on his dash before taking a blanket from behind the seat.

He folded the blanket even smaller and tucked it under his arm. After closing the door, he looked back at the limo and then at me. I shrugged my shoulders and smiled at him. Then he pulled one of the tiny white daisies out of my hair, using it to tickle my nose. I grabbed the flower, throwing it to the ground and pushing his hand away. With a twinkle in his eyes, he pulled me forward, kissing me softly.

Hand and hand we walked across an open field. And for the first time in my life I realized something about Steven. He was the best friend I ever had. The only one who had stayed with me since I was a young girl and he treated me the same as he always had. My fame and fortune had not changed his perspective of me in any way. I was safe with him and now all I wanted was for him to feel safe with me. Only trust would allow that to happen and only time would tell if I could regain his trust.

We reached the edge of the woods, entering on a well-worn path. He was walking ahead while holding my hand behind his back. He remained silent but I could feel anticipation surging through his body and mine. It was like electricity in the air, you can't see it but somehow you can sense its power. And if there was anything I knew about Steven Cross, he had the power to give me pleasure like no one else on earth.

Leaving the path, we pushed our way further into the forest. Steven stopped, letting go of my hand looking all around us. I could see a very large oak tree not too far away. When he took my hand again, I knew in an instant that was where he was leading me. Within a few minutes of holding branches and stepping over fallen trees we were close. He let go of my hand as we stepped under the limbs of the massive oak. I stood still, watching his every move.

He repositioned the blanket firmly under his left arm and began to clear a spot under the enormous tree of any debris. When he finished, he took the blanket by the corners, threw it up in the air and spread it on the ground. Then he looked around, as if to see if anyone was watching before turning toward me. Holding out his arms he motioned with his fingertips for me to come to him.

"What took you so long?"

"I don't know," I replied, walking into his open arms.

He pulled me forward, looking into my eyes, "You know I had given up. I was done…with the waiting."

"I know. And I don't blame you."

"Don't make me wait anymore."

Looking into his eyes, I could feel his pain. I wondered if there was any way I would be able to heal all of the damage I had done. Would he ever be able to trust me again? Over and over, I had let this man down. And still here he stood in front of me, willing to give me another chance, to give us another chance. The only hope we had rested on my shoulders. It was my choice whether we would build a future together or spend one last hour together.

My arms pulled him closer, as I closed my eyes and parted my lips. His hunger for me was apparent and I did not hold back my desire for him. Our lips met in a fury of pent up frustration, anger and lust. His hands pulled and pushed my flesh as I responded with the same intensity, touching and exploring his body. I pulled his shirt up and out of his jeans so I could feel his back. He lifted up the side of my pale yellow dress to caress my outer thigh. Our lips stayed firmly pressed together as our desire grew deeper and deeper.

Steven stopped for a moment and looked all around us again. We were surrounded by trees and bushes, thick enough to shield us from anyone walking on the trail but I guess he wanted to be sure we were still alone. When his gaze fell back on me, he picked me up and laid me down on the blanket. He took his shirt off, and lay down beside me. At first he just took me in his arms and I put my head on his shoulder. He held me tight then pulled me closer, turning on his side.

Kissing under the beautiful oak tree in Mississippi, under a spring sky almost felt like getting to experience a little piece of heaven right here on earth. For the first time in a very long time, I felt at home. So many years of running melted away like wax from the heat of a hot flame. What I had been running from, I didn't know anymore. But now I felt like I finally knew where I belonged and I never wanted to leave the embrace of Steven's arms, ever again.

He unbuttoned the tiny buttons on my dress one by one. It made me nervous with anticipation as he took his time. When he opened the fabric, exposing my skin, I closed my eyes. His hands warmed my cool flesh with each caress. His mouth no longer spoke words nor did it linger on mine. It touched, nibbled and lingered on my skin, bringing me closer and closer to surrender. Besides, what was I fighting? It was obvious that I wanted Steven and Steven wanted me.

Under the oak tree, beneath a perfect blue sky, our bodies united into one. No longer did he have to wonder or wait to know how I felt. My actions spoke louder than any words I could have verbalized. We made love, as nature had intended, wild and hot with the ground for a bed, the sky for a cover. The earth provided all the amenities, wind blowing, birds chirping, bees buzzing, and the smell of wildflowers drifting in the air. This moment was filled with the promises of forever.

2
Chapter

We sent the limo driver on his way and I slid into the passenger seat of Steven's truck. It wasn't long before we found ourselves back at his house. Neither one of us felt comfortable climbing into the bed that he and Hannah had shared so we laid down on the couch. We held each other tightly until sleep finally took over our minds and bodies.

When we woke up still in each other's arms, I knew this was real. It was exactly like Steven always told me it would be in his poetry. We were happy together. Time had passed us by but our love for each other had not. Our love was as strong today as any day in our past. I knew him and his ways and he knew me inside and out. Neither one of us could contain our happiness or keep our hands from touching the other. We wanted this closeness; we needed this time to adjust to finally being with each other. After making plans to fly back to California the next day we discussed going to see our families. Should we let them know our decision to be together again? But the thought of explaining anything to anyone kept us in that little house in Natchez all day long.

We had more than enough to keep our minds busy. Making love took up most of the day. We were content and peaceful that we almost forgot to book our flight back to California. In a way I think we both just wanted to stay hidden away in Mississippi. It would give us time to connect on a deeper level. The kind of deeper connection that only time alone allows. But before the day turned into night we realized that the world had not stopped just because we had and there was business that needed to be taken care of in Los Angeles.

We flirted with the idea of going to Italy after taking care of business in L.A. Then we could spend a month or two, just living in a small village. In a place where no one knew who we were or what we both did for a living. It would be our chance to run away, the way we should have done before Steven moved away to college. But we both knew that it was impossible for us to do that right now. So we settled on trying to free up our schedules soon and fly away to some exotic location for an extended vacation.

The next morning after packing his suitcase, we decided to go for a walk on Carter's trail. It was a perfect day, to be alone with someone you loved in the forest. The sky was the bluest blue without a cloud in sight. There was still a cool breeze that blew every so often to remind you it was still spring. Birds flew from limb to limb preparing to have a family and take care of their young. Flowers of every color popped in and out of view as the long and winding trail took us deeper and deeper into the woods. Steven held my hand in his, talking about his dad, his up and coming book and our trip back to California. It seemed his mind was jumping from subject to subject, I could hardly get a word in but I didn't mind. I was enjoying the sound of his voice mixed in with the sounds of the forest.

He pointed ahead and pulled me to a stop. His constant rambling ceased as he watched me look ahead. Just ahead of us on the trail was a wild rabbit. It had stopped hopping and was staring up at us. I smiled and looked into those hazel eyes that always looked back at me with love and admiration. He was watching me, as I looked back to watch the bunny hop back into the undergrowth. My eyes turned back to his and I noticed tears welling up in his eyes.

"What's wrong, Steven?"

"Nothing. It's just…"

"It's just what? Tell me."

"It's; you're just so beautiful. That's all."

"Thank you," I whispered, kissing his cheek.

He wrapped his arm around me and pulled me close. He pressed his lips against mine so hard, it almost hurt. I could feel his intense need to be close and sensed that he didn't want to let go, so I held on tightly, wrapping my arms around his body. I opened my mouth to kiss him deeply, letting him feel my passion. It felt like we were teenagers again and we could do whatever we wanted. For that moment we were free and unafraid of the world and its rules. All I could think about was being one with him. So this time, I took him by the hand and cut a path of my own through the thick trees off of the well-worn path.

It wasn't long before we were hidden from the eyes of any other hikers. My body was ready for his touch. Before I turned to face him, I pulled my shirt over my head and hung it on a tree. He reached out and grabbed me and pulled me forcefully into his arms. Our lips and tongues moved in unison as though we were born to kiss each other. He unfastened my bra and pulled it off my shoulders. Then while still kissing me, he unbuttoned my shorts and they fell to the ground.

"Do you want me, Tiffany?"

"Yes, I have to have you. Now!"

"Turn around," he said in a low voice.

Slowly, I turned to face the other direction and he pulled my panties down over my legs. I stepped out of my shorts and panties as he picked them up. I was naked, except for my tennis shoes, standing deep in the woods on a bright sunny spring day. I closed my eyes and waited for his touch. He bent down and started to kiss me right below my knee on my right calf. His hand traveled up my inner thigh as his kisses followed up the outer half of my thigh. I shivered from pure excitement and anticipation. Not even in the movies did they have such exciting love scenes. And now I was living them with someone I loved and desired so deeply.

He kissed his way up my body and lingered at the small of my back. With the knowledge that only one lover has of the other, he prepared my body to receive his. I let him be certain of my pleasure with the knowing moans and breathing patterns he had become use to. He caressed my stomach, inching ever closer to my breasts as I longed for his hand to touch me there. I almost took his hand and placed it where I wanted it to be but realized he needed to be in control. I kept my eyes closed, enjoying the moment and waiting until my desire was fulfilled.

It was at this very second in time, when we united and became one again, that I knew I had made the right decision. I knew that I would never leave Steven again. I wanted to be with him every day for the rest of my life. Whatever life may bring or take away, I wanted to be his from now to eternity. I could no longer see a life without him in it and began to dream of living with him. While we were making love, I dreamed of making love to him every day. I dreamed of wearing a beautiful white gown, walking down a flower lined isle, with him waiting at the other end.

He turned my head to kiss my lips and felt a tear that had escaped my eye. With the side of his hand he wiped it away and tried to look into my eyes. I turned to face him, to say I love you but the words did not come out.

"I know how you feel. I feel the same way."

"I don't think you do, Steven. I don't deserve you. I've done too many things wrong."

"I don't want to live without you anymore, Tiffany. We have spent a life time apart. Please, give me a chance."

"I am the one who should be asking for a chance, not you."

"Then let's take that chance. Let's both try to make this thing between us work," he said, holding my body close to his.

"I'm your girl."

"You've always been my girl. You're just now figuring that out?"

"No, yes, maybe. I don't know. I just know, I want to be yours. Now, and forever."

"You are and you will be. No matter what."

He knelt down and picked up my panties and held them for me to step in. Then he helped me put my shorts on and zipped and buttoned them up. Before he handed me my bra he pulled me close again, looking into my eyes. His lips softly touched mine and his eyes closed. It amazed me how easily he could forgive and accept me after I had been so selfish. So much of our separation throughout the years had been because of my anger. What a fool I had been, just a fool with pride and nothing else. Passing up on true love when it seemed the whole world was in search of the one thing I threw away, over and over again.

He stepped back, admiring my body in the sunlight and grinned. "You're still the hottest girl I have ever seen in my life, Tiffany."

"You're making me blush."

"After making love to me like that and you're blushing. You have nothing to be worried about, you're beautiful."

"I love you, Steven. Now, hand me my bra."

"Certainly, Ms. Starr," he replied, bending at the waist and lifting it toward me with both hands.

"Thank you, kind sir. Will you finish dressing me?"

"But of course," he said, taking my shirt down from the limb and pulling it over my head.

We weaved our way back toward the trail dodging limbs and thorny vines. It was enough to be together and words were far and few between as we held hands and walked further down the long winding path. The tall pines swayed with the breeze and the little bushes that grew beneath them were alive with new growth.

My mind raced with thoughts I had never had before in my life. I wondered how this man, that was so happy to be with me, could forgive me and truly love me again. I thought of how everything around me was dependent on the other for survival, that all the plants, animals and bugs lived in harmony together. At least it appeared to be harmony, but in truth there was always conflict. Somewhere, hidden deep within the bushes or behind my watchful eyes there was some kind of conflict being resolved. It was being resolved and that is what eased my mind. Whatever issues Steven and I were having or whatever might happen in the future, we could resolve it. Hate may destroy many moments in life but love always wins in the end.

"What are you thinking about, Love?" Steven asked, calling me by my middle name.

"That we will be okay," I said, looking down at our feet.

He reached out, lifted my chin, saying, "Yes, now that we are together, nothing will ever come between us. I have such strong feelings for you. I know we will be okay because I love you."

"It's so easy to do this…here, in Mississippi. We don't have to face the world or reality. Tomorrow is a different story. We'll be back in L.A. which is a completely different world."

"With love it doesn't matter where we are, we are the same people. If we let the world rob us of our destiny then we have no one to blame but ourselves. Tiffany…, I was destined to love you. From the moment you walked into my life I knew where I belonged. I knew my purpose in life was to be with you…to take care of you."

"Why didn't you give up on me?"

"I couldn't."

"I'm sorry I was such a fool."

"You were never a fool. I am the fool. I should have tried harder."

"Don't say that, Steven. Every other man I've ever known would have given up on me a long time ago. You are a rare breed."

"That's because there is only one you, my Love."

With my hand in his we walked in silence, under the perfect spring sky. I could feel his love for me. It felt as though it was traveling from his heart, through his body and down his arm into his hand. From there I could sense this energy surging into me, into my hand, which was Steven's love. It excited and calmed me at the same time and I felt closer to him than I had ever felt to anyone before in my life.

Without a word he gently guided me to turn around and we started to walk back. My hand in his and the memory of the love we had just made kept my mind at ease. It was as though the old Tiffany was missing. The girl who constantly had questions for everyone and needed the answers. The one who doubted that anyone could really love her unless she had something they wanted. The same person who denied her true feelings, all for the sake of accomplishing her goals in life. She was gone, silently I wished she was gone for good.

3
Chapter

With the morning sun came the first day we would travel together. It seemed strange that we were grown-ups, had known
each other almost our whole lives but had never really gone anywhere
together, had never been on a vacation or road trip. We had never been
on a plane or train together, not once. So we finished packing and got
ourselves ready before we sat down to eat our breakfast; a bowl of cere-
al, banana, with a cup of juice. When we finished, Steven cleaned the
dishes and called his brother.

"Blake will be here in a few. Do you want me to call for a driver or
do you want me to drive?"

"I hate for you to leave your truck at the airport. Who knows when
we will be back in Mississippi," I said, touching his cheek with my hand.

He pulled my hand down into his and pulled me close, "I know it
will be a while but I can always ask my brother to bring it back to the
house. He's done it before."

"That's okay honey. No need in bothering him, I already called for
a driver this morning while you were taking a shower."

"One step ahead of me, I see."

"Old habits die hard. It will take some time for me to get use to discussing what we should do. I'm use to making the decisions."

Steven pulled back, looking into my eyes before saying, "I don't mind about the little things but the big stuff is totally different."

"I agree, Steven."

"That's good, now, for the most important decision. When are you going to make me the happiest man in the world?"

"I thought you already were the happiest man in the world," I said, wondering what he was talking about.

"Now… don't get nervous. All I was talking about was a long, passionate good morning kiss. What did you think I was insinuating?"

"Well, I wasn't sure, Mr. Cross."

"I know exactly what is on your mind, Mrs. Cross."

"It certainly wasn't a big kiss."

"Do you like the ring of that? Or did you catch it?"

"It does have a certain ring to it. I remember very well what it sounds like. Remember, I was the girl who was madly in love with you when you went away to college."

"That was you. Oh yes, I remember."

"Stop teasing me, and give me that kiss."

His lips pressed hard against mine and I met his passion with my own lips. One hand pulled against his hip and the other found its way to his neck where I caressed his hair line. Each passing moment brought us deeper and deeper into a rhythm of pressing lips and bodies in a way that only lovers know how to do. He knew exactly what I needed, what I liked.

We found our way to the only kitchen wall that didn't have something hanging from it and he leaned back, pulling me forward. Somewhere in my mind I knew we needed to stop. We were getting carried away in the moment and there was little we could do to control ourselves. His hands started to pull at my clothes wanting to touch my flesh. I pushed his hands where I wanted them to go, where I wanted him to touch me and pressed my lips even harder onto his.

Steven reached down and pulled the side of my dress up to my hip and put his finger under the fabric of my panties. My lips left his and found their way to his neck which I began to kiss and nibble. His breathing became heavy as he gently tugged at my panties. I could feel them coming down my thigh as I began to move my legs there was a knock at the door. We both jumped and then giggled as we hugged each.

"That would be my brother."

"Yes, I think it is."

"Why are we whispering?"

"I don't know."

"Here, let me help straighten you up, Mrs. Cross," he replied pulling my panties up and straightening my dress.

"Why thank you, Mr. Cross. Now, go answer the door."

Steven was holding my hand, walking away and looking back. He winked and turned toward the door. I looked away, took a deep breath and felt like a little dizzy. I couldn't remember the last time I had been this blissful and gratified.

From the kitchen I could hear Blake and Steven in the living room. It had been many years since I had seen his brother but I could still tell it was his voice, just a little more mature. It struck me as odd that I wasn't sure what to do. Was I supposed to stay in the kitchen and wait for Steven? Or should I just walk into the living room and tell Blake hello? Instead, I just turned my back to the wall and took a deep breath before smoothing my hair.

I took a deep breath and walked into the living room. Blake looked me up and down and shook his head. My instinct was to hug him but instead I just sat down beside Steven.

"My gosh! I never thought I would see you again in person. What the heck are you doing here, girl?"

"I came home to see your brother."

"Yes, she did. And we have finally worked everything out," Steven said, taking my hand and pulling it up to kiss the back of it.

"You mean, you two are together?" Blake asked.

"Yes. In fact, we are leaving for California in about an hour. That's why I called you," Steven answered.

"Well I'm just blown away. Wish you would have told me Tiffany was here. I could have brought Vicky and we could have had a real reunion."

"You mean Victoria?" I asked.

"Yes, remember your best friend. At least that's what she tells anybody who will listen to her."

"I'm sorry Blake, I didn't know you were still with her or I would have asked you to bring her too," Steven said, letting go of my hand.

"We're back together. At least for now."

"How is she?"

"She's doing okay, Tiffany. She'd probably be doing a lot better if she had you for a friend again. Her life has not been easy, like yours."

"I wouldn't say that my life has been easy, Blake."

Steven interrupted, saying, "Hey, listen, I asked you to come over cause I need to ask a few favors, if you don't mind."

"Sure, what can I do for you?" Blake asked.

"I need you to come by once a week and check on the house for me. You still got the key?"

"Sure do, right here on my key ring."

"And will you drive the truck for me when you come?"

"If you leave the keys, I will."

"They'll be hanging on the wall in the kitchen. Just drive it down to Carter's Trail and back just like you did before. You know those old trucks don't do well if they sit around too long."

"I know. It's no problem. I like driving it."

"And one more thing."

"Alright. What else?"

"Would you mind taking all the food in the fridge and freezer home for you and Victoria? And will you pick up some baking soda to put in there?"

"Will do," Blake said, looking back toward the kitchen.

"Do you still have that bank account we opened up?"

"Yes, but there's not much in it."

"I'll wire you a little something every week for your trouble," Steven said, giving a wink.

"You hear that, Tiffany? Now that my brother has made the big time he thinks I am his errand boy."

"If it's a problem, Blake, I can get someone else to do it."

"No problem, big bro, I'm just making a joke. I'd be glad to do it. Every little bit helps now that the baby is coming."

"The baby? Are you and Victoria married?" I asked.

"Don't sound so shocked. No, we aren't married. Just having a baby."

I looked at Steven, wondering why he withheld all of this information from me. Then I turned to Blake and replied, "Then I guess congratulations are in order, to you and your brother. He'll be an uncle for the first time."

"Yes he will. And I bet he will be a good one."

"Look Blake, I really don't want anyone in my house except for you. I have a lot of stuff I don't want anyone plundering around in. I hope you can understand that," Steven said, ignoring our comments about him becoming an uncle.

"Yes sir. No one but me in the house. And knowing you, no one but me in the truck. That's fine. Victoria gets the message loud and clear, brother."

"I wasn't saying you can't bring her with you. I just don't want her nosing around in my house. Or anyone else for that matter."

"I got it. No problem. She's getting bigger and bigger every day and feeling less and less like getting out of the house anyway. But she'll be happy about the extra money."

"I really appreciate your help."

"So, how long you gonna be gone this time?"

"I don't know. We don't know. I'll call you in a few weeks when I have a better idea of when I'll be back. Or should I say when we will be back."

"Well, I wish you both the best of luck. It's kinda weird to see you two together. But then again, it seems like it should have happened a long time ago. This man right here really loves you, Tiffany."

"I know, Blake."

"You should. He has carried a flame for you for so long. I really hope you two can make it. Really. I'm not just saying that cause you're here in front of me."

"Thank you. I think we are going to be just fine," Steven replied, standing up.

"Yes, I guess I better get going. Victoria is going to wonder what took me so long to bring her some ice cream," Blake said, standing up, shaking Steven's hand.

"Will you let her know I asked about her?"

"Sure will, Tiffany. She will be sure enough mad that she didn't get to see you."

"Maybe you two can come out to California to see us."

"One day. By then it will probably be the three of us."

"Oh yes. You, Victoria and the baby. That would be awesome."

"Alright, good to see you, Tiffany. Thanks again, big brother. Ya'll have fun now. And don't do anything I wouldn't do."

"I don't think you have to worry about that, Blake. Thanks for coming over. And thanks for helping me out."

"Anytime, man. That's what brothers are for, right?"

"Take care, I'll call you soon."

"Sure thing," he said, walking down the steps of the front porch.

We both stood in the door, watching him walk to his truck. I was dumbfounded that he and Victoria were together and having a baby and not a word of this had come out of Steven's mouth. I knew I had no right to be angry. Truly it was none of my business what his brother and my childhood friend were doing so many years later. But still I could hardly believe Steven had not told me.

"I know what you're thinking, Love. It's written all over your beautiful face."

"Why didn't you tell me?"

"It didn't cross my mind. And you know I can't stand gossip."

"Telling me your brother and my ex-best friend are together and expecting a baby is not gossip, Steven. It's just the facts."

"I wasn't trying to hide anything from you. I just didn't think it mattered to you what was going on in my brother's life."

"Well, if you didn't tell me about that, what else are you not telling me?"

"Seriously, Tiffany...I wasn't trying to keep anything from you. All that is on my mind is you and me."

He took my hand and kissed it gently then slowly kissed his way up my arm. When he reached my shoulder, he stopped and looked into my eyes. I knew he was telling the truth but held on to my anger a moment longer until my smile took over.

"Now, where were we before that knock on the door?" He asked pulling my body next to his.

"We were getting ready to go."

"I know. But now I wonder which way we were heading."

"Whatever do you mean, Mr. Cross," I said sweetly, letting him kiss my neck.

"Are we heading to California or to the bedroom?"

"We are going home. I'm just not sure whose house we are going to.

"Mine is bigger," he said, hugging me close.

"Yes, that is true. But mine is on the beach."

"It doesn't matter to me, Love. I'd go anywhere to be with you."

"I guess we can decide before we get there. I think I just heard our car pull up. Will you go check?"

"Sure thing, baby," he said, kissing my cheek and turning toward the door.

Within minutes, the driver had our bags in the car and we were on our way to the airport. There had been so many trips to so many different airports and usually I wasn't nervous. But today was totally different. Today, I was traveling with the man I loved, had always loved, and we were beginning our life together. Being with him in Mississippi felt like coming home. It felt right but I wondered how it would feel when we were back in the City of Angels. When the flashes from the cameras hit our faces how would we look together? Would the public love our love story or would they try to tear everything we hoped to have to pieces? Only time would tell.

4
Chapter

With the salty air filling our lungs we walked hand in hand near the shoreline. The blue water rushed up to splash our legs and feet as we quietly strolled. Sunset was approaching yet we did not turn to look. Our focus was directly in front, on what was to come. And I felt that at just the right moment Steven would pull my hand, indicating he wanted to stop. Then we would walk away from the water's edge, where he would want me to sit in front of him. He would snuggle up to me and hold me like every girl in the world wants to be held. His gentle voice would comment on the beautiful shades of color the sunset made as he gently caressed my skin. Then he would press his cheek against mine as we gazed out onto the horizon.

It was just as I had envisioned. He pulled my hand to stop me; he led me away from the water, and sat down behind me. He moved closer to hold me in his arms. He pointed up to the clouds, commenting on the hues of blue, pink and yellow. He touched my arms, legs and face lightly with the tips of his fingers. Everything he did made me feel like

I was such a fool. Why had I waited so long to be loved by him? How many hours, days, weeks, months and years had I wasted on loneliness?

"You are my answered prayer, Tiffany. Do you know that?"

"No, I didn't."

"I feel complete when we are together. Like nothing is missing."

"I feel better too, but I'm still scared."

"What are you afraid of? I will protect you. I will take care of you. I will do whatever it takes to take away your fear."

"It still feels like you'll be leaving and I'll be alone again."

"I'm not going anywhere, Tiffany. Now that I have you in my life where would I need to go?"

"I don't know. It's just an awful feeling that you will be leaving and I don't want you to go."

"I promise you with everything in me that I will never leave you again. Never."

"Then everything will be okay?"

"Yes, everything will be okay."

His lips pressed against mine as sadness enveloped the moment. It felt like he was desperately trying to wipe away my fears with his kiss. But too many years had passed with too much heartache to cleanse away those memories with one kiss. Not even a hundred kisses would change the reality we had both lived. Only the passage of time and the devotion he spoke of would change the feelings we both held deep within our souls. He seemed unharmed when he talked but even I knew that he had scars from our past. My greatest hope was that the wounds we both nursed could be healed by the love we now shared.

As darkness began to fall we quietly stood up, dusting off the sand and began the journey back to my house. The lights from the beautiful homes along the beach shore were shining as we slowly walked the water's edge, hand and hand. There was silence between us but it was not awkward. I could feel his love, his desire for me and I hoped he could sense mine for him. I needed to make love to him. I needed to feel his body close to mine. I wanted to be one with him again and again and again.

We reached the stairs and I let go of his hand to take the banister. He reached out for my hips and squeezed for just a moment and let go. I looked back into his eyes giving him the smile he hoped for. Within a minute we were inside, kissing our way up another set of stairs. When we reached the top, Steven picked me up and carried me to bed. Our lips never parted as we lay down together and began to explore each other's bodies with our hands.

"Make love to me, Tiffany. Never stop…making love to me."

"Don't ever leave me again."

"I will never leave you," he promised, kissing my neck.

"Then I will make love to you…for the rest of my life."

"Then will you be my wife?"

I made him stop, looked directly into his eyes and asked, "Is that a proposal?"

"No, Love. I would never propose to you this way. You are way too special to me to do it like this. I just got carried away in the moment."

"I would be…"

"I know, baby. And you will be."

"I love you, Steven."

"I love you…more."

He gave me everything I wanted and never stopped holding, touching or caressing my body. This man, who I had known since he was a boy, knew exactly what to do to bring me more pleasure than I thought was humanly possible. It must have been the love he felt for me that made our bodies seem so perfectly matched for the other. The only thing I knew was each time we were together it felt like we were drawn closer and closer. Our passion soared, reaching new heights and I wasn't sure how much higher we could go but I was willing to find out.

The new morning found us in each other's arms, wrapped up tight with our bodies pressed firmly together. Neither wanted to move or let go and if given the chance we could have ignored the world for the rest of the day. It was the ring of the phone that pulled us reluctantly apart but only for a few minutes. He returned to my bed, letting me rest my head on his bare shoulder as we talked about what lay ahead.

We both had meetings to attend and work to be caught up on. But even though we talked about what needed to be done, nothing felt more important than what we were accomplishing in the moment we shared. We flirted with the idea of canceling all the appointments and playing on the beach all day. Our imaginations ran wild with what we would do and how much fun we could have. Then another ring of the phone and we were out of the bed. I was talking on the phone and Steven was in the shower and before we knew it, we were going our separate ways.

In a meeting that seemed to never end, my mind wandered through memories as everyone else talked. Memories of yesterday, last night and the past few days filled my thoughts with nothing but Steven. Staying focused was totally beyond my control and I wondered how no one else could tell. Was I always this removed from every meeting and they merely put up with my presence? Or could everyone in the world some-how tell or notice that I was in love. Yes, for the first or perhaps the second time in my life I was totally and hopelessly in love with the one man I should have always been with, the one I should have spent my life with. And even though I had wasted so much time, I knew it was time to stop regretting the past and start living in the present.

It was so wrong but it felt so right that I stood up and said, "I've got to go."

"What?" Some dark-headed man I had never seen before, asked.

"I'm sorry but you will have to finish this meeting without me."

"Why certainly, Ms. Starr. We hope you feel better soon," a young woman said, who I had never seen before in my life.

Without another excuse, I picked up my purse and walked out the door. There was only one thing on my mind. Quickly, I walked to the door and out to my car where the driver was holding the door open for me to get in. He closed the door and got in the driver's seat asking where he needed to take me. I asked him to take me to a park. Preferably one that might have some nice trees. After giving me a strange look, we were on our way.

As soon as we got there, I asked him to put a blanket on the ground under a tree that was not too far from the car. Then I searched for a pen and paper and grabbed my sunglasses before getting out of the car.

I sat on the blanket, opened the notebook and pushed the top of the pen. Steven had given me so many words. So many that I could never count them all. And I knew that I could never repay him for what his poetry and letters had given me all those years. But every fiber of my being wanted to write to him and even though I am not a poet, I would write from my heart and hope the words would be good enough for him to read.

My beloved Steven,

When I finally came to my senses and wrote you the letter that I should have written so many years ago, I could have never dreamed this is the way things would be. My love and desire for you are overwhelming, almost to the point that I am unable to concentrate on anything else. You are on my mind when I wake up and when I am falling asleep and throughout every hour during the day even when we are together. Never, ever have I felt such strong feelings for another human being except perhaps when we were teenagers. My maturity is the only reason I believe my feelings for you are stronger now. Where once I was a child in a woman's body I am now a woman with childlike feelings. Once again I feel like you and I can do anything, can have anything if only we stay together. In my heart, I believe we can have anything we want in this world if we truly want it and decide that it is ours for the taking. There is nothing I want more than to please you, Steven… in every way. If there is anything you want, anything you desire from me, say the words and I will give it to you. Do not go without what your heart desires and do not be slow or shy in asking. Finally, I can say without hesitation that I am your girl and now I know I always have been your girl. Please, let me be that. Let me be yours and please be mine.

The only thing I ask of you is to forgive me for letting you down so many times. That and to give me a chance to love you. Please let me love you the way a man like you should be loved. We have both been let down, used and lied to in the past by people who only cared about themselves. This is our chance to make our dreams come true. We owe it to ourselves to give this love between us every opportunity to grow. Just imagine, my darling, if we make it through these first few weeks in Los Angeles how much stronger our love will be. Then I beg you…let's get away for a little while. You pick the place. I don't care where we go as long as we are alone. We need this time to reconnect, Steven. Not to mention, I want to make love to you every day. And I am not talking about just making love in the physical sense. I mean I want to make love to you in every way. By holding you as you fall asleep and when I cook your breakfast in the morning and when I hold your hand as we walk together. In every way and with every gesture I make love to you in hopes that you will choose to stay with me. I don't deserve you…and I know that but still I must ask for the chance to love you, to hold you, to know you.

You once told me life is short. If only I had understood that, our history would be different. But at least now I realize how short it really is and I am willing to forget my foolish pride and plead with you to give this silly girl your heart. You have always had mine. Do you know that? From the very first moment we met and you introduced yourself, I have been your girl. And I am still your girl. No matter what you decide to do, I will always be yours.

Forever and a day,
Tiffany

4
Chapter

The words I had written to Steven drew us together like the tight stitching of an accomplished seamstress. We spent the first few days of May avoiding work and responsibilities just to be near one another. With each new memory added into our minds and hearts our love grew deeper. It was as though no one had ever loved another person more than he and I loved one another. We were the first and certainly would be an example for future lovers on how to love another person with all your heart.

The road between his house and mine became worn by our constant commuting. His house had the pool, hot tub and privacy where we loved to leisurely spend our time but mine had the ocean and views that set our passion for each other on fire. It was a never ending tug-of-war between his place and mine but somehow we managed to make it work.

Steven seemed content to please me in any way possible and I, for the first time in my life, was continually thinking of ways in which I could please him. We had it all...money, success, youth, health and love. We had climbed the mountain and now we were enjoying our triumph. Simply basking in the light of all our accomplishments and reaping the rewards.

It was no surprise to me that when given even a moment alone; I would find Steven with pen and paper. Then when he felt my presence, he would raise one finger, asking me to wait a moment as he jotted down another line or two before closing his notebook. And even though I was curious, I never pried or snuck behind his back to look at his work. I knew when the time was right he would share his words with me.

Then the day came where I could no longer put the studio off. In order to fulfill my contract it was time to make some decisions. So I put on my best Tiffany Starr act and faced the music. Steven walked me to my car with his hand holding mine. We lingered at the open door, kissing tenderly and passionately. He promised to be at my house that evening so we could enjoy the sunset together. Then I was sitting in the back seat alone headed for the Hollywood hills.

After the first hour of my meeting, it was obvious that the decision about what film I would do next had already been decided by the studio executives. My mind was so distracted that I barely cared what they were all talking about anyway. I just wanted the meeting to be over. I wanted to be free to go, to be with the only person on the face of this planet that truly loved and cared about me. Not Tiffany Starr the actress but Tiffany Crenshaw the woman.

When the meeting ended I quickly walked toward the door, not offering any proper goodbyes. Right when I was about to get away my agent spoke up, reminding me about our lunch date with the other lead actor in the film. My tongue betrayed my heart when it accepted the invitation. The thought of being tied down another moment made my stomach turn. All I wanted was to be free. Free to go home, be with Steven and live life without the heartache of business meetings. One look at their faces made me control myself, it was obvious that everyone had heard enough excuses from me over the past few weeks.

We arrived at The Abbey and with the flash of the cameras, made our way inside. It had been a while since I had to deal with the public so in a way I was happy to see there was still interest in my career. After being ushered toward the back, far from prying eyes and camera lenses, I was introduced to a very handsome actor by the name of Michael McFarland. Post introduction, my interest in our upcoming film began to grow.

Michael was originally from Dallas, Texas but had moved to New York when he was twenty-three. There he did several shows off Broadway until he finally got his big break, landing one of the leads in Cats. At the age of twenty-nine he moved to L. A., to be in his own words… 'Where the magic happens'. And even though Michael McFarland was a few years my junior, he had the wisdom of someone much older than himself.

Mixed with this wisdom beyond his years were the most mesmerizing blue-grey eyes I had ever seen. They were set in a face that looked like it had been chiseled from stone by some famous artist from ancient Greece. His body matched his face and if there was anything about him that seemed a little unfitting of his good looks, it was his hair. Some of it was straight and some of it was wavy. It was dark brown but the very end was lighter as though he had colored it a long time ago and then there was grey beginning to show at the temples. Still, all and all he was a fine specimen of a man.

Michael's charm and charisma matched his wisdom and I began to relax and enjoy lunch. We spoke about the movie and work but mostly about our adventures in life. Between the two of us no one else got a word in but no one seemed to mind. They knew that if we hit it off, the movie had a much better chance for success.

When lunch concluded, Michael insisted on walking me to my car which I gladly accepted. He was such a gentleman and I had enjoyed meeting him so I didn't mind spending a few more minutes in his company. It was not until we walked out of The Abbey that I realized that perhaps Michael McFarland had a little more on his mind than being a gentleman. As picture after picture was snapped of us together his motive became very clear to me. And how could I blame him? At one time in my life I had wanted the same thing to happen to me.

Once I was seated in the car, Michael looked into my eyes and winked with a devious grin. He slowly closed the door and turned back toward the crowd. He was as smooth as silk, the way he handled me and the crowd of photographers. As I sunk back against the seat I instantly knew this man was going to be a big star. And I knew I would be one of many people that would make that happen. There was a little part of me that knew I should feel angry for being used. But there was another part of me that was truly intrigued by this man, soon to become a part of my life.

The afternoon was filled with several meetings about my upcoming film, Fly Higher. It was a stretch to seem interested because my thoughts were somewhere else. Steven, and the memories of our rendezvous, stayed on my mind. Then occasionally, Michael McFarland would pierce through my thoughts with his little grin and blue-grey eyes. Besides, it was meaningless to listen to the endless chatter about who would do what and when it would happen. So many times in the past, these words had proven to be just that. It seemed like most of the plans in the movie business were just high hopes and the only thing that really happened is when the production actually started.

Finally the day was over and as the driver opened the door, I could see Steven waiting for me at my front door. He looked so handsome and happy, I almost wanted to run up the steps to greet him. Instead, I slowly stepped out of the car and turned to look up at him and gave him my best Hollywood smile from behind my dark sunglasses.

"Hello beautiful," his deep voice called out, bringing delight to widen my smile.

"Well, hello handsome. How was your day?"

"Very busy."

"Busy? I thought you'd be lying by the pool or at the beach all day. What have you been doing?"

"You'll see," he replied, taking me into his arms. "Kiss me, Tiffany."

There was an aching in his voice that prolonged our kiss and strengthened my grip on his neck. He pulled me closer, kissed me harder and let out a small moan. I asked, "Did you miss me?"

With his lips kissing my neck, Steven asked in a whispering low voice, "Did you miss me?"

"What do you think?" I asked, taking his hand to walk inside.

Steven led me to the sofa and as I sat down he kneeled in front of me. He put his hand out for my foot and began to unbuckle my ankle strap. Looking into my eyes, I could tell he had something on his mind. He tried to hide it with a carefree grin but there was something going on behind those hazel eyes that had me wondering. After taking off my other heel he wrapped his arms around me, giving me a long and gentle hug.

"I thought we might take a nice quiet walk on the beach," he said.

"Sure, I'd love to. Just let me go change."

"I laid something out for you to wear, on the bed," he replied, pulling me up for another hug.

"Now I understand why you have those clothes on. And now you see why I thought you had been at the beach. But you smell too good to have been soaking up some sun."

"I just wanted to be ready… to watch the sunset… with my favorite person in the world."

"What are you buttering me up for, mister?"

"You know it's true, Tiffany. You are my everything. You are my world."

There was a tenderness and truth to his words that stopped me from teasing him further. He pulled me close, kissed me passionately once again then he moved me forward toward the stairs that led up to the bedroom.

Lying on the bed was a sheer white cotton dress, perfect for walking on the beach. I vaguely remembered buying it but couldn't have worn it more than once or twice. How Steven found it in my closet is beyond me but as I stripped away the day's business suit I was glad he did. It was light and airy and made me feel young and carefree. With one look in the mirror, I knew he would love this dress on me.

"I'm ready," I said, turning around sharply letting the dress flare up.

"You look beautiful, Love."

"Thank you. And thanks for picking this out."

"It's perfect, just like you," he said taking my hands, stepping back to look me up and down.

"What is going on, Steven?"

"What do you mean?"

"Well, you are tearing up just looking at me. Are you okay?"

"Yes, I'm fine. Are you ready to go watch the sunset?"

"Yes," I replied taking his hand.

"I took the liberty of setting up a special place to see it from."

"You did?"

"I did. Hope you like it."

We stepped out onto the sand and I could see a quaint little table set for two in the near distance. Right behind it was a beautiful cabana, with gorgeous curtains in white and gold blowing in the wind. As we walked closer, I noticed a young man standing on the other side of the cabana with a silver tray.

"Thank you, baby but you didn't have to go to all this trouble. I know it's the first day we've been apart in a while…"

"Just enjoy it, Tiffany."

He pulled out my chair and I sat down feeling excited with the anticipation of what was to come. He took his seat and then the young man walked over to the table, sitting the tray down and lifting the top to reveal what lay inside.

Steven smiled as he picked up a large chocolate covered strawberry and brought it to my lips. I open my mouth, keeping his gaze as he moved it forward. After I took a bite and began to chew, he never stopped looking at me as he took a bite from the same berry. Then the waiter asked if he was ready for the champagne to be opened, to which he simply nodded yes, never leaving my eyes.

Next, he picked up a small heart shaped piece of watermelon and brought it to my lips. Then he smiled while winking before putting it in my mouth. As its flavor burst, he leaned across the table to kiss me.

As the waiter poured the bubbly liquid into our glasses, Steven picked up a cookie covered in white powdered sugar and broke it in half. Then he lifted his hand and put the halves back together. Slowly he pulled them apart, while I watched his every move, bringing one side to my lips. I let him put the whole piece in my mouth and he placed his finger on my bottom lip. As I began to chew, he took the other half of the cookie and put it in my hand. I lifted it to his mouth then let my finger linger on his bottom lip as he began to eat. There was something so sensual about feeding each other that I finally ended our staring match to see what else there was to feed him.

"Do you like your surprise?" He asked, leaning back in his seat, taking a sip of champagne.

"I love it! You always know just what I need. How do you do that?"

"It's simple. I let the love I feel for you guide me," he answered.

"I love the way you love me."

Steven picked up his glass and offered a toast to which I followed by raising my glass.

"To our future," he said slowly, lightly touching his glass to mine.

We looked out onto the horizon as the sun was slowly sinking toward the water. The waiter poured more champagne then stood beside Steven. Steven didn't seem to mind but I was curious to why he was just standing there.

"Will you eat one more strawberry with me, Tiffany?"

"Yes."

His eyes scanned the remaining berries to pick just the right one. He brought it to his lips and then grinned. "You first."

I took his hand and pulled it toward my lips, taking a big bite. He took a bite and laid the rest onto the silver tray, nodding his head. The waiter put the lid on top and carried the tray toward the house.

As we finished our glass of champagne, he said he was ready to sit in the cabana. He took my hand and we walked into the shelter of the curtains. There was a large bed style platform with dozens of pillows in every shape and size. He sat down in the middle and leaned back beckoning me to sit in front of him, between his legs.

When we were comfortable, he reached under a pillow and handed me a scroll tied up with a white satin ribbon. I looked at it and felt elated, imagining what words were written on this small piece of paper. I looked back at him just in time to feel his lips pressing against mine.

Slowly I untied the ribbon and unfurled the piece of paper. It was a poem. He had signed and dated it at the bottom. It had todays date on it. I began to read it aloud.

In a boyhood dream
you stand in the midst,
shining like a diamond
within my memories.
Deep longing, incomparable
to any craving ever known,
the years spent in prayer...
sending the words to be sown.
Mistakes in the loneliness
better left in the past
but you, my immortal beloved
your presence within my soul, never left.
As though I was always right;
our souls have become intertwined...
regardless of the space and time,
I am yours; you are mine.
So as the boy has grown to man
I once again extend my hand
and ask if you will be my girl
then we will finally live as one in this world.

"This is for you, if your answer is yes," he said, lifting his hand in front of my eyes.

Sitting in his palm was a gorgeous diamond solitaire engagement ring. I dropped the scroll and took the ring from his hand. It must have been two or three carets and sparkled like a fire burned inside of it.

"Please make me the happiest man in the world and be my wife," he whispered.

I looked past the ring, onto the horizon, noticing the sun was nearing the water's edge. The memory of the first time I met Steven entered my mind. And I knew he had been in love with me since that very moment. This made me realize I would be a fool if I didn't say, "Yes!"

He put his arms around me and hugged me tight while kissing my ear. At the same time I could hear the sound of a camera in the distance. I sat up, looking around and spotted a man near the water taking pictures of us. Steven turned my head to kiss me but I pulled away. This was not the first time that I had photographers at my house. And I wasn't going to let this one ruin our moment.

"Hey! You need to get out of here!"

"Tiffany, he's with me. I hired him so we can remember this night forever."

"I'm sorry, I thought he was one of those guys from the tabloids."

"I guess I should have told you. David, come over here and meet Tiffany."

"Hello, David. I am Tiffany Crenshaw, I mean Starr," I corrected myself with a giggle.

"Yes, I know who you are. Nice to meet you."

"Will you give us a moment alone, David? I will call you when I'm ready."

"Sure man, but the sun is going down and we're losing light."

Steven turned toward me and took the ring out of the palm of my hand. He took my left hand in his and put the engagement ring on my finger. "Do you mind if David takes a few pictures of this moment?"

"No, I don't."

"David."

"Are you ready now?"

"Yes, we're ready. Fire away."

As David began to take pictures, Steven and I began to pose. He pretended to put the ring on my finger. We kissed tenderly for the camera and I laid back against him with his arms around me. Before the sunset we walked to the water's edge to capture its beauty in our photographs. As the big red ball sank into the water out on the horizon, Steven whispered into my ear. He started telling me what he wanted to do later and how he wanted to make me feel.

We made our way back to the cabana where we sat on the edge of the bed while cleaning sand from our feet. We crawled into the pillows as David took pictures of us laughing, talking and cuddling. The waiter served us another glass of champagne as the photographer continued to take shot after shot. So I tried to pretend like he wasn't even there and enjoy the moment.

When our glasses were empty again, our waiter held out the silver tray for us to sit them on. Then we turned toward David, lying side by side and took our last picture of the evening. Without a word David walked away and Steven and I looked out into the night sky which was growing darker by the moment. A few minutes later, the nice young man appeared in front of the cabana and began to close the curtains from the outside. He never said a word, he didn't even look at us one last time before he was gone.

Immediately, Steven pulled my dress up trying to take it off. I didn't resist. I sat up on my knees and put my hands up to help him. My chest was bare and the only thing that stood between me and my birthday suit was a tiny pair of white panties. He pulled me onto his lap, kissing my lips and gently sucking my tongue into his mouth. I slowly spread my knees apart where my body was touching his. I could feel his desire growing and I could barely conceal my excitement for him to begin.

He stopped, leaned back and looked into my eyes, saying, "I have waited for this moment for so long."

"I know, so have I," I whispered.

"So much wasted time, Love. Let's not waste anymore."

"We won't. Kiss me."

Between kisses, he said, "I'm asking you to marry me. I want you to be my wife. I want to be your husband."

"I am yours….I always have been."

"I want you to have my baby."

"You want me to what?"

"Have our baby."

"You want me to have a baby?"

"Yes. And I don't want to wait."

"Well, it does take time."

"And I don't want a long engagement. We've waited long enough," he said, kissing my neck.

"Yes we have. And you have made me wait long enough too. You are driving me crazy."

He kissed me, pulling my body even closer to his, asking, "I'm making you crazy?"

"Completely insane…"

"That means you have made me insane for most of my life," he said in a low voice, as he leaned back to look at me.

"And now you want me to do it for the rest of your life? You are crazy."

"Only for you, Love. Nobody but you."

He quickly sat up and picked me up while still on his knees. He kissed me with great passion as he turned and laid me down onto the pillows. Then he looked down at my nearly naked body and smiled that handsome country boy smile. It was the smile that melted my heart and shattered all my inhibitions. His shirt was the first thing to go and I could hear his breathing becoming heavy with anticipation.

The sound of the ocean was the only thing that reminded me we were still on the beach, still outside. That and the gentle blowing of the curtains by the ocean breeze, bringing its smell as we began to make love. It had begun to grow darker and darker inside the little cabana. As Steven pulled his pants off, he leaned to the front of the bed and took something out from underneath a pillow. I turned to see what it was and thought to myself, he thinks of everything. It was a tiny lantern and he turned it on with the flip of a switch.

With one motion he freed my body of clothes. And in another moment his was free. We lay side by side kissing and touching each other like it was the first time. And in a way that is exactly what it felt like. Now, I was his fiancé, his future wife. And he would be my husband. It made everything different. It would make everything right. It would bring purpose to every moment we had ever spent together and somehow to every moment we had been apart.

Steven took my left hand and kissed my finger that the engagement ring was on. He kissed my ring and then my hand and pulled it up to his eyes which he closed. I could feel his emotions were mixed somewhere between passion, happiness and pain. I wanted to make him forget the past. I wanted him to think only of our future. I wanted him to picture me in white, walking toward him to begin the rest of our lives together.

"Please, I want to be with you, now."

"I'm right here, Tiffany."

"Please don't leave me again."

"I will never leave you."

"I'm scared…"

"I promise, I'll never leave. Not ever."

He rolled onto his back and pulled me on top of him. I looked into those eyes and he gave me that same country boy grin that drove me wild. I dove in for a kiss like the high divers in Mexico dive into the ocean from the edge of a cliff. It was at first a hard impact, followed by a long wet and utterly fulfilling experience. His hands began to roam my body, to heighten every sensual nerve within it. The desire Steven had for me was different. It was completely full, not lacking anything.

He sat up, scooting back against the pillows, bringing me with him. He pulled me into him and in one motion we became one. I closed my eyes and moved my body with the rhythm of the ocean waves. Steven took my hips in his hands and pulled and pushed me with the same rhythm, soft and slow. And the thought of him waiting for me at the end of a long aisle, wearing a tux, never left my mind. For the first time in my life, I knew without a shadow of a doubt that I had done the right thing. I had written him the letter. The letter that I should have written him so very long ago.

6
Chapter

Why in the world does everything take so long? You would think with fame and fortune one would be able to make things happen quickly. Not to mention, Los Angeles is one of the most fast paced cities on the globe. But every venue we liked, there was a waiting list, no exceptions. And caterers, that you think would be dying to have my business, act like I'm the crazy one for wanting them to feed us so soon in the future. In fact, the dress was the only thing that was ready for our special day.

Steven tried to convince me that we should just go back to Mississippi. There we could put together a nice ceremony in less than a couple of weeks and we would have plenty of help. When I finally put my foot down and flat out refused he tried to talk me into eloping in Las Vegas. When I finished with the reasons why we would never be married in Vegas, he suggested going to Italy. And that was the moment all of our plans changed.

With the wonderful memories of time spent in Italy fresh on my mind, I began to make phone calls. It only took a few hours before I had reserved a church, the Church of Santa Sofia, in Capri and made a date for our wedding. Then I called The Grand Hotel Quisiana and planned the reception at their restaurant Rendez Voriz, including the menu. I also reserved the honeymoon suite in one of the finest hotels in Florence called The St. Regis Florence, for two weeks. Finally, I felt like everything was coming together and it would only be a couple of months before I became Mrs. Steven Cross.

When Steven got home, I couldn't wait to tell him the good news. He sat down and listened about the church, the food and the honeymoon suite with enthusiasm. He seemed delighted that I changed my mind about having the ceremony in Los Angeles. It was a dream come true for me that I didn't even know was a dream. But the thought of marrying the man I love in a country that I had grown to love felt like it was meant to be.

With the computer surfing from picture to picture, I showed Steven where we would go and what we would see. Then I remembered I had not told him that I picked a date. A twinge of guilt pulled at my heart but I knew now was the time.

"After the reception at Rendez Voriz, I thought we would fly by helicopter to The St. Regis Florence. And I hope you are ready to do this because I booked the church for August twenty-third."

"Now that's what I wanted to hear."

"Which is?" I asked, cautiously.

"No more wasting time. You're ready to officially be my girl."

"Mrs. Steven Cross."

"Those are the sweetest words you've ever said to me."

"And you're not mad at me?"

"No. Why would I be mad at you?"

"For picking our wedding date without you."

"I've been married to you for just about as long as I can remember. All we're doing is making it legal."

"Come here, lover," I said, reaching out for him.

"So, where did you say we would be for our honeymoon?" He asked, sitting down beside me, putting his arm around my shoulder.

"The Saint Regis Florence, in Florence. It's one of the most luxurious hotels in Italy."

"That's exactly what we need to begin our life together. How long will we stay?"

"Two weeks, darling," I answered, resting my head on his chest.

"Do you think that's enough time?"

"Of course. What? Did you want to stay a month?"

Steven turned to face me, saying, "I want to stay with you forever, throughout eternity."

"Then two weeks is long enough?"

"Yes, and I will cherish every moment with you, my love."

I sat up, saying "Then I will get busy with the rest of the arrangements. I'm sure Diane would help me."

"I think you're right. And last I heard she was taking some time off."

"So…it's perfect timing. Do you think she'd be my maid of honor?"

"What about your sister?"

"I haven't thought about that."

"Don't you think you've done enough for today?" He asked, getting up to look out the window.

I followed him, putting my arms around his waist and peering out the window beside him. "Yes, I do.

"It's been a long day for both of us. Why don't we relax and enjoy the evening, and each other."

"What are you suggesting, Mr. Cross?"

"Maybe, order some dinner or maybe a massage and then dinner."

"A massage sounds good. There's that place that will come to your house and…"

"If you call them, I will call and order dinner. Italian sound good?" He asked with that handsome country boy grin.

"Sounds perfect. I love you, Steven."

"I love you, too, Tiffany Cross."

"You said it!"

"Yes I did, and I like the way it sounds."

He took me in his arms and pulled me close. Our lips touched so softly at first and then the intensity grew with each passing moment. He reached down, grabbing the edge of my skirt and pulled it up to caress my thigh. I pushed my body against his and could feel his passion growing. Then I pulled away and looked into his eyes.

"I can see everything, when I look in your eyes."

"What do you mean, Steven?"

"I see the past. All the days spent with you and all the days without you. I see the present because here you are right in front of me. And I see our future. Here we are planning our wedding. And somewhere in those crystal blue eyes of yours, I can see our children."

"Our children?"

"Yes, a little bit of you and a little bit of me, all blended together. And I already love them."

"You better order dinner or we might begin working on this family you're talking about."

"Yes, so massage at six and dinner at seven?"

"Sounds about right."

"Okay, I'm on it, Love."

He turned to walk out of the room with a wink and I winked back at him. I knew the night would end with passion and the thought made me have a strange sensation deep inside. If there was anything I could say about my future husband it was he certainly knew how to satisfy me. And that was in more ways than one.

After I made the call, we passed each other in the hallway. Kissing only for a second and reaffirming our plans for the evening. He was on his way to chill a bottle of wine and I was going upstairs to take a bath. His hand held on to mine until the last second as we went our separate ways.

I turned on some soft music and began to fill the tub with water and poured in some bubble bath. When I caught my reflection in the mirror, I was surprised at how young and vibrant I looked. It could have been the result of the wedding plans coming together so smoothly or perhaps simply the night that lay ahead. Whatever it was, I wanted to bottle it and sell it. Then I would never have to make another movie ever again in my life.

As I soaked in the warm water, I began to fantasize about what might happen later tonight. A soothing massage as Steven and I held hands. Then a candlelit dinner with the sound of the ocean waves in the distance. He would feed me a bite of pasta and I would feed him some prosciutto. Then maybe we would share a moonlit walk along the shore and beautiful words to comfort and calm our hearts.

Somehow, I lost track of time as my thoughts of the night took over. The next thing I heard was the sound of Steven's voice telling me it was time for our massage. I quickly dried off and put my robe on. I took my shower cap off and let my hair fall loosely around my shoulders. One quick glance in the mirror and down the stairs I went to be with my future husband.

He stood at the bottom of the stairs looking up at me. After all of these years, his stare still had a way of making me blush. Even at my age, Steven had a way of making me feel so young. He extended his hand and that was when I realized that he was wearing a robe too. We walked into the living room where two young men waited beside two massage tables. The back doors were open which allowed the ocean breeze to blow into the room. I could smell jasmine and roses and salty air all blended together.

Steven untied my robe and helped me onto the table. Then the young man covered my bare bottom with a small thin sheet of cotton. Very exotic and beautiful music began to play as Steven unrobed and joined me on the other table. As the young men began to massage our bodies we joined hands. It was just like I had imagined and the smell of flowers mixed with the ocean breeze and the music were a perfect addition.

With each passing moment, I became more and more relaxed. Steven and I were no longer holding hands but I could still sense his presence. We had grown closer over the past few months and I had begun to feel him in a much deeper way. At times I knew what he was going to say even before he said the words.

Then I was drifting, drifting ever so slowly toward sleep when I felt a kiss on the back of my neck. I turned to look up into those hazel eyes and he whispered, "shhhhh….don't talk." Gently, he slid a blindfold over my eyes and suddenly my other senses came back to life. He pulled the sheet off of my bottom and began to kiss and caress my feet moving his way up my legs. My body shuddered beneath his touch as my mind wondered what he would do next.

When he reached the top of my left thigh, I let out a long soft moan. I moved my hips, arching my back. Then suddenly his hand came down upon my bottom.

"I told you to be quiet," he giggled.

Steven had never been anything but gentle and a gentleman. As his love pat began to sting, I wondered what in the world had gotten in to him. And then I wondered why in the world it had turned me on so much. Then I realized that it must be the blindfold.

He rubbed my bottom where it was warm from his love pat and then he began to kiss the bottom of my back. I tried to lay perfectly still, like he asked but when he began to lick my skin I could not help but squirm a bit.

"Be still," he said firmly.

"I'm trying."

His hand came down hard against the other side of my bottom and against my will another moan escaped my lips. "What am I going to do with you? You are being very bad."

No answer was given but I could tell he was enjoying this little game. And even though we had never done anything like this before so was I. It made me remember the thought I had about Steven earlier. He knew how to satisfy me in more ways than one.

He moved his mouth slowly up my body until it was beside my ear. I lay perfectly still eagerly awaiting his next words. He brushed my hair back with his hand, holding it against the back of my neck.

"Are you ready?"

There was a part of me that thought whatever he is doing is crazy. But I was so excited, waiting to see what he would do next, that I went along with his plan for pleasure. I wanted to speak but instead I nodded my head yes.

"Turn over."

Rolling onto my side, I grasp the edge of the table. Steven took my hand and held my back as I got into my new position. He quickly repositioned my blindfold so I couldn't see anything, then he kissed me. Then there was silence. Maybe a minute or two passed and I wondered where he was and what he was doing. The smell of jasmine and roses intensified as I listened for any sign of him being close to me.

Then I felt him leaning over from above my head, kissing my lips again but this time, upside down. They were tender kisses, soft and gentle and heartfelt. Then he ran his hands down the length of my arms, taking my hands. He pulled them up over my head and put my hands together with his hands over them. Then he leaned over again nibbling my ear.

"Keep your hands together. I want you to feel me, not touch me."

As I lay upon the massage table, completely naked and blindfolded with my hands grasped tightly together above my head, I began to shake from the inside. It was not from the temperature. It was not from the ocean breeze. It was from the anticipation of Steven's next move, his next touch, his next kiss and where that kiss might be.

He put his hands on my knees, pushing my legs slightly apart. As his hands slid down to my ankles I wondered why they were headed in that direction. Then he took hold of my ankles and in one swift motion pulled me toward the end of the table until my legs were completely off. It was so unexpected that for a second it took my breath away and left me breathing heavily.

Steven pulled my left leg until it was straight up in the air and began to playfully kiss it. I twisted under the touch of his tongue and he stopped. He grabbed my left hip and pulled me even closer to his body where I could feel his skin against mine. I was ready for him to make love to me. Maybe more ready than I had ever been in my life and then the doorbell rang.

Steven gently put my leg back down and walked to the head of the table. He unclenched my hands and took me under the arms and pulled me back upon the table. Then he took my arms and lay them down by my sides as the doorbell rang again.

"Don't move a muscle," he commanded.

This was the first time he had ever been so in control but it certainly was a turn on. Then I realized he was about to open the front door. Here I was, lying on a massage table, completely naked and blindfolded. It was already bad enough that the back doors were open and someone walking down the beach might see us but now he was opening the front door to a stranger. But I didn't move an inch.

The sound of the door shutting relaxed my body once again and I listened for his every move. First he went to the kitchen, then to the dining room where I could hear him fixing our plates. Then I could hear his footsteps coming toward me until I could feel his hand touch my face.

"Dinner is served, Love," he spoke softly, pulling the blindfold from my face.

Taking me by the hand, he helped me sit up on the side of the table. I pulled him close, hugging him tightly. He began to kiss my neck and I responded by kissing his. Soon our lips found each other's lips and we were lost in a wild embrace. I wanted him so badly, needed him so badly that only one thing could satisfy my hunger.

"We better eat before it gets cold," he whispered, picking up my robe.

"You are driving me crazy," I whined, pulling him back to me.

"If making you wonder what I am going to do to you next is driving you crazy...you ain't seen nothing yet, baby."

"What has gotten into you, Mr. Cross?"

"You set the date of our wedding today without me. So... you're in trouble. And you're gonna pay and pay."

"I will gladly pay that bill. And maybe I should get in trouble more often."

"You are about to if you don't put this robe on and come eat dinner with me," he said, smiling while helping me down from the table.

"Are you going to put me back on this table and finish what you started?"

"I wouldn't miss it for the world, Love."

We held hands, intertwining our fingers while walking to the dining room. He pulled out my chair, helping me sit as I looked down at my plate of food. Prosciutto with spaghetti and meatballs filled the plate to the edges.

"All of this is for me?"

"Yes. You're going to need your strength."

"Why don't we share?" I asked, noticing his plate was empty.

"Food is not what I'm hungry for," he answered, picking up my fork.

He stabbed a meatball and raised it up to my mouth. I opened wide for him to put it in while raising my foot and laying it on his lap. He moved his legs letting his robe move to each side as my foot rested between them. My mouth was full as he picked up my napkin to wipe sauce from the side of my mouth.

Twirling the fork into the spaghetti noodles he brought a large mouthful to my lips. I barely swallowed my meatball when he put the noodles inside my mouth. Again, my mouth was way too full as he wiped both sides of it because the sauce began to drip down the side of my lips.

My foot rubbed the inside of his thighs as my mouth moved to the same motion, chewing up the noodles. Steven put the fork down and picked up the prosciutto, waiting for me to swallow. When I did, I closed my eyes and opened my mouth wide.

"Damn, girl. You have never looked finer," he said, pushing at least half of the prosciutto into my mouth waiting for me to bite.

With my eyes closed and my foot touching him, I chewed my food as seductively as possible. It was strange how for many years I had been paid large sums of money to be sexy on screen but in real life it was a different story. I wasn't sure if I looked sexy but all I was trying to do was keep him turned on because all I wanted was to get back to where we were a few minutes earlier and the way it felt.

"Open your eyes, Tiffany."

He held up a glass and I took it, drinking deeply. I sat the glass down, looking into his eyes and picked up the prosciutto bringing it to his lips. He shook his head no and took the fork, got another meatball and brought it to my mouth. My head shook from side to side as I closed my eyes. Steven suddenly stood up, leaned over and took my face into his hands.

"Come on blue eyes, let's finish what we started."

"Beat you there," I teased, jumping up to run into the living room.

He took me by the wrist, pulling me into him and said solemnly, "Let's go together," while picking me up.

With Steven's arms under my back and knees he carried me close to his body. I nestled my mouth against his neck, closing my eyes. He would never know how much I needed him or how much he meant to me. But I would do whatever it took to let him know he was wanted. Whatever that meant, I was willing to do it.

Laying me back upon the table, he took his robe off. His body was not the body of a teenage boy or a young man like I had replayed in my memory so many times over the years. He was grown. He was one hundred percent man and I could hardly wait for him to make love to me.

Untying my robe, he helped me pull it out from under my body and put it with his on the other massage table. Then he took the blindfold and held it before my face. He hesitated before putting it back on and I wondered why but didn't ask.

His kiss surprised me, as his hands began to explore my body. I reached out to pull him close but he pushed my hand back down to my side. I bent my knees wanting to move back down to the edge of the table like I was before we went to eat but Steven gently picked up each leg and laid it back down.

Working his way down my neck so slowly that I felt like I was going to explode, he reached up and lifted my blindfold. I peeped out as he smiled. Then he put it back again and continued kissing until he reached my breast. I took his head in my hands guiding his mouth to where I wanted it to be and he stopped.

"I thought I told you...no touching, only feeling."

"That's right. Sorry."

"And no talking!"

"Yes, sir!"

"That is talking," he said, pulling my leg up and swatting my behind.

We both laughed and he took my hands and put them together again. He moved to the end of the table and pulled me close to him, putting my legs on his body. In one movement we were one and all of the tension flew out of my mind and body. We moved in rhythm to the beat of the music as he took my hips in his hands.

It was strange how I couldn't see anything. I was completely blind. Yet somehow I could see better than I ever had before. For the first time, I trusted another person without doubt. And I had let him do what he wanted without judgment or my opinion.

Steven brought me to a peak of pleasure that I had never known before this night. We had made love so many times but this time was more explosive than ever. My entire body relaxed as he found his own rhythm. After basking in the overwhelming joy and exhilaration, I took a few deep breaths and began to match his rhythm again.

Time seemed to be moving in slow motion as I moved my legs and wrapped them around his waist. Steven seemed to be mumbling but nothing was clear and I dared not speak. My hands were still clasp above my head when I could feel we were both reaching a deeply satisfying conclusion to this moment.

"I love you, Tiffany," he said reaching out for me.

I took his hands, as he pulled me up into his arms, I whispered, "I love you, too."

7
Chapter

After many hours of preparation and planning we were finally on the plane, heading to Capri Italy. Diane was sitting across the row from us with her new boyfriend, George. She had agreed to be my maid of honor and without a doubt I was thankful to have her coming to Italy with us. George seemed like a nice enough guy. He worked as a screen writer and loved to drop names trying to impress Steven and me. It didn't bother me because my thoughts were focused on our approaching wedding day.

Oddly enough after all these years Victoria would be attending our wedding. And it seemed only right since she was the one that was with us at the beginning of our relationship. She would be coming to Italy with Blake, Steven's brother and their parents.

My sister, Cheryl, her boyfriend Kenny and mom would be joining them on the same flight when they reached New York. It would be the first time my mom would meet Steven's parents and I hated that I would not be there to introduce them. But it couldn't be any other way because we had to arrive a few days before anyone else. I had to make certain that everything was ready for the special day.

Dad would be the last to arrive because he decided to stretch his journey out over a few days. He planned to keep himself busy with sightseeing in between stops. Traveling overseas was a new experience, one that he said he may never get the chance to do again so he was taking full advantage of the opportunity.

Steven and I had invited numerous friends and relatives to our grand affair but with it being so far away from home, our wedding party would be very small. And that was exactly what I wanted from the beginning, a very intimate affair with just a few friends and some of our family to share the moment. Of course, I also wanted the best of everything. We deserved the best church, the best restaurant and food, the most beautiful gown and a very lavish honeymoon. After all the years of waiting, I wanted this to be something Steven and I would always remember so I also hired the best photographer in Capri, Italy.

It was only after Steven took my hand that I remembered where I was. I had been so deep in thought about what needed to be done that I completely zoned out. For the first time I wished I'd hired a wedding planner. But back when we started this I didn't want anyone trying to tell me what I needed or telling me what to do. Now, in hind sight, I could see how much easier it could have been to have someone here to help me through the next few days.

"Tiffany, are you okay?"

"Oh Steven, she's fine. Just the last minute jitters. Right Tiff?" Diane interjected, leaning across the aisle, touching Steven's arm.

"Yes, but no jitters. Just deep in thought."

George looked around Diane, saying, "You're not thinking of being a runaway bride, are you?"

"No she isn't, you silly man. She would never do that to Steven," Diane said, sounding unsure.

"No, I have no intentions of running away."

"And I'm not going to let her. Besides, she can't run faster than me," Steven said, making Diane and George laugh.

"I just want this day to be special, that's all."

"We know that, Love. And it will be. Don't worry, Tiffany," Steven said, taking my hand and pulling it up to his lips.

"It's going to work out just fine, girl. I'll be there to help," Diane said, trying to reassure me.

"And if it's a total bomb, who the heck is going to know anyway? You'll be half way around the world...far, far away from Hollywood," George added.

He was right after all. We would be far away from home. It would be far from the cameras, far from the lights and far from the reporters and their prying questions. I had to learn a long time ago to have thick skin when it came to what I saw on the front covers of magazines about me. Most of the articles were flat out lies but sometimes they hit on the truth. Somehow I had managed to keep our wedding under wraps but by the time we got home I knew everyone in America would know about our wedding.

Shortly after the plane landed in Rome we were in a car headed for the coast. From there we would take a boat to Capri and check into the Grand Hotel Quisiana until the wedding. It had been a very long flight and everyone was exhausted and we still had a very long way to go. It didn't take much to convince us that we should rest before we headed out to sea.

It was just before sunset when we set sail for Capri. Steven held me tightly in his arms as we looked out over the Tyrrhenian Sea. Diane and George sat nearby softly talking where their words were not recognizable. It had been so long since I had been in Italy but still in some strange way felt like I was coming home. My soul found rest in the quaintness of the people and the history of the towns. The water on the coast was like nothing you could ever see in America. The colors, the boats, the faces and even the sunset seem to be very different from what the rest of the world looked like.

Purple, pink, blue, yellow and white filled the western sky as though a famous and talented artist were up there painting a masterpiece. We held each other tight as the waves brought the small boat up and down. Neither of us spoke. There was no need for words. My soul was at peace and I knew Steven could feel it. The only question in my mind was already answered. I could tell he loved Italy too and I determined within my own mind that we would have to make plans to visit each year to celebrate our anniversary.

As the night grew darker, the lights on shore became brighter. When the captain docked the boat I was surprised at the welcome we received. There was at least ten people from the hotel there to help us with our luggage. Their English was a little rough but their genuine kindness and excellent service crossed all language barriers. They ushered us into small vans and sent us on our way with big smiles.

We held on as the driver weaved his way through the tiny roads up to the hotel. It was so much grander than it looked like in the pictures. There was lots of people enjoying the night as the lights beckoned us inside. The staff treated us like royalty as we entered the hotel lobby. Without as much as a signature we were directed by a stately gentleman into the elevator and up to our suite. We barely had a chance to take the tour before a group of young men were carrying our things inside and placing them in closets, cabinets and drawers.

After tipping each of the young men, Steven and I stepped out into the hallway to bid Diane and George goodnight. We both took our shoes off and sat down on the sofa. Steven leaned back pulling me into his arms. Our surroundings were so luxurious that I found it hard to relax, after our extremely long trip I should have been exhausted but instead I could not sit still. I walked over to the large window, pulled back the drapes, and looked out upon the town. It was incredibly gorgeous, romantic, and full of life. Something deep inside of me knew without a doubt, this was the right place and time for Steven and I to finally become husband and wife.

Only the thought of making love to the man I loved in the fanciest bed and bedroom I had ever laid eyes on got me away from that window and the view. He enticed me with words and the touch of his skin upon mine. After he undressed both of us we crawled up onto the bed that was covered in a gold and scarlet blanket that looked like it belonged on a queen's bed. I took him into my arms and whispered the words he wanted to hear until we were both completely spent and satisfied.

As we began to drift off to sleep, I reminded him that this would be our last night together until our wedding night. Tomorrow we would part ways and only see each other briefly for the rehearsal and rehearsal dinner party. The thought of barely seeing him for three days almost brought tears to my eyes. But if there was anything I knew, the old saying 'absence makes the heart grow fonder', is certainly true.

The sun began to filter through the towering windows of our bedroom as we woke up in each other's arms. My first thought was how much I wanted to make love to him, how I wanted to feel his love for me over and over again. Then I remembered where we were and what day it was. I crawled over him to look at the clock and couldn't believe my eyes. It was eight-thirty already and we had not even got out of bed. I yanked the covers off and jumped down to the floor, telling Steven it was time to get up.

"What's the rush, Love? Is the hotel on fire?" He asked, reaching his arms out for me.

"It's already eight-thirty and we haven't done a thing to get ready."

"Come here, darling. Let me hold you."

"Seriously, Steven, you've got to get up. There is a million things to do."

"Okay, what can I do to help?" He asked, sitting up on the side of the bed, stretching.

"You can get outta here," I said, pulling the covers back.

"And what am I supposed to do for the next few days?"

"Explore, meet the locals…have fun and get ready for our wedding day. Don't worry, I've got everything under control."

He pulled me closer, whispering, "I'm not worried, Tiffany Cross."

"Can you stay in your suite, on your floor of this hotel until I really am Tiffany Cross?"

"I can if you can."

"Then I will see you tonight for the rehearsal?"

"By now you should know I would go anywhere just to see you. Tell me when and where and I'll be there."

"It's at five o'clock at the Church of Santa Sofia. Ask anyone and you'll find it easily."

"Okay, Love. I will see you tonight," he said sadly, getting up to walk to the bathroom.

"I'm going to call the front desk and tell them you are ready to move to your room. I ordered your breakfast too. It should be there shortly."

"Well, you are on the ball, aren't you?"

"Yes, I am. Now get going…I have a lot to do today."

"Yes, Ma'am. "I'll be outta your hair in just a few minutes. You don't want me to walk through this hotel naked, do you?"

"No."

"Alright then, call the front desk and I'll get dressed. But one thing before I do."

"What is it, darling?"

"I want to know, do you love me?"

His words stopped me dead in my tracks. I turned to face him, saying, "Yes. Why would you ask me that?"

"Because after all this time and all we have been through, I want to make sure you are marrying me because you love me, not because I love you."

"We love each other. We have always loved each other from the beginning and we will love each other until the end. It's just, I'm not afraid anymore."

"Good. Then we can finally begin."

"Yes, but first you have got to leave. I've got to get going if I'm going to have everything ready for our big day."

"I wish you would let me help," he said, walking back toward the bathroom.

"Diane is here for that."

With a few goodbye kisses and the closing of the door, my day began to speed up. First I made a phone call to the front desk then to Diane who crossed paths with Steven as he made his way to his new suite just two floors down. Then soon we were off and running, attending the last minute details of the wedding.

She began the phone calls as I pulled out my Vera Wang dress to give it space to breathe after being boxed up for so long. It was the most gorgeous gown I had ever laid eyes on. She had made it especially for me and even though it was a rush job you could never tell by looking at it. The style was mermaid with a sweetheart neckline and cap sleeves. We chose an ivory satin, then she and her team of seamstresses embellished it with lace and sequins and beautiful tiny beads that sparkled like diamonds when it was in the light. The back laced up from the top of my hips up to my shoulder blades which accentuated my waist. It had a court train, only about two and a half feet long which I thought was a perfect length given the location and the fact this was going to be a very small and intimate wedding.

Diane surprised me with the most beautiful wedding gift, a cathedral bridal veil. It was ivory, to match the dress and made of tulle with lace appliques. It was simple, just one-tier, a drop style veil. She stood behind me holding the veil on my head while looking at my reflection in the mirror. Then she looked at me in the mirror and smiled.

"What do you think?"

"I think Steven is a very lucky man," she replied, looking over her shoulder at my wedding gown.

"It is beautiful, isn't it?"

"Absolutely gorgeous and you will look so beautiful in it. Thanks for inviting me to come and share this special time with you."

"You know, I wouldn't have it any other way."

"Thanks, girl. Now, I don't mean to end this special moment so quickly but we have got to get a move on. I can see I need to add one more thing to our to-do-list."

"What's that, Diane?"

"Have someone come up here and steam the wrinkles out of your wedding gown."

"Thank God you're here. What would I do without you?"

"Glad to be here. Now, where is that list of yours?"

The day was filled with handling all of the last minute details and taking care of things that I had not even thought about. Steven and George spent the day together visiting the tourist sites and meeting some of the locals. The rehearsal went just as we planned and then the four of us went to a small local restaurant that Steven and George had heard about to have dinner.

After dinner we all walked back to the hotel to have a glass of wine and dessert before calling it a night. Both of our families would be here tomorrow so we decided to part ways early and get some rest. Steven and I lingered after saying goodnight to Diane and George so we could say goodnight privately. We both knew this would be the last time we saw each other before our wedding day. Steven walked me to my suite and after a very long and urgent kiss, he went walking down the hallway as I went inside, closing the door behind me. It was the first time since I said yes to his proposal that I wondered if we were doing the right thing by getting married.

With the beginning of a new day, came the gifts. They seemed to be arriving more frequently as the hours of the morning passed by slowly. There were small boxes, big boxes and baskets full of fruit, food and chocolate. Then there were bouquets of flowers, bottles of wine and champagne with a mounting stack of cards and letters. I had no idea that this many people even knew we were getting married and it made me wonder what was going on back in L.A.

When Diane arrived she began to look at the names on some of the gifts in amazement. Her voice merrily called out in surprise who sent this gift and that bottle of champagne. It was her childlike enthusiasm that kept me from making her stop. And I didn't want her to think I didn't appreciate the gifts, I just felt like this was not the time to deal with them. Then she spoke out a name that stopped me dead in my tracks.

"What did you say?"

"This one is from Steven."

"Will you bring it here?"

"I think you'll have to come over here, honey. It's a little big to move," Diane said, picking up the card and waving me over with it.

"It says...

This gift I bestow...
To the one I love,
And take to wed
To share my life.
May it hold
My words of love...
I promise to write,
All the days of our lives.
Love forever and ever,
Steven (aka: Your Future Husband)"

"What do you think it is?" Diane asked, kneeling down in front of the large box.

"I know what it is. I just wonder what it looks like."

"Well, are you going to keep me in suspense?"

"No, let's open it now."

Kneeling down beside her, I began to untie the white ribbons that encircled the box. Diane began to carefully pull at the taped edges of the beautiful pale pink wrapping paper. I gave her a moment, watching how she seemed intent on keeping the paper in perfect condition then I ripped the other side, making her laugh.

We both opened one side of the box lid, only to expose another thick layer of tissue paper, still hiding the present. She grabbed a handful, tossing it on the floor as I held the box open. After another handful we both gasped at the exquisite beauty our eyes beheld. She took one side and I took the other and we sat the chest on the floor in front of us.

It was wooden, beautifully and skillfully carved by an artist. On the top, in the center was a large Oak Tree. I knew in an instant what that Oak Tree represented and the tears began to well up in my eyes. On the right side was an open book with words of poetry carved with great care. On the left side the masks that represent drama, one happy and one sad. I knew instantly that these carvings were about the poet and the actress. All along the edges were daffodils and roses, creating an elegant border.

The front had a large waterfall in the center with the forest on the left side and a peach orchard on the right. I moved so I could see the right side panel and was happy to see a perfectly wonderful sunset on the beach. How could anyone be so skilled at wood carving to make such a masterpiece was beyond me. I moved to look at the left panel and there it was, the Hollywood hills with the Hollywood sign. Then I moved to the back, it was thick, yet to be carved and I wondered why. Why would Steven go to all this trouble to have this made yet leave the back of it undone?

Diane and I admired the craftsmanship of the piece as I took out the key and opened it. Inside was another card. I started to pick it up but I could see the words written on the outside. *Do not open until our wedding night.* So I gently closed the lid, locked it with the key and put the key in my purse.

The day turned to night and with it came our families, travel weary and hungry. After we all had a chance to say hello each of us went our separate ways for the night. As everyone settled in, room service was delivered so no one would have to be bothered with going out. After dinner, if they chose to, they could have massages in the privacy of their rooms. My hope was they would all spend some time unwinding and get a good night's rest. I wanted everyone to be at their best for the big day.

It was a little strange to find myself alone so early in the night. There was nothing left to do. Nothing left to arrange or order and take care of and I felt restless. I missed Steven like crazy. It had only been one night and a day since I had seen him but it felt much, much longer. I picked up the phone to call but knew that would be breaking my own rule. Then I began to second guess the rule in the first place. Did it really matter if you didn't see each other before the big day?

After a long debate with myself, I finally decided that a massage would also do me good so I called for one. Within thirty minutes, I was face down and all my concerns melted away with each touch of the masseurs' hands. Then just when I was about to drift off further into deep thoughts, the phone rang.

"Hello," I answered, slightly irritated by the interruption.

"I was just about to hang up," Steven said, softly.

"I thought we were not going to see each other."

"I can't see you through the phone."

"I wish I could see you," I said, suddenly full of emotion.

"Tomorrow, my love. I just called to say good night and to see if you got my present."

"I did. It is the most beautiful gift anyone has ever given me but one question. Why didn't you have the back carved?"

"I will. After our children are born and we have a family portrait."

"Okay," I answered, swallowing hard.

"Good night, Love."

"Good night…" Before I could add anything else I heard him hang up. I let the receiver fall out of my hand back to its resting place. Then I thanked the young girl with a generous tip and sent her on her way. It was time for a long bath and then a good night's sleep.

The morning began with the sound of thunder outside my window. I stumbled from bed, pulled back the drapes, looking down onto the street. The rain poured down in sheets while only a few brave souls hurried along with their large black umbrellas shielding their heads from the drenching. When I looked back to the clock, I expected to see perhaps seven or eight but to my astonishment it was already nine-thirty.

The phone was flashing with a red light which indicated that I had a message. I called the front office and in fact, I had three. When I asked why the phone had not rung they explained that someone had placed a do not disturb notice on my room. I knew in an instant that only one person would have been able to do that. It was Steven and even though I was a little upset, I knew he only wanted me to sleep in. So I put a smile on my face and decided that is exactly how I wanted the whole day to be, easy. Then I went and checked the door for a do not disturb sign then went back to the phone to order breakfast.

It was after eleven before anyone dared to ignore the sign on the door. After putting on my robe, I answered the door. I fully expected to see Diane's face but instead it was my sister, Cheryl. She looked beautiful, better than I had seen her look in a long time, I asked her to come in and sit down. She reached out to hug me and I gladly accepted her embrace. We stood in the doorway, hugging for a few moments longer, then she followed me to the sofa.

"So, how was your trip?"

"Very long but totally worth it. This place is awesome, Tiffany. How in the world did you and Steven decide to get married here?"

"I was having a hard time putting things together in L.A. and didn't want to get married in Mississippi then Steven mentioned Italy and that was it. Remember? I did a film here a few years ago."

"Yes, I remember. But you weren't here, were you?"

"No, but Capri is famous for weddings."

"I see someone got you a new chest to put all those love letters in. Let me guess...Victoria?"

"No, it was Steven."

"Well, he better get to writing. Don't you think?"

"He always finds time to write something for me. And I understand you have plans to get married, too?"

"Kenny has been asking me almost from the first week we started dating."

"How long is that?"

"We have been together about a year now."

"Are you going to marry him?"

"I bet that's mom," Cheryl said, going to the door without answering my question.

"Yes, she's here. Come in. Tiff, it's your friend, Diane."

"Good morning," I said, standing up to give her a hug.

"What do you mean morning? It's almost afternoon. It's time to get you in the tub."

"She's right. And it's time to get everything ready for tonight. Do you have your things packed for your honeymoon?"

"Yes, I kept all of that stuff separate and it's already in Florence."

Diane nervously walked toward the window to see if it was still raining. She peered out, saying, "Looks like your luck is good. The rain is tapering off. I'm going to go run you a big warm bath. Okay?"

"Yes, that's fine."

"I'm so excited", Cheryl said in a way that reminded me of her when we were young girls.

"And I'm excited you're here," I said, hearing another knock at the door.

"Now that's gotta be mom," she said, walking back to the door.

My mother made her grand entrance, with her head held high and her eyes taking in the scenery with an air of royalty. I had seen her do this all my life but still it never stopped amazing me how she could make even a place as luxurious as this unable to meet her high standards. I stood, waiting for her to make her way to me, which she did gracefully, taking her time.

"Tiffany, it's so good to see you again, darling," she said slowly, leaning out to kiss my cheek.

"Good to see you too, mom. Thanks for coming. It means a lot to Steven and me for you to be here."

"I would not have missed it for anything. Isn't this the young man you have been involved with all these years?"

"Yes, mom. We have known each other for a long time."

"Well, I am happy that you are finally settling down. Are you going to start a family soon?"

"Are you telling me you're ready to be a grandma?"

"I will never be a grandma, my dear. I have decided to be a Me-Me."

"Come on, Tiffany. It's time for your bath," Diane shouted from the bathroom.

"Coming. Please make yourselves comfortable. I won't be long."

"We'll let you get ready. Be back here in let's say an hour?" Mom asked, standing up.

"To help get you ready," Cheryl added, standing up too.

"Okay, we'll see you two later," Diane answered for me, taking my hand and leading me toward the bathroom.

She shut the door behind me and I took my robe off and stepped into the tub. I sank down in the bubbles, and tried to contain my sheer delight by sighing softly. In the history of the world, I don't think there had ever been a happier bride. Today truly was the beginning of the rest of my life and I could not be more ready for it to begin. Steven was my one true love, my other half, the man of my dreams all rolled into one. Somehow I could see that so clearly now and it made me wonder where was my mind and what was going on in my heart for all of those years?

As I began to wash my body, I felt an urgency to be extra clean. My skin was turning a bright pink but I kept on scrubbing, if only I could get clean enough, I could wash the past away. Besides, I had to be ready to receive my husband, the husband that I had dreamed of when I was a young girl. Slowly, my happiness faded as I found so many faults with my body, with my mind and with my soul. Doubt began to creep in like an old friend that did nothing but get me in trouble. And I had almost convinced myself that there was no way I could go through with it when someone knocked on the bathroom door.

"I don't want to disturb you, but they just brought lunch," Diane told me, through the door.

"I'm really not hungry."

"Tiffany, you need to eat, honey. And I can tell by the sound of your voice, it's time for you to get out of that tub."

"I'm almost finished."

She stuck her head in, smiled and said, "I'm waiting for you."

With one look, she took my mind off the negative and guided me back to the positive. After rinsing off I dried my body, put deodorant and lotion on and slipped on a clean gown. My reflection showed a woman with mixed emotions so I quickly looked away and walked back into the other room to join Diane for lunch.

We had only begun to make our plates when mom and Cheryl came back. After a few minutes of awkward conversation, it suddenly felt like all the tension left the room. Maybe it was the food or Italy or maybe it was just having Diane as a buffer between us. Whatever it was didn't matter. Because it felt like all of my fears and doubt left too as the tension melted away with our laughter and chit-chat.

"Cheryl, will you call down and get someone to clean this up so we can start getting your sister ready?"

"Sure mom, but I could put everything on this table and roll it into the hallway."

"No honey, they have someone to do that. Besides, we need your help," mom answered, looking over at me like I was a project.

"Well, I was thinking that we get her completely ready to go except for the gown. Then we could take turns getting ready and all meet back here to put her gown on right before we leave," Diane added, like she had this all figured out.

"That's exactly what I was thinking except I thought we might all get ready here if that's okay with my daughters," mom said, a little more bossy than normal.

"Okay, someone from room service will be here soon to pick everything up. So, what's first?" Cheryl asked, sitting the receiver down.

"If you and Diane will go and get our things we have decided to all get ready together. Is that okay with you, Tiffany?"

"Yes, I would like that."

"Good, then it's settled."

"We'll be back soon," Diane said, ushering Cheryl out the door and looking at her watch.

"Thank goodness they left."

"Mom!"

"Well, I thought I wouldn't even get a minute alone with you before this evening."

"Oh, I'm sorry."

"Nothing to be sorry about, baby, I just have something I want to give you."

"You didn't have to get me anything."

"I know that. I wanted to."

She pulled a small heart shaped box out of her purse and handed it to me. I looked at it wondering what could be on the inside, knowing it was some kind of jewelry. Mom sat back down on the sofa and I walked over and sat across from her before opening the lid.

"They were your great grandmothers. I thought you could wear it for your something old. You know, something old, something new, something borrowed, something blue. That's if people are still doing that sort of thing these days."

"Thank you. They are so beautiful. I would be honored to wear them," I answered, looking at the diamond and pearl earrings thinking they would look perfect with my wedding gown.

"They are yours to keep. Maybe you can hand them down to your daughter on her wedding day," she said, with an obvious strain in her voice.

"Did you wear them when you married dad?"

"Of course I did, darling."

"Have you seen him yet?"

"Who, your father? Yes, last night I ran into him for a minute or two," she replied, sounding distant and cold again.

"I haven't seen him yet. He left a message for me. Guess I should give him a call."

"That's a good idea. I forgot to get something out of my room. I think I will go down and get it while you make your call."

As Mom was walking out the door, I was surprised to hear her speaking to another woman. When I recognized the voice, I walked back toward them just in time to hear Mom tell Steven's mother good-bye.

She strolled into the room, taking a seat on the sofa before looking directly at me. The smile on my face must have made her uncomfortable because she grimaced and sat up, pulling her shoulders back.

"Well, you won."

I crossed my arms, saying, "I didn't know we were competing."

"There's no need for you to be coy, dear. You are finally getting what you always wanted."

"Mrs. Cross, there is no need to be defensive."

"You're right, Tiffany. And there is no need to beat around the bush. You will never satisfy him. You will never make my son happy. And once he realizes that, you'll be gone…forever, out of his life for good."

"I really don't know what to say to you."

She stood up, smoothing her skirt and said, "There's nothing else to be said."

"Why have you always hated me? I've never done anything to you?"

"Everything you've ever done wrong to Steven, you might as well have done it to me," she said, her voice full of hatred.

"I had hoped you would let bygones be bygones."

"Then you hoped wrong," she said, walking toward the door.

"Why did you even come here?"

"For my son! Certainly not for the likes of you," she snarled, walking out the door.

My heart raced with memories of her unkind words. Now there was no way of denying her distaste for me. Steven had always tried to downplay it to save my feelings. I had always tried to talk myself into believing maybe it was just me. Maybe I was imagining Mrs. Cross wanted me gone, out of his life. Before the tears started to fall, I picked up the phone to call dad. Maybe he could help me make heads or tails of what was happening.

Dad and I barely began to talk when Cheryl and Diane walked back into the suite. They cut our conversation short, not giving me a chance to talk about my future mother-in-law. But after we hung up I was thankful that I hadn't said anything. It would have only upset him too.

There was no reason what so ever to ruin the mood so I bit my tongue, keeping the peace. It was hard, swallowing the mean words she had spoken. It was even harder not to share them with Cheryl and Diane. And if it would have done any good, we would have talked about it until it was time for me to walk down the aisle. That's when I became determined that the old witch was not going to ruin my day. I didn't care what she did or what she said. Besides, she was right. I did win. Which meant she was the loser.

After I had my mind made up, things began to move very quickly. First they did my hair, then makeup and finally my fingernails and toenails. While they were drying and I couldn't do anything but sit still, Mom went to my room and began getting ready. Then Diane looked at her watch and grabbed her stuff and headed for the bathroom. Cheryl sat down across from me, folded her arms and began tapping her foot on the floor like she couldn't stand waiting for her turn.

My eyes closed as I snuggled back against the softness of the over-sized chair. The tapping of Cheryl's heel on the hardwood floor had a nice soothing rhythm to it and it made me feel calm and sleepy. If my mind hadn't been wondering so wildly I could have easily taken a cat nap. But before I could completely drift away my mother's voice had me sitting straight up again.

"Tiffany, are you sleeping?"

"No, I was just thinking."

"What do you think of this dress?"

Not once in my entire life could I ever remember my mom asking me if I liked her outfit. So I shook my head, trying to shake off my sleepiness and said, "Yes, you look very nice."

"You don't sound so sure of yourself," mom answered, pointing toward the door, indicating to Cheryl it was time for her to go and change.

"Sorry, guess I was drifting a little. You really do look good and that color is perfect with your skin."

"Thank you for saying so. You can't imagine how many dresses I tried on before I found this one."

"It's Tiffany time," Diane sang, as she strolled into the room.

"I know. Guess I'll put my slip on first then the shoes. How much time do we have?

"About half an hour," Mom said, looking at the clock.

Between the three of them, I was dressed, laced up, made up, bedazzled, looking like I had twice as much hair on my head and smelling like a rose. Mom stood back, admiring my wedding gown and had to take out her handkerchief. Diane never slowed down, she just kept making sure everything was taken care of and that nothing, not one last little detail had been overlooked.

Cheryl began to show that little green monster that lived deep down inside her. All of the attention I received from Mom made her so uncomfortable that she squirmed in her seat. It reminded me of Mrs. Cross and her wonderful blessing she had given earlier. Now, it all felt so dream-like that I simply let my emotions flow like the tide of the ocean. Not the least bit of animosity came from within me as I waited peacefully for the last few minutes before I would say I do.

We made it down to the car that would take us to the church without a single problem. I listened to the sounds of the small town and to the voices in the car but my mind was very far away. There was a boy waiting for me. It was the boy I fell so deeply in love with so many years ago that waited for me. It was the only boy who had ever truly loved me and he was waiting for me in a man's body.

As the car pulled to the front of the beautiful Church of Santa Sofia, I looked at the inviting and happy yellow building. The church was steeped in history, being originally built in 1510, that I could feel the energy when I stepped out of the car. There were several local women to greet us and then they led us to a small room near the entrance for us to wait for the ceremony to begin.

It was only a few minutes before mom and Cheryl left Diane and me to take their seats inside. And only a few more seconds before dad came in with big hugs for both of us. Tears welled up in his eyes which caused me to cry. The older Italian women that were still in the room with us did not approve and handed us both handkerchiefs. They were shaking their heads no and speaking a language neither of us understood but we understood that was not acceptable.

"Must be bad luck to cry before the wedding," dad said, drying his eyes and trying to hand back the handkerchief which the woman refused to take back.

"Then let's stop. I don't need any bad luck."

"I know I have told you how beautiful you are so many times, Tiffany, but you are the most beautiful bride I have ever seen. I hope you will both be happy. I feel so blessed to be here, to share this time with you."

"I'm glad you're here, dad."

"I still brought you a little something but I figured your mom would give you the earrings and I was right. Everybody gets new things for their weddings but I figured you hadn't thought of anything blue," he said, pulling a small piece of blue cloth from his shirt pocket.

It was a brilliant blue and as I unfolded it, I realized it was a small handkerchief. It was embroidered with small white daises and little red hearts. I held it up to my eye, to wipe away the last tear, saying, "Thanks, dad. I will keep it forever."

"I love you, Tiffany. I'll see you in just a few minutes to walk you down the aisle."

"Okay. I love you, too," I whispered, hugging him before he turned to leave.

"Let's see…where shall we put this? Oh, I know. I brought safety pins just in case. Let's pin it to your slip. Sound good?" Diane asked.

"Yes, that sounds good," I said, as she took the small piece of blue cloth from my hand and got down on her knees to lift up my gown and pin it onto my slip.

Right when she finished, there was a small knock on the door. The Italian women motioned for me and Diane to come, it was time. It was about six o'clock on Saturday September 20, 2003, almost exactly six months since Steven had asked me to marry him. I stood behind Diane, took three deep breaths and told her I was ready. She turned, kissed my cheek and walked out the door first. One of the ladies held it open for me and dad was standing with his arm out for me to take. I slid my hand under his arm as we began to walk toward the sanctuary.

There was a young girl standing to my right who handed me a bouquet of flowers. Beautiful white roses and small daises bound up with peach and white ribbons filled my right hand. Dad stopped, right when the wedding march began, kissed my cheek and then lifted the upper veil up and over my face. He held his arm out again as Diane turned and began to walk down the long aisle.

Everything seemed like a dream as dad and I slowly walked forward. There was another young girl motioning for us to slow down and then to come forward. We turned to make our entrance and everyone stood up, looking back. I was surprised to see the entire room full of people and in an instant I knew what Steven had been doing while we were apart. It looked like nearly every man, woman and child from this small town lined the pews with their nicest clothes on and their most inviting smiles. I couldn't help but giggle when I thought of Steven and George in Italy, inviting people who they couldn't even speak to, to come to this wedding.

"Are you ready?"

"I'm ready, dad."

"Me too," he said, taking one final glance at me, giving me a smile then taking a step forward.

Steven was far away but not too far for me to see his very black tux fit his body like a glove. His face was beaming with pride as all eyes were on his bride and his bride's eyes were only focused on him. The pews were decorated just as Diane and I had asked, white roses, tiny daises with white and peach satin ribbons to match my bouquet. The arches in the church were brilliant and majestic, casting shadows in the most mysterious ways. The sunset cast shimmering light through the stained glass windows that caught my attention as we slowly made our progression toward my groom. Then it was the ceiling, with its awesome frescos painted with such love and care. I only looked up a moment or two for fear of falling but even in those brief seconds, I could see angels and one was a picture of Christ.

We drew closer and the music grew louder as familiar faces came into view. Mom, Cheryl, and George sat to my left, along with a few familiar faces from the hotel staff. To the right was Victoria, who waved when she saw me and Steven's mom and dad. Then I looked straight ahead, only to be caught in those unforgettable hazel eyes staring back at me. Blake and Diane were there but I only saw their forms not their faces. All of my concentration was on Steven, the look on his face and in his eyes. They welled up with tears as my dad stopped, kissed my cheek through the veil and walked back to sit beside my mom.

He reached out his hand, which I took and we stood before the priest together waiting for the music to stop. Everyone sat down in the pews and Steven squeezed my hand gently. The ceremony began and we both followed the instructions given to us. Words were exchanged, then a ring for him and a ring for me. With all eyes upon us, we took individual candles and lit a unity candle together, as a sign of our two lives becoming one. Then with the lifting of my veil and one very special kiss, we were announced husband and wife, both in English and in Italian.

As we walked forward, the entire church stood to their feet and began to clap. Then everyone began to file out of the pews behind us, cheering us on and following us out into the square. A beautiful red convertible sports car sat out front with a waiting driver beckoning us to get in. Steven went first and then helped me get in and sit down. The square was full of on lookers and the many guests from the wedding. As we drove away slowly, the crowd began to follow behind us on foot and the bell towers rang out in a musical melody.

We were followed by the kind people of Capri the entire distance between the church of Santa Sofia and the hotel. Once there, we were greeted by several members of the hotel staff as though we were royalty. I held Steven's arm as we followed the staff members to the reception. And what seemed like half of the town, with a few of our family members and friends, followed behind us.

Two smiling men opened the double doors to reveal a vision I had only seen in my mind. Beautiful white flowers of every shape and size seemed to be not only on every table but in every place they could be. The contrast of all the greenery against the white flowers made it feel almost like we had walked into a garden. However, it wasn't a garden, it was a luxurious, gorgeous room in the fanciest hotel I had ever been to in my life.

The dance floor was directly in the center of the room. A stage was set up on the edge of the floor at the far side of the room. Several band members were already sitting at attention, waiting to begin the music on cue. Steven and I were led to two large chairs where we sat down to greet our many guests.

Steven leaned over, whispering in my ear, "I had to do something to keep myself occupied."

"I guess that's when you invited everyone from Capri, to our wedding?"

"I just wanted to show you off. You didn't buy that expensive dress just for me, did you?"

"No, well yes, I guess kind of."

"Make up your mind, Love."

"Stop picking on me."

"Okay," he said, taking my hand to kiss it.

More and more people filled the room as the band begin to softly play. Our family and friends were all seated at a large rectangle table and I could see where Steven and I would sit. His mother glared at me, rolling her eyes but all I did was smile. Then the locals began to take their seats at the many beautifully decorated round tables. I looked around realizing that soon it would be standing room only and that's when waiters came into the room, carrying large trays of food.

We took our seats and dad went up to the stage. The band stopped playing and a very short and bald man went up on stage and stood beside him to translate. Dad waited for the crowd to quiet down, looked over at me and winked then cleared his throat.

"Good evening ladies and gentlemen. Thank you for coming to celebrate this blessed event with me, my family and our friends. I hope you feel welcomed because we all greatly appreciate your presence here tonight."

Dad paused, waiting for his words to be translated. After the short bald man finished speaking, the crowd roared with approval, words that only an Italian speaking person can understand, and clapping. Dad nodded his head waiting for enough silence to speak again.

"God has blessed me with a son. This is something I have waited for my entire life. And He gave me the son I wanted, the son I prayed for…," he choked up, stopping to gain his composure but before he could finish, the translator started speaking.

"Everyone, please bow your head. Lord, please bless this food for our bodies, we are thankful for Your gifts. Bless everyone here, Lord. And most of all bless Steven and Tiffany and let them have a very long and happy marriage."

Dad sat back down after kissing my cheek and shaking Steven's hand. The band started playing beautiful soft music as we began to eat. Waiters seemed to be moving in every direction. They were pouring wine, water, and making sure everyone had what they needed.

After we finished our meal, everyone was taking turns on stage, making toasts. Even Steven's mom took a turn, surprising us with her heartfelt words of encouragement. Cheryl was the funny one, bringing up our first date and our great fashion sense. Victoria and Blake took the stage together and needless to say their toast was more like a train wreck than words of wisdom. It was Diane that rounded out the toasts and of course hers was very well planned. They were also the words that really hit home and made me realize marriage was not a sprint but a marathon.

It was time to cut the cake, I couldn't wait for them to bring it into the room. When I had shown Diane a picture of what it would look like she asked why in the world would I want a five tier layered cake at such a small wedding. I didn't have a very good answer but now I was happier than ever that I had ordered such a monstrous cake. It was vanilla and cream, two of his favorite flavors. I just knew it was going to blow Steven's mind when he saw it and when he tasted it, it would be like a little slice of heaven in his mouth.

Steven stopped a waiter that was walking by our table and he walked over to the stage. Then I noticed several other waiters talking and they all started walking very fast out of the room. I wondered what Steven had up his sleeve and how he stopped them from bringing in my big cake surprise. A few moments later, a man handed Steven a microphone and he stood up.

As the room began to quiet down, he leaned over whispering in my ear, "I love you, Tiffany."

Kissing his neck I said, "I love you, too."

"I have waited a lifetime to say this and now is the moment."

"What?" I asked, but knew he would not answer that question directly to me. He would show me.

"I would like to thank you all for coming tonight. I know it was short notice and you are all so very gracious and kind to be here with Tiffany and I as we begin our lives together. I would also like to thank the Grand Hotel Quisiana for sheltering us and the Church of Santa Sofia for marrying us and the restaurant Rendez Vouz for feeding us. Now, that I have properly thanked everyone, I have something very important to say. I have waited an entire lifetime to introduce you to the love of my life, my soul mate, my everything. This is my wife, Mrs. Steven Cross."

He took my hand and helped me stand up in recognition of the loud applause. He put his hand around my back and onto my waist, pulling me closer. We turned, giving each other a kiss, which only made the applause grow louder. Then we hugged, while the crowd began to settle down.

"I have a little something I want to read to my bride. It's not a toast," he said pulling the piece of paper from his pocket, unfolding it.

"You walked into the room
and thus began a boyhood dream.
We played our roles so perfectly,
young and in love
so sure the world would be ours.
You walked out of my life…
and I followed a few steps behind,
never losing sight
of what I would never find… again.
You pursued your dreams
and I watched you fly,
only wanting to be the wind
that would keep you safe and high.
You turned back to me…
barely in the nick of time…
to save me from the misery
of desperately wanting you
for the rest of my life."

There was silence in the room. His words had created an imaginary canvas that a masterpiece had been painted on that held everyone's attention. Or perhaps it was more like a trance had fallen over their minds and thoughts. Most of them, I presumed, didn't even know what he had said but I guess emotion translates regardless of what language you speak. I, too, was left without words. This person standing in front of me had never ceased to amaze me with his talent to write poetry. He was the poet of my heart and for lack of anything better to do, I began to clap. The whole room followed my lead and everyone turned their attention from Steven to the beautiful wedding cake as it was brought into the room.

We walked over, hand and hand, as a young lady handed Steven the knife and I placed my hand on top of his. Cameras were flashing away as we cut into the first layer. Together we finished cutting it and put it on a plate without too much of a mess. Then we followed tradition and fed each other a generous portion, making sure to get a little icing on each other's face.

While our guests enjoyed wedding cake, another waiter poured us a glass of champagne. We took another cliché picture of intertwining our arms to drink the bubbly substance. It was the first moment since we had said I do that I really got to look into his eyes. And it was the first time in my life that I would see the pride that another human being had for me, besides my mom and dad. That one look reaffirmed that I had done the right thing by writing Steven the letter that had brought us to this special day.

One of the musicians announced in English and Italian it was time for our first dance. We walked to the center of the dance floor, turned to face each other. Steven took my hand and put his other arm around me and placed his hand on my lower back. Then I realized the one thing I forgot to do, pick out a song.

"You can wipe that worried look off your face," he said, reassuring me with his eyes.

"But I forgot…"

"I know, they asked me what to do so that's why the band will be sitting this one out."

The instant the music began, I knew the song he had picked. So sweetly the voice came through the speakers that moved our feet around the dance floor while everyone watched.

The first time….ever I saw your face. I thought the sun rose in your eyes and the moon and the stars were the gifts you gave to the dark and the end of the skies. And the first time…ever I kissed your mouth. I felt the earth move in my hand like the trembling heart of a captive bird that was there at my command, my love. And the first time…ever I lay with you. I felt your heart so close to mine and I knew our joy would fill the earth and last, till the end of time, my love….

It was as though we were completely alone even though many eyes were watching our every move. When the melody ended, we stopped dancing and stood staring into each other's eyes. My tears were falling as one beautiful tear fell from his left eye and found its way down his cheek. I pulled him closer, kissing his lips with great emotion. As soon as our lips parted, there was the familiar sound of happiness and applause.

The band played several songs, some in English and some in Italian. Steven and I didn't care what language it was as we danced. We danced with each other, we danced with our family, and we danced with strangers. It was a great time of celebration and we were happy to dance and sing and laugh.

Diane interrupted me and dad, asking me to come with her to the bathroom. I knew it was time but I asked her to wait until the song was over. She stood by the double doors and patiently held my bag in her hands.

When the song ended, I told Diane, "I know I'm late but I want to throw my bouquet first."

"See, that's why they say two heads are better than one. I totally forgot about doing that. And is Steven going to throw the garter?"

"I think so," I said, turning to see if I could spot him."

"I see him, just go back to your table and I will get everything ready. Your honeymoon will have to wait a little longer," she said, teasing me with every word.

Diane was a wiz at making things happen and even better at making them happen quickly. In no time, Steven and I were in the middle of the dance floor. He was helping me lift my gown up for him to take a beautiful lace garter from my left thigh.

He lifted it high above his head twirling it around as all the bachelors gathered in a circle. Dad came over to help him, and Steven asked why he wasn't joining the single men. He laughed, gently guided Steven until his back was to the crowd and told him to throw it hard. Men jumped and scrambled in every direction trying to catch the small piece of lace and elastic. In the end, it was his brother Blake who came out with it, smiling as though he had just made a touchdown in football.

Diane came, handing me the large bouquet of roses and daises and took the chair away. The single ladies began to gather in front of me in all shapes and sizes. I was not surprised to see Victoria standing right in front, telling me to throw it to her. But I was surprised to see my mom, standing almost dead center, smiling as though she was having the time of her life. Diane came back to help guide me but I told her to join the crowd which brought the whole room alive with laughter and coaxing. After she was ready, I turned my back to the ladies, closed my eyes and gave it a good toss. It was one of the local Italian girls who caught the flowers and she rushed up, giving me a big hug and kiss on the cheek.

Diane and I quickly went to the restroom and she helped me get out of my wedding gown. I put on a very elegant peach colored dress for our trip to the honeymoon suite in Florence, Italy. We would be staying at The Saint Regis, a world famous hotel, known for its romantic setting and outstanding service.

"Don't worry about anything. I'll make sure everything gets back to California safely. Including all of your unexpected wedding presents from your unexpected guests," she added, sounding a little perplexed.

"I can get somebody from the hotel to take care of it."

"No, I want to do it for you."

"You are so good to me…and Steven."

"That's what friends are for, Tiffany."

"Then thank God you're my friend."

"You look beautiful but you're running late. You'll need to make your good-byes short and sweet."

"Do you think a wave will do?"

"Yes, and maybe a few hugs," she said holding the door open, hugging me with one arm.

"Thanks again, Diane. I couldn't have done this without you."

"You're welcome. Now go have fun with your husband."

We walked back to the reception room and Steven was standing on stage, waving at me to come up and join him. I took my time, giving everyone who was near, a hug, kiss or handshake. He watched me with admiration and helped me step up on stage while complimenting my new dress.

"We would like to say good night and farewell. We enjoyed having you here tonight and hope everyone had a good time. We hate for this evening to end but we must be on our way to Florence," Steven said, waving goodbye and pulling me behind him, off the stage.

Dad hugged us goodbye and wished us luck. The crowd parted and we walked out the door, into the hallway. The noise faded as we walked with a young man to the elevator and got inside. Steven turned and pulled me into the corner, kissing me as we went higher and higher. The ding of the elevator door stopped us, then the night air invited us to step out. I could hear the distant roar of the helicopter and felt giddy about our flight to Florence.

Steven helped me get on board and buckle up. It was only a few minutes later and we were ready to go. I sat back, took a deep breath as Steven loosened the tie on his tux. It was hard for me to ever remember him looking sexier than he did at this very moment. I pulled him closer by the ends of his neck tie and kissed him, to send a very distinct message. After this kiss he would know I wanted him and could barely wait to be in Florence, to be in his arms, and to be in our honeymoon bed.

Chapter 9

Florence at night, from the seat of a helicopter, is a spectacular sight to see. There were so many large buildings, businesses and homes compacted so closely together and a large river running through it that I began to wonder if I chose the right place for us to spend our honeymoon. Steven seemed full of interest and intrigue as the pilot was giving us an impromptu tour of some of the area attractions. It's not that I wasn't interested. I just couldn't help but think that I wish he would just stop talking. We were here to enjoy each other and the beginning of our lives together, not go sightseeing.

Finally, we landed and just outside the helicopter door, on the outskirts of the landing pad sat a black limousine. Steven and I half ran and half walked to the car and as the driver opened the door we got inside. He barely shut the door when both of us at the same time turned to kiss. It felt like we were drawn, by some strange magnetic force, to press our lips to the others.

"I could barely wait until we were alone," he whispered, while kissing my neck.

"And I thought I was the only one who felt that way," I said, kissing my way up to his ear.

"Now why would you say that?" He asked, not giving me a chance to respond before kissing my mouth again.

"Because...," I mustered out between kisses, "you were so interested in the pilot."

"Oh contraire, my sweet. My only interest is in you," he spoke softly, changing his voice while unbuttoning the top button on my dress.

"I am so ready to make love to my husband."

"I was wondering when you were going to call me that," he said, kissing his way down my chest into my cleavage.

"Now you know," I answered, leaning back, laying my leg across his lap.

His hand slid up the length of my leg, resting on the top of my thigh as he slipped a finger under my garter belt, "Tonight, I make you mine....forever."

"Sounds like you have big plans for me, lover boy."

"I am going to make love to you all night and then," he paused, kissing my lips, neck and chest before saying, "and I am never going to stop making love to you, not ever."

"So when we're sixty?"

"Still be making love."

"And when we're seventy?"

"Yes, I'm still going to make love to you."

"What about when we turn eighty?"

"If there is any way, I will still be making love to you, Tiffany."

"I hope we make it there to find out," I said, taking his hand into mine.

"You know, there are many ways a husband can make love to his wife."

"Really?"

"Yes," he said, pulling me up to sit across his lap. "He can take her to exotic locations and admire the color of her eyes. He can cook her dinner and clean the kitchen while she relaxes. And he can buy her beautiful jewelry."

"Well, you do have a point, Mr. Cross," I said, watching his expression as he spoke of making love without ever laying a finger on me.

"And the wonder of it all is why it took so long for me to get that point across to you," he said, turning me until I was sitting between his legs.

"Glad you finally did," I said, between moans, as he opened my legs with both hands placed between my knees and upper thighs.

Closing my eyes, I turned my head back and caught his mouth open to my kiss. His hand moved up my thigh as his tongue moved with perfection, dancing with mine. Then we were lost, in each other's arms as the driver weaved his way through the Italian streets of Florence to our hotel, The St. Regis.

Greeting us in broken English was a gentleman, dressed in a most unusual uniform at the front entrance of the hotel. We stepped out of the car, feeling the swift breeze that blew toward us from Fiume Arno River that was just a few steps away. As the tails of his long jacket whipped in the wind, Steven tried to shield me from the wind and I held my dress down with both hands while walking inside.

Another gentleman greeted us inside the door, handing me a bouquet of flowers and giving Steven a gift box wrapped in white paper with a big, stunning red bow. The inside of the hotel was glamorous and shiny with its marble floors, high ceilings and sensual lighting. It felt like we had walked onto a movie set of a romantic film and Steven and I were the stars of the show. Several staff members bid us hello and congratulations with smiles and happiness. The young man who had given us presents beckoned us toward the elevator and it opened, right on cue as we approached.

We reached the top floor and the doors of the elevator opened onto a hallway. Steven and I followed the smiling young man down the hall holding hands. He reached out, opening the door while using his other hand to beckon us inside with a bow of his head.

The suite was just as I remembered from the pictures. It was elegantly decorated with lavish furnishings that you would see inside a castle or a mansion. In fact, it looked more like a mansion than it did a hotel room. As he gave us a tour of where we would be staying for the next two weeks I noticed a few unusual things. There were extravagantly wrapped gifts in every room. Fresh flowers that followed the theme of our wedding were also adorning every table in each room. In the bathroom and bedroom were large baskets full of gifts. But to me, the most unusual thing was the sheer white lace nightgown I had planned to wear that evening was laid across the bed with a long stem white rose on top of it. It was not the first time my bags had been unpacked for me but how would anyone have known that was the gown I had chosen to wear tonight?

When the bellman left Steven closed and locked the door, turning to look at me. He smiled, closed his eyes and took a deep breath. I sat down on the sofa and patted the seat beside me where I wanted him to sit down. He tilted his head and strolled over, picking up the red box before sitting down.

"What do you think is in there?"

"Let's see. It must be from the hotel because there isn't a card," he said examining the outside.

"Open it."

"Yes, Ma'am."

"Look at that, baby," I said, reaching over to pull one of the huge chocolate covered strawberries from the box.

"If you give me a moment, I'll open a bottle of champagne."

Before Steven got up, he turned toward me and kissed my lips with passion and fire. He moved to stand and I pulled him back down kissing him again with the same intensity. For a moment, I thought we would not get to taste the fruit of the bubbly but he resisted my grasp and walked over to the table where he lifted the bottle out of the ice.

"We have time, Love. There is no need to hurry."

"Let me get the glasses," I replied, as he popped the top off the bottle with a loud bang.

He poured us both a glass as I went to sit back down. I picked up a strawberry, ready to put it in his mouth. His eyes drew me in as I took my glass of champagne from his hand. I lifted the berry to his mouth and he bit off the end, staring into my eyes as he did. I put it to the edge of my lips and pressed it just inside my mouth, keeping his gaze as I took a small bite. I sat the berry down and we lifted our glasses.

"To my beautiful wife...may we always be this happy every day and night for the rest of our lives."

"I am your wife."

"Yes, and I am your husband."

"I will drink to that."

We brought our glasses to our mouths and drank to each other. Steven got up to move the ice and champagne closer to where we were sitting. I walked over to the window, pulled back the drapes to look outside. Down below was the Fiume Arno River, still alive with people, lights and boats. I turned to look at my husband because I could feel his eyes watching my every move. He lifted my newly filled glass, inviting me to come back to his side.

"Is it okay if I take a short bath before we go to bed?"

"Of course, baby. Why would you ask?'

"I don't know."

"We have plenty of time, no need to hurry."

"Do you want to get in with me?"

"I would love that."

"I'll go start the bath," I said, kissing his cheek and picking up my glass.

"I've got the champagne. I'm right behind you," he said, caressing my behind.

We lay in each other's arms in the enormous bathtub with millions of bubbles. Very few words were exchanged as we both finished off the bottle of champagne and enjoyed the warmness of the water and the touch of wet skin on skin. He helped me out of the tub because I was feeling a little tipsy. He wrapped a towel around my body and began to dry his. I opened the door, ushering him out so I could put on my nightgown.

"I'll be waiting for you," he said, through the closing door.

"I'll be right out," I replied, starting to dry off.

The moment we had been waiting for since we were teenagers had finally arrived. For the first time in our lives we would be making love as husband and wife. In my mind I had always imagined it to be in a fury of rush and passion. But this was completely opposite. I felt nervous and I could tell Steven was too. It was strange how this time it was so personal and intimate. We had made love so many times before but this was different. It was special and I wanted to make it memorable. For a moment I felt awkward because I didn't realize I would feel so unprepared. All of the hours spent on planning the wedding and not once did I think about the wedding night, other than this night gown.

When I saw my reflection in the mirror, I smiled. The jitters were gone and I knew I was ready to receive whatever Steven had to give. And I knew he was ready to receive my love. From behind the bathroom door I could hear music and I looked into my eyes one last time before walking out. In the mirror, I saw a woman ready to make love to her husband, for the very first time.

He was lying across the bed at an angle watching me walk toward him. His eyes lit up when I smiled and he smiled back, moving his head from side to side. I stopped, short of the bed and shrugged my shoulders as if to ask what.

"You are the most beautiful woman I have ever seen, Tiffany Cross."

"You're not looking bad yourself, Mr. Cross," I replied, climbing up on the bed, into his arms.

As we kissed, he rolled me over onto my back. His lips never left mine as he slowly undressed me. His body was already bare and now we were touching each other from head to toe with nothing between us. He moved down my body, using his lips to prepare me for his love. Closing my eyes, I completely let go of every thought, purely feeling his touch and living in the moment.

After kissing his way back up my body, I opened my eyes to look at his face. There was such a calmness and gentleness to the way we were making love that it gave me a sense of floating on air. He pulled my arm up, placing it on the back of his neck as he positioned his body over mine. He stopped short and touched my face until I looked at him again.

Steven kissed me gently, held his body above mine, looking into my eyes. Slowly he moved until we were one again, never looking away from my eyes. It was then that I felt a tear fall to my face and I eagerly lifted my head to kiss his lips. Our eyes closed at the same time and the movement of our bodies intensified. We were on a ride that was completely of our own making. Almost like addicts, we were each other's drug of choice. He took his time, making sure I was high on his love before he gave me any relief, allowing me to melt into his arms. Then he held me so close, so tight, as if he were afraid I might vanish, I held on to him as tightly as he held me. Then I drifted, after the long day, from thought to thought remembering all that had happened, occasionally tingling inside.

Then it was like a dream, a very good dream. A very strong and handsome man was lifting me up into his arms and gently laying me back down onto my side. Then he laid down beside me touching my body with his strong hands from my waist down to my ankles. Rolling over onto my stomach I stretched out, yawning and again felt the pressure of hands on the back of my thighs. Then just as I realized I wasn't dreaming, lips pressed in on the back of my neck as Steven's body pressed against mine.

In a moment, he was inside of my mind and body, whispering of his love and desires. As the sleepiness left my body I crawled to my knees as he lifted his body keeping pace with mine. I was no longer silent, even though my eyes remained closed, he knew the pleasure I felt from his touch. We were deep, deep in love and our bodies needed another dose of the drug the other gave to it. His strong grip on my hips gave me another reason to verbally explain the way he made me feel. And just when I felt I couldn't hold on a moment longer, we both reached the peak of ecstasy at the same moment, collapsing onto the bed.

After covering me with his body like a blanket for a long time, he rolled over pulling me up on his shoulder. I placed my head where he could hold me and put my leg over his. His arm wrapped around me and pulled me even closer to his body with a soft moan. My other hand found its way to his cheek, then to his lips which he gladly kissed. Then we drifted off to sleep in each other's arms, completely content and satisfied.

Then it was the familiar feeling of too much to drink that woke me up. My dizzy head made it a little hard to steer my body straight to the bathroom but I made it just in time. When I walked back to the bed, Steven was gone. I looked around and saw him standing behind me by the door.

"Wait for me right there," he said firmly.

"Right here?" I asked sitting on the bed.

"No, stand back up. I'll be right back," he said, going into the bathroom.

My feet hit the floor and my arms stretched high in the air over my head. I yawned a big loud yawn, feeling very naked. I turned back toward the bed, looking for my gown and Steven snuck up behind me, grabbing me by the waist from behind.

"Mmmm, baby...I do love those muscles of yours," I said, leaning my head back on his shoulder.

"And I love everything about you, Tiffany," he said, pulling me back into him.

Arching my back, he slid his hands down my waist onto my hips. He gripped them tightly, making me moan out loud. In an instant we were one again and I didn't hold back my feelings anymore. I told him how he made me feel. I told him what he was doing to me. I told him how much I loved him. How I had loved him all my life and how I would never stop loving him.

He made it difficult not to talk, moan and even squeal with delight. If he was my drug, certainly this was my first overdose. I felt like he needed to stop but those words never left my mouth because I was afraid he would listen. If I could have handled it I would have begged him to never stop making love to me.

It was reaching the point of no return when he let go of my right hip and stepped backward, pulling me back with his left hand by the hip. Then he pushed my head down toward the bed making me lean forward. If there was any way for him to quicken the pace he certainly did and within just a few minutes we were both breathing hard and calling out each other's names. Sweat was dripping from his body onto mine and my body was wet with its own sweat.

We separated only to fall down upon the bed, trying to catch our breath. We were laying sideways, holding hands until I rolled onto my side to kiss his stomach. He touched my back, wet with sweat and leaned over to get me a pillow. I rested my head on one side, turning over with my back to him. A minute later he rolled onto his side putting his head on the other side of the pillow and his hand over my waist. Then everything faded as sleep took over again.

Steven was holding me and true to his word, he was making love to me all night long. We were still on our sides, as he gently kissed my neck and touched my breasts, arousing me out of sleep. I started to turn over but he slid his left hand under my body and held onto my stomach, keeping me in the same position. Then down my body his right hand touched and caressed my skin until it found the spot it wanted to be.

My breath became quicker with each touch of his fingers. His mouth began to kiss every part of me it could find with more and more fever. His tongue tickled my flesh as his hand prepared me for love. My legs parted to his will and once again we were making love. This time it was slow and easy as he held onto my lower stomach with his left hand and my right hip with his other hand.

"I want to make love to you every night," he said, kissing my neck.

"And every day?" I asked, reaching behind me to pull him closer.

"Yes, and every day. I want to make love to you in every way a man can make love to a woman," he replied, burying his head into my hair, pushing against me harder.

"And I want you to. Please don't ever stop making love to me," I pleaded with him as he held onto me tightly.

"I promise, I will never stop..."

Slowly we climbed together, higher and higher, our love being our guide. Time was irrelevant, neither was reaching the end of our mission. The only goal was being one. He was inside of me, in my heart, in my soul and I was his girl, completely and totally his girl. I had given myself to him willingly, he had accepted me and in return given himself to me. We had given each other a new beginning. As the sun began to filter through the draperies announcing a new day, we were beginning our new lives with the hope of a bright new future as husband and wife.

10
Chapter

The room was bathed in light, seeping through the open draperies. My legs automatically kicked the cover off as my temperature began to rise. Soon my eyes focused on the empty space in front of me. Then I reached behind me, fully expecting to feel Steven. Rolling onto my back, still laying sideways on the bed, I searched for his form but saw nothing. I sat up, looking out the door of the bedroom only to see even more light in the other room. Then I glanced at the clock, shocked by what I saw and jumped up out of bed to go to the bathroom.

Quickly, I washed my face and brushed my hair and put on a little make-up. Then I tiptoed to the closet to put on a dress. When I entered the living room section of our suite, I noticed that food had been delivered but it appeared untouched. The door to the balcony was slightly ajar so I crept up to it and peered out. My husband was sitting with his back to the sun, looking out toward the river and tapping his pen upon a pad of paper.

"Never in a million years would I have dreamed I would wake up alone this morning."

"You didn't, Love. You didn't wake up at all this morning. Good afternoon," he answered, charming me with his words.

"Well, I was awake this morning. In fact someone barely let me sleep all night long," I said, moving his paper onto the table to sit in his lap.

"I am a man of my word."

"That you are, Mr. Cross."

"So…how is Mrs. Cross this afternoon?" He asked, leaning back, pulling me with him and holding me like a baby.

"I'm happy."

He reached up, stroking my cheek with the back of his hand. We reached for each other, kissing deeply then hugged each other tightly. There was no need for words. The cool September breeze of the Florence afternoon made our embrace even more meaningful. His love for me came through his touch as I became putty in his strong hands.

"Why did you leave me in bed?"

"I had to write the words, darling. Remember?"

"Remember what?"

He touched the end of my nose playfully then traced my lips with his fingertip more seriously, saying, "You inspire me."

"Will you read it to me?"

"Yes. Will you sit beside me so I can see your face?"

Closing my eyes, I kissed his mouth one last time before moving to get up. He pulled me back, hugging me hard like it had been forever since the last time he had seen me. It was strange how he had just asked me to sit beside him yet he didn't seem to want to let me go. When I relaxed and just waited for his signal he relaxed and helped me get up and sit down across from him so we were face to face.

"How can words begin to describe the way I see you,
the way I behold you in my mind's eye?
You are my purpose for living this life.
You are the reason I wake up after night.
Yours is the soul that's the mate to mine.
I am certain God brought us together,

to share in this very moment in time.
You are my life…my princess and my world.
I've fallen madly in love…
because now… you… are my girl.
You are the only one for me,
my beloved destiny…
whom I will cherish
now… and throughout eternity."

"Can I have this one?"

"Of course," he said, pulling the piece of paper from the pad and handing it to me.

"I will put this in the chest you gave me."

"Are you ready for some brunch?"

"Yes, I'm starving," I said, walking toward the door.

He walked up behind me quickly and stopped me by wrapping his arms around my waist. "Do you remember making love on the balcony in Texas?"

"How could I ever forget?"

"Tonight…we make love on a balcony in Italy," he said, releasing me from his grasp.

"I can hardly wait," I replied, walking inside with him right on my heels.

We sat down beside each other and began to fill our plates full of delicious food. He poured water into our glasses of melting ice and handed me a napkin for my lap. After bowing our heads for a small prayer of thanks we dug in. Our appetites were hearty and our words were few. Occasionally he would put his hand on my knee or squeeze my hand between bites. It reminded me of when we were in high school and he would take me out to eat. Even back then he could not stop touching me, even when we were eating.

We finished brunch and he went to draw a bath while I took a moment to pick out clothes for the day. After a very long and sensual bath, Steven and I dressed in casual clothes. He called for a limo and we made our way down to the lobby. Several people working at the hotel stopped to speak, asking how we were doing and telling us congratulations.

When the limo arrived, a young man escorted us outside, opening the door. We gazed out onto the Fiume Arno River, with its many boats and lively people traveling its waters. The sun broke free of the clouds, pouring light down upon the streets as we turned back into the city. After a few turns and twists down the winding roads we stopped at our destination.

Boboli Gardens had caught our attention months ago as we researched where to stay in Florence for the honeymoon. We learned it has a lot of sculptures, some dating back to the 16th century. The Italian style gardens were full of statues and fountains, some semi-private and some public. From the pictures, it looked like the perfect place for us to make special memories.

When we entered Boboli Gardens, Steven took my hand, letting the path lead us where it might. Fragrant smells captivated our senses as we strolled hand and hand looking at the plants and flowers. Occasionally we would see another person or a couple but for the most part, the garden felt like our private oasis. It felt like this day had been made just for us to be at this place with each other at this very moment in time. And I could not have thought of a better way for us to spend our first day as husband and wife. We were virtually alone, in one of the most beautiful gardens in the world, enjoying nature.

When we saw an arched walkway in the distance, both of us instinctively walked toward it without saying a word. The arch was at least ten feet tall and covered by several different types of vines. One had an almost heart shaped leaf in a deep green color while another was a small pale green rounded shape. There were still a few flowers even this late in the season and Steven reached up to pick one for us to smell.

At the other end we could see the tunnel of plants ending as the light opened up the pathway. I loosened my hand from his and took off, jogging at first until I felt him passing me. We both started to run and giggle at the same time and I let the flower he had picked, fall to the ground. When we reached the end of the archway, Steven picked me up off the ground in a strong embrace and spun me around.

"I'm so glad I married you," I said, pulling back to look at him.

"I'm glad you finally wrote me a letter."

"Alright, alright, I took way too long to do it. But maybe this was perfect timing."

"Yes…like now or never."

"Mr. Attitude."

"I was done, Tiffany."

"And now we are just beginning," I said, trying to steer the conversation back into the present.

His body let go of mine and he walked forward, looking toward a fountain on our left. When he didn't notice I wasn't beside him, I hurried to catch up. There was no way I could imagine what he had been through all of these years. He was one of the strongest people I had ever known. How he held on to the thought of us being together when I rarely gave him any hope was beyond me. A much weaker person would have given up so very long ago. Now, it was my turn to give him confidence in a future with us happy and in love for the rest of our lives.

The fountain had a seat all the way around it and what appeared to be a step leading down into the water. After taking off our shoes, we turned toward the water putting our feet in the clear cool water. Then our eyes examined the statue that was bursting with water from every angle. It was a very old fountain and we could see where there should have been repairs made but were left untouched. It was the same story in every part of Italy I had ever seen. The artists and people here made things of great quality that would last for a long time to come. Which made me think at least the people here may have a little bit of American in them after all. Wasn't it our country that had the ole saying, 'If it ain't broke don't fix it'?

These were also the words that changed my attitude after the last words we had just spoken. Nothing was broken between Steven and I. I didn't have to try and fix anything. So I relaxed, took his hand and stood in the water, reaching up with my other hand to let some of the water rain down on it. Steven opened his legs and pulled me back toward him, wrapping his arms around my waist. Instantly, I could feel my passion for him growing as his hands started to wander around my body.

Off in the distance was another pathway that led into a group of evergreens. I sat down on his lap, kissed him with passion and eagerness then pointed toward the path. He helped me sit down to put our wet feet into our shoes. Our hands came together and we were walking very swiftly toward the path with one thing on our minds, finding somewhere private where prying eyes could not see.

Halfway down the evergreen lined path, we entered into a dense small forest of fifteen to twenty foot evergreens that were on the right hand side. Steven did his best to hold the branches as we worked our way deeper and deeper into the sea of green. He stood still for a moment, looking around to see which way to go. Then he took my hand, pulling me behind him as we walked a little further until we came to a small clearing in the overgrown bushes.

Steven took off his shirt and opened it up laying it on the ground like a blanket. Then he took his pants off and laid them beside his shirt. I started to take off my dress but he stopped me. He looked around in every direction and so did I. There was little chance of anyone seeing us much less finding us in here because we could not see anything but green. If we could be very quiet then we wouldn't get caught.

My heart was racing as my husband kneeled down, putting his hands under my dress and pulled my panties down to the ground. I kneeled down in front of him and we began to kiss like it had been a lifetime since the last time our lips had met. Our passion and desire began to build and build with each passing moment of kiss after kiss.

"Lay down, Love," he said, standing up to make room for me to move.

"Do you want me to take my dress off?"

"No, leave it on, just in case," he said quietly, looking around again.

Slipping my shoes off, my panties fell on top of my left shoe. I sat down on his clothes and waited for his direction. He took his underwear off, making me smile, then kneeled before me helping me pull my dress up. Steven took my legs and put them on his shoulders while looking into my eyes. And even though we went slowly, I made too much noise causing him to cover my mouth with his hand.

"Last night," I said softly, when he removed his hand.

"I know, me too," he said, pulling me closer by my thighs.

My hand grabbed his while the other one covered my own mouth. Closing my eyes, I let him have his way; I let him have exactly what he wanted. It might have been the long night of lovemaking or perhaps the fact we didn't make love before we left this morning but whatever it was we were both more than ready for the deepest pleasure a human being can have.

We didn't stick around in our little evergreen love nest very long, just a kiss or two and we were getting dressed, then searching for our way back to the path. Steven took my hand and we tried to go back the way we had come. We passed the fountain, walked back up the arch-way, past the statues and out the entrance. It had been a long couple of hours of exploring the gardens and we were both tired so we decided to return to our honeymoon suite.

After a long leisurely nap, we awoke to find the sun setting over the city of Florence. Steven asked if I wanted to go out for dinner but the thought of making love on the balcony was the only thing I could think about. So, I told him I would rather have room service bring our food and serve it alfresco on the balcony. He smiled that knowing smile and picked up the phone to order dinner and asked for it to be delivered around seven.

We soaked in the tub, washing each other's bodies and talking about the past. It was easy to reminisce about the times we had shared over the years. His memories were always a little different than mine but it was still fun to talk about. It was the future that always made us silent. He would start with questions I didn't know how to answer which made him make vague suggestions about what our plans could be. It was time for us to make plans and I knew that but there was something deep inside of me that made me clam up when he started talking about the future.

Steven dressed while I lingered at the mirror putting on make-up. He politely excused himself to the living room of the suite to wait on our dinner, closing the door behind him. He didn't know it but I wanted to surprise him with a new negligee instead of clothes tonight. So after I finished my make-up, I locked the bedroom door and began to put it on.

A light tapping on the door told me he was ready for me to come to dinner. After looking in the mirror, I hoped this negligee wasn't too much. It was hot pink and very sexy. The sheer robe that went over it did very little to hide the body parts that were not covered. I took a deep breath, reminded myself that he told me all the time that I was beautiful and put on my high heels.

Tap, tap, tap my high heels went across the floor as I approached the balcony door. From where Steven was sitting he could see me and stood up when I opened it wider. His eyes smiled with delight when I stepped out into the night air.

"Damn, girl," he swore, walking toward me with the biggest grin.

"Do you like it?"

"That's a crazy question," he replied, taking my hand and pulling it up over my head, moving me to spin around. "Hot damn!"

"Really, Steven, you sound like a redneck."

"And you look like every redneck boy's dream," he said, pulling me close and kissing me.

"Are you hungry?"

"Not anymore," he said, running his hand under my sheer robe to touch my bare bottom.

"We haven't eaten since brunch," I said in broken words, in between kisses.

"Who needs to eat when you feel this way?" He asked, lifting my leg off the ground, pulling it to his waist.

Steven picked me up with both hands holding onto my bottom and waist. He carried me over to the table and set me down. We pushed a few things on the table back so I would be comfortable and got back to kissing. When I unbuttoned the top button of his shirt, I pulled him into me by wrapping my leg around his waist. Then with the second button, I pressed my lips harder into his. It was the third button that sent my nails into the flesh of his back which caused him to make a very primitive noise.

His hands pulled me forward, to the edge of the table before they took his shirt over his head. He dragged the chair over behind him and sat down. I leaned back, closing my eyes and opening my mind for what was to come. His love for me gave him an unquenchable hunger for my flesh that I readily gave to him. It was his delight to fill me with ecstasy and joy as the pink negligee was performing its duty.

When I recovered in his embrace, the tables were soon turned. His pants hit the floor and I patted the table for him to sit down. After taking my seat I found it very easy to see why he had me in this position. His patience had paid off because now I was his, completely his. I was willing to try new things and go to places we had never gone before. He found it easy to let me know how he was feeling with each passing moment. And in my mind I could think of nothing else except giving him the same pleasure that I had just received.

After resetting the table and a few long passionate kisses, we sat down to dinner. Our appetites were rather small after such a long day but we lingered at the table, nibbling and talking about much of nothing. It seemed like we were both on the same track and no matter what the subject it turned back to sex. Sometimes it was about the sex we just had or sex we had had in the past or sex we wanted to have in the future. It made me wonder if all newlyweds were like us.

One thing led to another and who wouldn't have thought so with all the sex talk over dinner. The next thing I knew we were making love again. This time it was on the balcony's edge, looking down toward the river. The people below never even looked up as he stood behind me, slowly bringing us both to heightened pleasure. One minute he was standing me up to kiss my neck and the next he would push me forward, taking me by the hips. The gentle cool breeze blew my sheer robe in the night air as I whimpered from the painful pleasure of our lovemaking.

It made me wonder, how could making love to one person seem to get better and better each time? Could people really be on to something with this soul-mate theory? It really did feel like our bodies had been formed to fit together perfectly. And even though I had had more than my share of lovers over the years, no one had ever made me feel the way my husband did.

He picked me up, carrying me to the bed, laying down beside me. We covered our bodies with only the sheet because we were still warm from making love. I placed my head on his shoulder and caressed his body while he held me close to him. We whispered good night and fell fast asleep in each other's arms.

10
Chapter

Minutes, hours and days flew by as we allowed our bond of marriage to strengthen and grow. Mornings were usually late ones with brunch or an early lunch to start the day. Then we would wander through the streets of Florence, holding hands and enjoying life. We hired a boat and spent a day on the Fiume Arno River learning of its history and experiencing it in its present service to the locals. Then there were museums, full of art and history which seemed to captivate Steven's imagination the most. But my favorite thing was the hours we spent exploring Boboli Gardens and the timeless moments we spent exploring each other at our love nest in the evergreen garden within its perimeters.

Steven woke up early one morning and quietly got up, going into the bathroom. At first I thought something was wrong but then I heard the rush of the water, beginning to fill the tub. Stretching my body to its fullest length still did not give me the energy to go and see what he was doing. I rolled back over, closed my eyes and tried to fall back asleep but my mind was full of questions.

"Good morning, darling. Did you sleep well?"

"Mmmm," I moaned, turning toward him.

"I'm running us a bath," he said, leaning over to kiss my arm, working his way up to my shoulder.

"Why so early?"

"Because I have a surprise for you today."

"A surprise?"

"Yes, and we need to get going."

"But…"

"I see that. You are naked."

"And ready for you."

"If you don't get in the tub with me, we'll be late."

After pouting like a child for only a minute or two, I took his hand and led the way, saying, "We wouldn't want to be late."

It was a quick bath, then we ate some bagels and drank some exotic juice. Steven and I were dressed and ready to go when one of the young men from the hotel knocked on the door. He announced our driver was waiting downstairs and asked if we had any luggage he could carry down. Steven said no but the question sure had me wondering what in the world he had up his sleeve,

We followed the bell man out to the elevator and down to the lobby. Then walked with the driver to the car and climbed in as he held the door open. Steven pulled me close and put his arm around my shoulder, taking my hand with his other arm. He was so giddy, just like a child, I could sense his excitement so I kept the twenty questions I had to myself. Instead, I relaxed in his arms, knowing that whatever he had planned for us today, it was certain to be full of fun and pleasure.

The driver twisted and weaved the little car through the streets of Florence as Steven held me tight. We watched together as the many buildings and faces flew by our window. There was something about this man. It was the same way when he was a boy and I was a girl. No matter what day it was or where we were going, it always seemed to be an adventure. He had a way of being excited about each new experience and it was contagious. It is one of the things I admired most about him.

It wasn't long before we turned onto a road that looked vaguely familiar. Shortly after that, out in the distance I could see the airport where Steven and I had flown in from Capri. It looked quite different in the daylight but I remembered it all the same. When I turned to search Steven's face, asking a question with my eyes and not my lips, he returned with a blank expression. But within the next few minutes of looking out the car's window my question was answered. We were going to the airport which could only mean one thing. Whatever his surprise was we had to fly to get to it.

Instead of pulling up to the front doors our driver took us around the side of the building and out onto a small dirt road. For a moment I wasn't sure what was happening and then I saw it. A helicopter sitting on a pad with two pilots waiting by the door. This time when I looked at Steven he smiled, which meant the pilots were waiting for us to arrive.

The driver quickly got out of the car and opened the door for me, giving me his hand to help me out. Then he opened the trunk, handing Steven a large white bag. It was stuffed full and I could not imagine for the life of me when Steven had found the time to arrange everything. We had been together nearly every waking moment since the moment we said I do. My mind raced with questions that needed to be answered. They were building up inside, causing me to become anxious with desire to know. It was at the exact moment that I thought I would explode with words that he stopped me cold in my tracks.

"Kiss me, you beautiful girl," he demanded, turning to face me.

"Right here?" I asked, with all eyes on our every move.

"Right here, right now," he spoke slowly, setting the bag down, taking me into his arms and kissing me like it was the first time his lips had ever touched mine.

He put his arm around me, to steady my feet, leaving the bag behind us. Both of the pilots smiled and one of them turned to open the door for Steven and me to get in. The driver picked up the mysterious white bag and handed it to one of the pilots, waving goodbye. Once we were all in our seats and safely buckled in they started the engine and soon we were in flight.

Higher and higher we rose above the great city of Florence, making it appear even larger than when we walked the streets. The white buildings, the many church steeples and the tan bodies reminded me we were still in Italy. Steven moved closer to share my view as the younger pilot of the two began to give us an impromptu tour of the attractions of Florence that came into view. Part of me was listening and part of me could feel Steven's desire. It was there, in the way he touched my skin, the way he sat so close and caught my eye whenever he could. If the men flying the helicopter couldn't have seen us, I am certain we would have made love right then, right there.

Out over the horizon, in the distance was the beautiful blue water that surrounded the Italian coastline. Suddenly, I could feel great anticipation for the water, wanting to see it more clearly, wanting to be near it. As we got closer and closer, a calming ease came over me and my soul felt like it was coming home for the first time in a very long time.

"How did you know?"

"Because I know you, Love."

"Thank you," I whispered, hugging him gently, kissing his cheek.

"I love you, Tiffany. All I've ever wanted to do is love you and make you happy."

He turned his face back toward the window, not wanting to show his emotion and I did not force him to look at me. His words had been charged with feelings, feelings that were deep and heartfelt. Who was I to ever understand or think I could understand how he felt? My life had been full of regret, sure but never-the-less I had lived it to the fullest. Steven, on the other hand, had spent most of his life waiting. Which was something I could never understand.

We flew down the coast for a few miles and watched the tourist and locals swimming and sunbathing. Then darted out over the open sea where water and a few boats were the only thing in sight. The helicopter's blades were the only sound as we continued our journey to Steven's big surprise.

It was the younger pilot that broke the silence by pointing out an island in the distance, called Island di Capraia, with great enthusiasm. My husband took my hand and squeezed it tightly in his. His secret surprise was not so secret anymore. As the day progressed so did my theory on who, when, where, and what this little surprise held. Steven appeared to be oblivious about my wondering mind and intent on making lasting memories for us to share for many years to come. So I tried once again to put the questions out of my head and focus on the here and now.

The tiny island grew as we flew closer. Soon a small clearing came into view with a white house nearby. The pilot hovered above it for a moment before setting down. Then a man and two women came out to greet us. He opened the door and helped me out of the helicopter. Then the two women hugged me and each one took a hand and pulled me toward the small white house. I looked over my shoulder just in time to see Steven getting the mysterious white bag. He smiled and shook his head as if to say yes…go with these women.

We entered the very familiar looking Italian villa and the ladies guided me into one of the back rooms. Inside were several dresses hanging along the wall and some swim suits laying across a chase lounge. It didn't take a rocket scientist to figure out what they wanted me to do.

When I walked back into the living area of the house, my husband sat at a table, watching me walk toward him. His eyes showed approval for my choice in dress. He too had changed from jeans and t-shirt into swim trunks and flip-flops. So as a matter of deduction, I assumed we were going somewhere to swim.

Now, the large white bag made perfect sense. It was a beach bag and was probably full of beach towels and sunscreen. Steven picked it up with one hand and took my hand with the other and led me outside without a word. This time an old Italian man stood beside an old jeep that looked like it needed a paint job. He gestured with his hand for me to climb in the muddy old truck. And I think I surprised him with a smile when I climbed in and sat in the back seat. Proving there was still a little bit of that Mississippi girl in this Hollywood woman's body.

We rode down the winding little roads, holding onto the roll cage most of the way. The old man barely said anything the whole way and what little he did say was hard to understand. Steven was happy, it was written all over his face and as we approached the shoreline, I was feeling happier too.

The old man stopped the jeep just short of the dock and got out to help me down. I took his hand, giving him another smile and jumped to the ground. A beautiful young girl came running up to say hello in English but it was the only word she knew. We exchanged hellos and smiles before Steven took my hand, bringing me closer to the dock where many boats sat along its length. Without a doubt, part of his surprise involved a boat and the sea and I was more than curious to find out where he was taking me next.

A man about our age stepped up onto the dock from his boat and happily said hello. For a moment, I thought he was an American, just by his accent and the way he looked. Then as he continued to talk to Steven, I realized he was not American. He was definitely Italian, but somewhere or somehow he had learned English and it certainly wasn't in a classroom or out of a book.

We stepped aboard his antique wooden boat that had almost as much charm and charisma as he did. Then he introduced himself as Albert but we could call him Al if we wanted to. The name of his boat was Grey Swan, which in my mind didn't make a bit of sense. It was beautiful and shiny and where he came up with such a dull name for such a nice boat was beyond me. He explained that it would only take about fifteen minutes to get to Cala della Mortola Beach. It was the only beach on Island di Capraia and could only be reached by boat. When he said this, Steven raised his eyebrows up and down which made us both smile.

Those fifteen minutes crept by as we motored along the coast in search of this isolated beach. Something deep inside me began to feel strange with anticipation. The thought of finally being alone with Steven made erotic sensations travel throughout my body in waves. He was right here beside me but he might as well have been a hundred miles away. I needed him now, and the only thing that stood between me and my desire was a slow moving boat and a long winded captain.

"Have I ever told you how beautiful your long red hair is?"

"Maybe once, or twice."

"It is, Tiffany," he replied, ignoring the captain, watching it whip around in the wind.

"Thanks, now how did you find out about this place?"

He turned back to see what I was looking at, saying, "A little birdie told me about it."

"It's awesome."

"I can hardly wait to be with you… alone," he said quietly, raising my hand up to his lips.

"Whatever are you proposing, Mr. Cross?" I asked in my best southern belle accent.

"Just a little rendezvous, Scarlett, and then I'll let you get back to your draperies," he replied in his best impersonation of Rhett Butler.

Our boat came to the shoreline and the captain jumped off. First he took our white bag and ran it up to the beach. Steven jumped down into the clear blue water looking back at me. His hazel eyes danced with light as his words coaxed me to trust him and jump. Captain talk-a-lot came over and began to add his words and arms into the equation. I sat down on the edge of the boat and lifted myself enough to fall into Steven's arms with the Captain helping to catch me too.

It was awkward as the two men carried me to shore walking sideways with their arms under my body, carrying me like a huge baby. The only thing I could think was the captain must have thought I didn't want to get my dress wet which couldn't have been further from the truth. Why Steven didn't tell him to let go was the biggest question in my mind. But for the first time, the chatter bug was quiet so I guess Steven just let it ride.

The men set me down on the sand and I immediately took off my shoes. The sand was soft and warm even on this late day in September. Tears began to sting my eyes as I turned back toward the sea, feeling a great longing to be near the water's edge and being so full of gratitude that someone loved me enough to bring me here. And that someone was my husband, the man I was falling madly in love with, all over again.

Steven and the captain stood together talking near the rocky landscape where the white beach bag sat. Gazing out into the sea, I could barely make out their conversation and really would have preferred not to hear the words at all. It was in my heart to hear only the lapping of the waves upon shore and the gentle breeze pass over the sand. Walking away from the guys, I noticed that the cove was very secluded. The beach was small, surrounded by rocks that had fallen from the hillsides that climbed out of the sea. It was the perfect location to spend an afternoon with someone you loved.

When I looked back, Steven and his new friend had hiked up into the rocks and both were pointing down at something that I could not see. They were beyond the point of hearing me so I turned back toward the sea and began to talk aloud, "I want to come back here someday, with our children. I want to let them swim in this very spot, in this crystal clear water."

That's when I saw it, slowly slipping back out to sea. Then I called out loudly, "Hey....guys!"

I ran to the edge of the rocks, shouting louder, "Steven! Captain...!"

"What?" Steven yelled back, turning to look at me.

"The boat!" I yelled, turning to point in its direction.

The captain ran across the rocks with great skill and Steven came behind him a little slower and with caution. The once joyous and extremely English sounding captain had now become a full blooded Italian right before our eyes. Not a word he spoke was English and even though I don't speak Italian, I don't think most of what he said was very nice. His boat had slipped out to sea far enough to have him running into the water and splashing head first into a dive. He swam with enormous vigor for a man his size and quickly reached the small vessel. In a few moments he had pulled himself onboard and shook the water from his head like he was part dog.

"Well I guess that is one way for you and I to get some alone time," Steven said, laughing, and putting his arm around my waist.

"I was beginning to wonder if you had invited him to stay."

"I'll be back!" The captain yelled before pulling the cord to start the engine.

Steven waved in recognition, as the captain turned the boat back toward the sea and waved goodbye. He let his hand slide down from my waist to just below my hip. And the second the captain of many words slipped from view, he forcefully took me in his arms and kissed me like we had not seen each other in a very long time. I returned his fervent kisses, matching his passion ounce for ounce. He pulled at the island frock the natives had dressed me in, nearly ripping it apart. I helped him remove it, kissing and touching until it hit the sand beneath our feet.

The bikini held little resistance to his unyielding hands until I was left with nothing but a smile between me and the warm Italian sun. Steven stepped back, to look at me, as though he was taking a mental picture. There was no reason to, but I blushed under the heavy stare of his mesmerizing hazel eyes. He extended his hand which I took then lifted it into the air and turned me round. Once, I spun for him, feeling his eyes all over my body then I darted into the sea with laughter. I turned back before going any deeper into the water to see if he was following me but he wasn't. He stood there on shore, fully dressed, watching my every move. So I dove into the cool clear water and skinny dipped alone for the first time in my life.

When I came out of the water he was waiting with a towel. He had laid a blanket on the sand which we both laid on. We didn't speak. No words needed to be exchanged. We both knew what we wanted.

With one final look around to make sure we were alone, Steven took his clothes off and pulled the towel wrapped around my body loose. His lips touched mine more gently now as our skin soaked up sunshine and was cooled by the salty sea breeze. We had made love so many times since we had said I do but I wanted this time to be special. I wanted to take it slow and easy, I didn't want to rush. And as if somehow Steven and I could communicate without speaking that is exactly what he did. We spent the next moments of our eternity, making love on the shore of Cala della Mortola Beach.

We explored our bodies under the glory of an Italian afternoon sun. With hands, fingers and mouths our senses were heightened and hearts renewed. When it was time to stop playing and get down to business, I let Steven take control.

He guided my body into position. My head lay on a make sift pillow with my arms outstretched, ready to receive him. When he paused, I almost demanded he stop toying with me. It was his eyes and the way they stared that kept me from speaking. Then the weight of his body and the touch of his skin brought sound from my lips. He loved to bring my body to the edge with a perfect rhythm, then slow down, making me need more. It was his way of driving me crazy.

If making love could be an art form, Steven Cross would be considered a master artist. His words, sounds and touches were perfectly timed to bring excessive satisfaction. He used his paintbrush with blissful skill and great precision, taking his time with every stroke. The paint he used was one color then another, each making me unsuitable for any other man.

As the waves crashed harder and the sun sank lower in the sky, he concluded his day's work. Steven's labor of love was complete; a masterpiece. If my body had not trembled, I would have been concerned. I was putty in his hands. Steven had worked me over, broken the mold and reshaped me. And I had never felt more freedom in my life than lying naked in the sand.

After holding each other for a long time, Steven got up and put his swim trunks on then retrieved my clothes from the shoreline. While I was putting my suit on he pulled a bottle of wine from the white bag along with water and sandwiches. We were both quite hungry and ate our late lunch quickly, washing it down with water. Then we raced to the water for one final swim before the captain arrived to put an end to this frolicking by the sea.

We thanked the captain with a generous tip and the bottle of wine that we didn't get around to drinking. He repaid our generosity by offering to take us home with him tonight. His wife had prepared a beautiful meal in our honor and we were welcomed to come and stay as long as we liked. It was so hospitable but Steven did the right thing and refused. We had to get back to Florence because in just a couple of days we would be flying back to Los Angeles.

Chapter
12

Italy had a way of slowing the world down, letting each breath flow in and out of your body with purpose and at a pace that made the body feel alive. It filled you full of imagination and dreams that life could be exactly the way you live it when you are there. That somehow, when you left the white buildings, old churches and cobblestone streets behind some part of the tranquility would come with you. And you would be able to carry on in your old surroundings with this newfound calmness, this new way of living.

The first few days, it's a cinch. You even influence others around you to slow down and smell the roses. Your niceness rubs off on them and everyone seems to benefit from your time in the old country. Then slowly but surely everything begins to speed up. Weeks of letters, emails, phone calls and missed meetings are hunting you down. Everyone is wanting an answer to their questions. There are bills to be paid, duties to perform and at least a thousand wedding gifts to open. And let's not forget a thousand or more thank-you notes to be sent out.

However, Diane deserved much more than a simple thank you note. She had gone above and beyond the duty of a friend during our time of need. Not only was she a fabulous bridesmaid but she basically became a wedding planner without the pay that goes along with it. Then after we were long gone from Capri, it was her hard work that had brought back all of our luggage, gifts and memories from our wedding ceremony.

Steven and I contemplated what to do for our friend. We knew she would never accept cash plus she didn't need it any way. We considered giving a generous donation to her favorite charity, but we wanted her to have lasting memories from our gift. So we paid for our friend to spend a week on the beautiful Island di Capraia and for a special boat ride to a secluded Cala della Mortola beach from an English speaking Italian boat captain. We knew that out of all the people we know, Diane would enjoy this little island perhaps even more than we did and make special memories that she would never, for the rest of her life, forget.

Life has its way of pulling and pushing one to adapt to its whims and Steven and I were no exception. First, our days were divided between being in each other's arms and working as little as we could get by with. But with his latest deadline pushed past the breaking point and the studio suggesting that they find another actress for Fly Higher with Michael McFarland we both knew it was time to get back to work. And we both knew that would mean time apart.

We had only been married for sixty-eight days when I boarded a plane for New Zealand. Michael and his entourage sat across the aisle from me in first class. It was at least thirty minutes into the flight before he even said hello which I barely acknowledged. He had gone from a humble and polite man, just a few months ago, to a hot-headed, loud-mouthed obnoxious man. It was as if he thought his bad attitude would give him an edge or something. But even I knew that having a bad attitude in Hollywood only labeled you as hard to work with. Which certainly would not help his career in the least.

Steven had decided to spend the next few months back in Natchez working on his long overdue book. He wasn't use to not meeting deadlines and felt that he produced his best work when he could be outside, in nature. I supported his decision and we agreed not to let more than two or three weeks pass without seeing one another. It was an agreement that we both knew would be hard to keep.

He assured me that writing would keep him busy and promised that he would go see my dad and his family. We had not heard much from anyone in Mississippi since the day we had married so I was wondering how they were all doing. Steven had been talking about becoming an uncle more and more and I felt that was another reason he wanted to be there. Victoria and Blake could probably use any help they could get to prepare for parenthood and even though Steven wasn't a father yet, I knew there wasn't anything he wouldn't do to help them.

When we finally arrived in New Zealand, the old Michael McFarland awoke out of a deep sleep. He followed me out of the plane, paying me compliment after compliment. Even though I was momentarily confused, I wasn't going to argue with this man. Whatever had caused him to be so bossy and disrespectable earlier was gone now and all I could think about was I hope to never see that part of him again. There were two limos waiting to take us to our hotel. One was for me and the other was for him and his group of friends.

"Looks like there's plenty of room in your car. Care to have some company?"

"No, thanks. You need to entertain the masses," I replied, getting into the car.

He poked his head inside, saying, "What about dinner? Can I interest you sharing some food with me?"

"Thank you, Michael but I will not be going out to dinner tonight. It's room service for me."

"Room service in your suite sounds good to me," he said, lowering his glasses to look at me through his blue-grey eyes.

I looked down at my wedding rings and looked back up into his eyes. "Maybe another time."

"Yes, another time," he said, pushing his glasses up and turning his attention to his entourage.

The driver closed the door with a whoosh turning my attention to the small gift box on the seat beside me. The card was tiny and took me a second to get it open. In a flash, I recognized the words from a poem, a poem my husband had written to me so long ago.

These are wasted days and lonely nights until I take flight.
I shall think of you by day and dream of you at night.
When the sun shines, I will see your hair.
When the wind blows, I will hear your voice.
When the rain falls, I will feel your heartbeat with mine.

Steven had a way of making me feel like the only girl in the world. What lengths did he have to go to for this package to be sitting on this seat beside me today? When did he find the time in his busy schedule to always think about me and special things to remind me of his love? How did I ever live without him in my life, making me feel so admired and cherished?

As the driver pulled away, I ripped the paper exposing what was inside. It was a jewelry box made of glass, decorated with colorful flowers on top and tiny white daisies on the sides. When I opened it up, I was surprised that it held no jewelry, just another small piece of paper.

I promise to love you whether near or from afar.
I promise to be faithful from now… to eternity.
I promise to hope only for the best for you and me.
Let this box hold these promises held within your wedding rings.

Tears filled my eyes like so many times before when I read the wonderful words he had written for my eyes only. Then the same old feeling of why me, what did I ever do to deserve to be loved like this came over me. It was ever present, just under the surface of my skin or perhaps my heart. It was the same thought that had kept me from having more in life. And right then, that very moment, sitting in the back seat of that limousine in New Zealand, I made a promise to myself. I promised to hope for only the best for Steven and me, as I wiped the tears from my eyes.

The sun was setting against a multi-colored sky in shades of pink, purple, orange and blue. We rode for several miles down the coastline and I watched from my window all of the people living life. Walking along the shore, hand in hand, moms and daughters, husbands and wives, young lovers. So much peace and beauty made me long for Steven even more than I thought was possible. I needed, I wanted him here to fill this void, this empty feeling, this big hole in my heart.

The first few days were tough, full of missing everything I had left behind. Then as more days passed and I focused on work, my mind would drift less and less on memories of me and Steven. Fifteen hour days on a movie set pass by in a blur of costumes, make-up and 'let's shoot that again'. It was only at night when I'd lay in bed, exhausted from the day that my thoughts would consume me. It was why Steven and I usually talked until I fell asleep. He would tell me about his day, where he had gone and what he was writing. Occasionally, he talked about seeing his mom and dad, Victoria and Blake and my dad. Sometimes we talked about what was happening on the movie set but mostly we talked about us. How much we missed each other and how many more days it would be until we were together.

For our first visit, Steven was flying out to spend a week with me in New Zealand. He knew my schedule and promised to go and enjoy nature and possibly get some writing done while I was working. Then we made plans to make love every night when I got back to the hotel.

When the day finally came for him to arrive, we had an early day on set so I was able to be there when his plane landed to surprise him. Without even thinking, I showed up at the gate completely empty handed. No present, no flowers, not even a sign to hold in my hands.

The guilt of not being more thoughtful began to really take over my thoughts and began to steal the joy of seeing him again. For a moment I contemplated leaving and going back to the hotel so I could buy him something nice before we saw each other. But as I turned to look back, he was walking toward me.

At first, Steven didn't see me. I stepped back behind a man so it would be even harder for him to spot me. From a distance, I watched him walk, carrying a small bag over his shoulder which most likely contained a computer, paper and pen. He greeted the people waiting for their loved ones as he passed by and said goodbye to a few of his fellow travelers as they went on their way.

He was so handsome, rugged and manly. He spoke volumes of southern hospitality and lived out the simple values that his parents had instilled in him. Suddenly, I was hit with an overwhelming feeling of pride. Steven made me proud to be his girl, his wife and the fact that he was my husband, my other half made me emotional enough to dab my eyes. I told myself to get it together, put a smile on my face and that's exactly what I did. Then I stepped out from behind my hiding spot just before he walked past me.

"Surprise!"

He half ran, half walked and picked me up into his arms, burying his head into my hair, whispering, "Tiffany, Tiffany, Tiffany…"

My eyes were closed as I felt the power of his embrace. The noise of a busy airport seemed to be muffled against the whisper of his words. Slowly, he kissed his way between saying my name from my neck to my cheek until his lips met mine. Without ever opening my eyes, I remembered what it felt like to be the most important person in the world to another human being. Steven reminded me of my worth to him and his desire for me with the touch of his hands and the taste of his kiss.

We lingered, not wanting to let go. My emotions were not so easily held at bay in his arms but being ever the gentleman, he simply wiped the tears away and didn't let me go. He loosened his hold and his bag slipped from his shoulder to his forearm. Taking a step back, I touched his cheek and looked into his eyes. He looked tired, perhaps weary after such a long flight and I remembered how I felt when I first got here.

"Come on, let's get out of here."

"I'd go anywhere with you," he said, giving me a wink.

"Let's start with a ride to the hotel. Then it's straight to bed for you, mister."

"Now that's exactly where I want to be," he replied, taking my hand.

"We don't need to go to baggage claim. I sent the driver to get your stuff," I told him, pulling him in the other direction.

"You are so good, Love. So, which way to the magic bus?"

"You really do need some sleep, don't you?"

"I need a lot more than some sleep, honey."

"That's good. Because I have a lot to give you."

He stopped, pulling me to a stop with his hand and turned me back to him, saying, "What do you have for me?"

"I have what you need. Come on, let's go!"

He smiled and took the lead. We were out the door and into the car in just a few minutes and headed toward the coast amid a barrage of kisses and hugs and I missed you. His hands traveled the contours of my curves as my hands recalled the definition of his muscles. We were deep in the throes of passion when the driver rolled down the separation window to ask if we wanted to stop at the hotel or did we want him to continue down the coast. Steven sat up, straightened his shirt and told him we wanted to stop.

We hurried into the hotel, barely caring about his luggage or the stares of passer-bys. Knowing we must have looked like a hot mess did not bother either one of us. It had been much too long since we had seen the other smile or received the great pleasures we were able to give. The thought of entertaining anyone else at this point seemed, well, pointless. We both had only one thought on our minds and that did not involve anyone or anything except him and me, alone.

When the door shut to my hotel room, Steven turned and locked it. With the twist of a switch, I turned the lights down low and with the push of a button turned on some music. He took his shirt off and hung it on the back of a chair.

"Maybe I should get cleaned up," he said, sounding nervous.

"If you want to, baby. But you look clean enough for me," I said, slowly unbuttoning my top.

"It will only take a few minutes," he said, walking toward the bathroom.

"Okay, I'll be right here waiting," I replied, as he closed the door behind him.

For a moment, I felt a twinge of sadness. Steven usually couldn't wait to make love to me. Had I done or said something wrong? Or had something happened in Mississippi that I didn't know about? The questions ran through my brain as I heard him in the shower. When he turned the water off, I knew that I was probably overreacting. He just wanted to be fresh and clean before we made love and I was being foolish to think otherwise.

He came out of the bathroom with a towel wrapped around his hips. After lying sideways on the bed he turned to look at me from tired eyes. He patted the bed beside him as if to say come here. When I walked toward him, he turned on his side and propped his head up on his hand. Instead of sitting, I stood in front of him and started to sway to the music while I undressed myself. His eyes took in my every move and watched intently as I slowly became more and more naked.

When I crawled in bed, he put his arm under my neck and I rested my head on his shoulder. His hand moved softly around my back as I kissed his neck. Just when I thought things were beginning to heat up, Steven began to breath deeper. With one push, his eyes fluttered open as he apologized for drifting off.

This time Steven lay in my arms and within just a few minutes fell fast asleep. As his breath began to slow to a perfect symphony of sleep I longed to get up. It was dinner time, I was hungry, not sleepy and I needed to go to the bathroom. But another part of me wanted to linger and hold him close a little bit longer. There was a stillness that filled my soul when I was this close to him that I could not find in anyone else or in any other place on this earth.

Sliding out from underneath him, I quietly left the room. After taking care of my needs, I went back and sat down in the chair beside the bed. While letting my dinner settle, I watched this man sleeping so peacefully. I wanted to be disappointed, even angry that he had fallen asleep on me. Instead, I crawled into bed beside him and closed my eyes.

It was the rising of the sun that brought my husband back to life and fulfilled both of our desires. He woke me with his body pressing into mine, a gentle and surprising way of starting the day. When I was fully awake, he changed positions, burying his head into my hair, turning only to kiss my neck. My hands stroked his back while our legs fought to kick off the covers.

"Is this what you wanted to give me last night?" He asked, teasing.

"No," I replied, crawling out from under him. I pushed him hard, onto his back and crawled on top.

"So this was it?" He asked, pulling my hips into his body.

"No," I said, digging my fingernails into his chest.

"Tell me, no, show me..."

"You will never know," I said, standing up quickly, looking down at him.

He reached up, pulling me back to the bed with a thud, saying, "You better tell me."

"Never!" I yelled, as he began to tickle me.

"You better tell me right now," he teased, turning me over onto my stomach, sitting on my back to hold me still and tickling me harder.

"Okay," I gasped between laughter.

He stopped for a moment, and put his head beside my ear. But before I could say another word he was inside of me, giving me his love and letting me feel his desires. I pushed back as hard as I could, letting the weeks of loneliness melt away moment by moment. We climbed to the peak of ecstasy together and laid naked in each other's arms, catching our breath.

When the alarm began to ring, I reached across the bed, turning it off. Another day of being apart was not what I had in mind but with production in high gear playing hooky was out of the question. He followed me into the bathroom and turned on the water to draw me a bath. He grabbed the bubble bath and gave me a grin. Then he sat down on the edge of the tub, waiting for me to come over and join him.

We immersed ourselves in the water and sat soaking for a while. He stroked my arms and chest as I rubbed his thighs and knees. It was an exchange of love that we both needed and wanted that kept me lingering far too long in the warm soapy water. He turned to kiss me but only on the lips to avoid exchanging our bad morning breath. Things were getting heated between us again when the phone rang and I excused myself, getting out dripping wet, trying to catch the call.

It wasn't a surprise to anyone that I was running late when I finally made it to the set. My mind and heart was on Steven and what he would do today. If there was anything I knew about him it was he would find somewhere picturesque to be alone so he could write the words that the world loved to read. And as the hours of the day passed my hope was somehow I could be some part of the inspiration he needed to make those words flow.

After work, we joined each other at our favorite place to be together, the bed. It was an oversized king with plenty of room to eat and play. He had found some candles during his outing and had put them near the bed creating a romantic glow in the room. It only took a few minutes to discuss our day and what we wanted for dinner and then we were back in each other's arms, making love. This time he was rested and fully awake and alive. I was the one that was weary from the day but I did my best not to let it show.

When dinner arrived, we stayed in bed, watching T.V. and talking about our plans for the only day we could spend alone together before he had to go back to Mississippi. On Sunday, we would go to Lake Matheson and have a picnic. We also planned to find a little spot in the woods where we might be hidden from prying eyes.

The week flew by in a haze of long days on set and long nights in that king sized bed devoting ourselves to enriching our relationship. We talked, made love, and ate some of the most delicious food room service had to offer. As Saturday night came and went, we both fell asleep excited with the anticipation of the fun Sunday would hold for us.

"Wake up sleepy head," Steven said, sitting beside the bed.

"What are you doing?"

"Watching you wake up."

"Don't you mean watching me sleep?"

He kneeled beside the bed, pulling the covers back to expose my body, saying, "Yes, I was watching you sleep."

"That's a little creepy, don't you think?" I asked, stretching and yawning loudly.

"Not when you're in love," he replied, tenderly touching my stomach.

"It's Sunday!"

"Yes, all day long," he said softly, moving his hand lower.

I stretched again then let my body relax with his touch. My eyes closed as he affectionately whispered compliments and words of love while preparing my body for his. Every word, every touch made my heart fuller and my body ache. By the time he joined me on the bed I was fit to be tied. My begging did no good. He was taking his time, making me crazy with desire. He knew how to make my body crave his and how to make my mind long for his words. For a moment, the realization that I was in too deep to ever walk away from him entered my mind. Then with another touch it left just as quickly, as the fire within me grew.

We wrestled with love between words and promises for over an hour before falling into a heap of tangled arms and legs. Holding on to each other with sweat and tears like we would never let go felt like the only thing we might do today. But there was a lake, with our name on it out there waiting to be claimed so we dragged ourselves out of that king sized bed and set our sights on preparing for the adventure that lie ahead.

As usual, Steven had planned ahead to make our time together extra special. When we went downstairs to the lobby there was a driver waiting with a picnic basket in hand, leading us outside to his van. It was about a half hour drive to Lake Matheson so we settled in the back and buckled up for the ride. A beautiful red checkered blanket lay on the seat in front of us with a beautifully wrapped present. When I asked what was inside of the box, Steven only smiled teasing me with his eyes.

I looked out the window, taking in the sights of the New Zealand country side as we drew closer and closer to our destination. Then for a while it seemed we were climbing higher and higher then slowly began to descend as the trees became larger and dense. With one sharp turn the lake came into view and what a breath taking view it was. The water's reflection was unlike any other lake I had ever seen. It was like a mirror, showing Mount Cook and Mount Tasman within its frame. Along the lakes' edge were tall beautiful trees that towered over the water but shrunk under the majesty of the mountains. It was a calm and serene vision that almost looked like a picture-perfect postcard. Steven squeezed my hand and pointed at a lush green hill in the distance.

The driver knew exactly where to go cutting a path through what seemed to me to be unpassable land. The closer we got to the water the more my heart yearned to be near it. I began to picture Steven here, all alone, writing his latest novel. No one to interrupt him, no phone ringing, just him and Mother Nature to feed his imagination. In that moment, I wished I had spent those hours here with him instead of on a movie set.

When the van stopped, the driver got out and Steven stole a quick kiss. The side door slid open and the man picked up the blanket and gift before letting us get out. Behind us was a picnic table which he set the blanket and present on before opening the passenger door to retrieve the basket. Steven helped me down and when my feet touched the ground I took a deep breath of the freshest smelling air I had ever smelled.

"It smells like a dream, doesn't it?" Steven asked, watching my reaction.

"Actually that's the Kahikatea trees," the driver said, putting the basket beside the blanket.

"I was wondering what made it smell so good out here," Steven replied.

"Well, that's the culprit. You'd most likely know them by the common name of white pine."

"They look a lot different than the pine trees we have back home," Steven said, looking up at the tree.

"Meet you back here...around five?"

"We'll be here," he said, shaking the driver's hand.

He turned to get back in the van and with one final wave we were alone again. The huge grassy hill lay in front of us and the only thing I wanted to do was exactly what Steven did. Without hesitation, he took his shoes off and ran toward the lake. I kicked mine off with so much force, one flipped up in the air almost hitting me in the head, then I took off after him. We were laughing like a couple of kids and racing down the hill to the water's edge until he suddenly stopped right before stepping into the water.

"Look, Love."

"Wow, I've never seen one that color before."

"Me either and I've been out here all week."

"What kind do you think it is?"

"Maybe the purple and gold spotted wing master?"

"Are you serious, Steven?"

"No. But I do know one thing," he said, putting his arm around me.

"What's that?"

"That butterfly is here just for you."

It flew up, passed right in front of our faces and I said, "Why do you say that?"

"Because I do."

We watched the butterfly flutter its wings, carrying its little body across the enormous lake. Arm and arm we stood taking in the glory of Lake Matheson with its mirror imagine displaying Mount Cook and Mount Tasman. As far as we could see, not another living soul was in sight. It was just us two and the wonder of the beauty that surrounded us.

Steven walked into the water beckoning me to follow and I couldn't resist. It was so calm and tranquil with the golden amber water revealing the white sand beneath. It was only after the water touched my feet that I screamed, "It's cold!"

"The lake was formed by Fox Glacier," he said, in a matter-of-fact way.

Before I thought about it, I kicked the water, splashing Steven and wetting his clothes. He turned back toward me and bent down to splash me back with his hand. Not wanting to get wet, I ran back to dry land but not without some of the ice cold water hitting me. When I reached a safe distance, I looked back toward Steven but he had turned his attention back to the mountains and lake. So I sat down on the grassy hill and watched my husband.

His tan body stood perfectly still allowing the ripples to die down rapidly. It was only a few moments until he was standing in the edge of the mirror and becoming a part of the picture. With one sharp motion, his head turned to the right as a stunning large bird flew from one of the white pines. Steven watched the bird until it had landed near the water several hundred feet away.

"Did you see that?" Steven asked, walking out of the water toward me.

"Yes, I did."

"I love it here," he said, sitting down.

"I bet you got a lot of work done in your new office."

"This place did make a good office," he said, staring back at the lake.

"Better than Mississippi?"

"Now you know, there's no place like home."

"Yes, I do. So, you've barely talked about what's going on back home."

"I know."

"How's Victoria? Is she getting big yet?"

"She's starting to show. And Blake seems to be happy about it. He's real proud. I've been meaning to tell you something."

"What's that?"

"Amber moved back."

"Really? Have you seen her?"

"We ran into each other a couple of times," he replied, leaning back on the grass with his elbows.

"How's she doing? Nice as ever?"

"She's fine, just trying to put her life back together."

"Oh, my gosh! What's happened to her? Did she break a nail?"

"No, she lost her husband, she's a widow."

"I'm so sorry, I didn't know."

"It's alright, I just hate it for her."

"Does she have any kids?"

"She has a little boy, Myles. He's seven."

"Poor thing."

"He's doing alright. I think he's too young to really understand what happened."

"What happened?"

"Car wreck."

"That's such a shame."

"I know," he said, standing up and extending his hand.

We climbed the hill hand in hand without another word about Amber when we reached the table Steven picked up the present, handing it to me. With a gentle shake and smile, I tore into the paper.

"Why do you buy me so many presents?"

"Because I love you," he replied, taking the wrapping paper from my hands.

"What? A camera…what a perfect gift, thank you," I said, hugging him.

"I wanted us to be able to remember this day forever."

"Why are you so good to me?"

"Because I love you," he said, pressing his lips upon mine.

Without hesitation, I kissed him back with desire that there was no denying. My appetite for his flesh was a hunger that could not be satisfied. We were both craving the gratification that only he and I could give to one another. And I wanted him to indulge me, to spoil me with his love and attention right then and there.

"Do you like it?" He asked, nibbling my earlobe.

"Like what?" I asked grabbing him from behind, pushing his body into mine.

"Your present," he said, turning to face me.

"Yes, I already said thank you."

"Do you want to take a picture?"

"Sure, why not."

"What's wrong?"

"Nothing."

"Why don't you turn your back to the lake, so I can get it in the background. Smile! Not like that. Give me that… I can't live without you smile."

"Okay, now let me take one of you," I said, reaching out for the camera.

Steven posed for the shot and then for another. With the camera still in my hand, he took the blanket and spread it on the ground. He lay down, patting the spot beside him. I sat down and took another picture, this time a close up. He pulled me toward him, and I held the camera up to take a picture of us together. He took the camera, turned it off and put his arm under my shoulder.

"I was thinking that maybe…"

"What were you thinking?" he asked.

"That maybe, you might stay here in New Zealand. It's so beautiful here. You said it's a great place to write."

"I can't do that, Tiffany. There's so much going on in Mississippi right now and you're working all the time. We would barely get to see each other even if I did stay."

"We'd see each other every night and on Sundays."

"I know but you only have what, about a month left here?"

"About a month or so," I said, sitting up.

"That will give me just enough time to finish the first draft, if I get to work. I'm already behind schedule, Tiffany. If I stay here, I'll never finish in time."

"Okay, Steven. I was just asking. For some strange reason I thought you might want to stay here with me."

"Look, the only thing on my mind is finishing this book."

"It seems to me that you have something else on your mind. Or maybe someone else."

"You're wrong," Steven said, getting up.

"A few months ago you would've done anything to spend even an hour with me. Now you can't wait to get on that plane tomorrow."

"You're wrong, Tiffany."

"I knew something wasn't right from the moment you got here," I said, shielding my eyes from the sun with my hand.

"I don't know what you're talking about."

"You've been different. Like you're a thousand miles away."

"I have a lot on my mind," Steven replied solemnly, coming to stand in front of me, casting his shadow over my body.

"Let me guess? Amber," I said, moving my hand to look at his face.

"She is the least of my worries."

"This is supposed to be the happiest time in our lives. What are you worried about?"

"It's my mom."

"What about her?"

"She's sick."

"What do you mean?"

"They're running a bunch of tests."

"I'm sorry. Why didn't you say something?"

"I didn't want to cancel the trip. Plus we really don't know anything yet."

"Well, what's wrong? Is she just feeling bad?"

"She's been running a fever off and on and is in a lot of pain."

"That's not good. If you would have told me…"

"Look, I didn't want to ruin our time together."

"I know, but…"

"But nothing, Tiffany. In case you didn't know, you are the most important person in my life."

"I know that."

"My mom is important too but Amber is just somebody I use to know."

"Who is probably still in love with you."

He knelt down in front of me, looked in my eyes and said, "It doesn't matter because I am in love with you."

"Are you sure?"

"Why would you ask me that?"

"I need reassurance," I said, pulling him toward me.

"After all this time and all that we've been through and all that I have done, you still don't know that I'm desperately in love with you?"

"I'm sorry, again. I just can't get anything right today."

"Really, Tiffany, there's no need to say you're sorry. But look," he said, turning slightly, pointing at the awesome view of the lake and mountains.

"I know, it's breath taking."

"Just like you," he said softly, leaning in for a kiss.

"Thank you," I said, reaching up to touch his cheek.

"Let's not waste this, baby. I'll be leaving in just a few hours."

"Okay. What do you want to do?"

"I want to make love to you."

"Where?"

"There's a place in the woods I found a few days ago."

"Sounds good," I said, taking his hand as we both stood up.

He picked up the blanket, folded it then put it under his arm, saying, "Follow me."

We walked up to the top of the grassy hill until the white pines towered above our heads. Then he walked down toward the lake until he found a small foot trail. We walked hand and hand and I could feel the energy and excitement rising between us. Just minutes ago, I thought I would not want to touch him again for a long time. And after learning that it wasn't me or Amber that had caused his mysterious aloofness, my body tingled with a deep yearning for his affections.

The sun glinted through the trees giving us a virtual light show from the sky. As the minutes passed, we found ourselves, deeper and deeper in the forest that surrounded the lake. Soon, the water was no longer in sight but up ahead I could see an open field of green grass, bathed in sunlight. Steven walked a little faster and I followed with enthusiasm. His smile widened as we came to the end of the trail and stood at the edge of the meadow. With one movement, he turned my body to his and kissed me with a forceful enthusiasm that felt a bit awkward. It was my strong feelings for him and the trust we had that kept me from asking him to take it easy.

He moved my hair to the side, revealing my bare neck which he began to kiss softly. His lips brushed my skin while chills began to form all over my body. It should have been excellent, exactly what every girl wants but I felt like I was about to explode. Now, more than ever before, I wanted Steven to shatter every rule we had, every preconceived notion about what was right or wrong. If he was burning the way I was, I wanted him to prove it. I wanted him to tear down the walls that restricted our actions and make me feel and do things I had never felt or done before.

"Stay right here, I'll be right back," he said, nervously brushing my lips with his.

I watched him walk out toward the center of the pasture, looking around in all directions. When I looked around, I didn't see anything or anyone. There was nobody here but us and the birds and the trees. He spread the blanket out, looking around again and then ran back toward me.

Without a word, he swept me off my feet and into his arms. When I tried to get down and walk, he held on tighter. So I relaxed and held on to his neck as he carried me through the tall grass and flowers. It might be the last time we made love for a while and I knew we both needed to savor the moment.

Before we reached the blanket he put my feet to the ground and helped me stand up. He didn't speak, except with his eyes which told a story of happiness and sadness. His eyes made me yield to his appetite for my flesh. With an unforeseen raging urge to have me unclothed, he wasted no time in exposing my skin to the afternoon sunlight.

There I stood, not a piece of clothing on in the middle of a meadow and Steven walked backwards, leaving me alone. At first I looked around, hoping no one was watching. Then I realized he was watching. His eyes were glued to me, searching every inch of my body from my head to my toes. When I blushed, he ignored it and circled me from a distance like I was his prey, making me feel unusually awkward again.

Something inside of me wanted to disagree with his inspection but I kept silent. Instead, I turned against my own shyness and an overpowering boldness came over me. My shoulders pulled back erect and strong as my back arched with surety. One hand rose up to my waist as the other flipped my hair back over my shoulder. Now his eyes sparkled with delight as they took in my frame from every angle.

"You are one fine-looking sight, Tiffany Cross."

"How long are you going to make me stand here?"

Without a verbal answer to my question, he took my hand and led me to the blanket. After I helped take his clothes off we kissed in the warm autumn sunlight. A cool breeze rushed across the tall grass causing us both to hold each other closer. We knelt down together in the midst of a long kiss when he pulled away from me abruptly.

"I'll never leave you, Tiffany," then he paused before adding, "and I'll never be unfaithful."

"Those are hard promises to keep. I'd rather you'd promise me something more realistic like you'll always love me no matter what happens."

"I'll always love...I've always loved you and that will never end... no matter what."

It was time for words to cease and for our hearts, minds and souls to be reunited. Every touch of his hand on my skin raced throughout my body like lightening. Each caress felt like it made contact with almost every nerve in my body setting me on fire. And though he spoke no words, the sounds that he made touched a chord deep within that affected my thoughts. He held me captive, I was a slave to his love that needed no chains or rope to bind. There was no escape and even if there had been I would never have taken it now.

My mind began to fill with questions that should have never entered it at such an inappropriate time. But no matter how I tried to live in the moment and push them aside they kept wandering through my thoughts.

Why did I wait so long to be with this man? Had I loved him all along and only held a grudge because he moved to New York for college? What I felt for him now...was it real love?

Steven was making love to me, under a beautiful fall sky, surrounded by a picturesque green meadow arrayed with flowers in hues of orange and yellow. I did my best to push the questions out of my mind and make myself present for his affections. But each time I tried to focus on us, a familiar face from the past crept into my minds' eye. It was Amber and her wicked smile that would not let me relax and enjoy my husband's devotion. It was the same wicked smile she had at the bon fire the first night Steven and I kissed. I was afraid it would be the same wicked smile I would see when I got back to Mississippi.

13
Chapter

It was doubt that ruled my mind and filled the waking hours with unending questions. Try as I might to focus on the movie, Fly Higher, the plot and the character I was hired to portray, the same face kept creeping back in my mind. A spoiled rotten southern belle with an offensive scowl glaring straight at me. Amber even made her appearance in my dreams with the same dirty look from so many years ago. It was me. I was the one who had caused such a pretty girl to become so ugly-faced. Without even knowing what I was doing, I had stolen her boyfriend, her true love and her future. And now looking back, it seems she should have been mad at Steven. He is the one who left her behind. He moved on without looking back or feeling any remorse over ending their relationship. Who was I but an innocent girl? The new kid in town just looking for some new friends and a way to fit into a new school. But without a doubt, I knew she was mad at me again. I had married the man she always wanted. What I didn't know, what I couldn't get off my mind was why was she back in Mississippi and why was my husband back there too?

Michael McFarland proved to be more than just a handsome face when he showed concern for my state of mind. In fact, he was about the only one who noticed that I had become distracted and disinterested in finishing the film. He was smooth in his approach, asking only simple questions at first while digging for the truth. It took me a few days to figure out where he was going with the whole twenty questions thing but soon he had captured my attention. However, anyone or anything that could distract my attention away from my rambling thoughts about what was happening back in Mississippi was a welcomed relief.

At first, we hung out together a little more on the set, quizzing each other about where we grew up and what we had done during our lives. Then we began to eat lunch together and discuss our careers. The ups and downs of being an actor was the main topic. Within just a few days, Michael and I had become friends. When we shared time together, my mind wandered less and less to Natchez and Amber's frowning face.

After a long day on set, I was surprised to see a letter sitting on my desk in the hotel room. It was addressed to me, with no return address but instantly I recognized the handwriting. It was Steven's and I eagerly ripped at the paper to open it. Then I remembered all of the times I had savored his letters in the past so I sat it back down on the desk and went to make myself more comfortable.

A quick shower and change of clothes brought me back to the desk. I picked up the envelope and walked to the big bed, crawling under the covers. When I pulled the paper from the envelope I was surprised to see that there was only two pages of paper. One was blank and the other had a single poem. I sat up, cleared my throat and read it aloud to myself.

> *My soul longs to look into blue*
> *that I can only see*
> *when looking at you.*
> *So far away…*
> *the distance now,*
> *it plagues me somehow*

like a poisoned thorn
from the gift of a rose.
Why were we given everything,
even our heart's desire
only to catch glimpses
of the fire
we've created within our souls?
How can fate be so cruel
and take me from you
planting my feet
on the other side of earth?
Will you ever look back
on this day
remembering the words I say
and wished we had both freed
ourselves
from this world
and it's tangled web…
to truly become one?

There was no signature, no I love you, no explanations…nothing. I skimmed back over the words, trying to get some idea of what in the world this meant. Was he missing me? Was he saying he would never leave Mississippi again? What in the world did he mean when he asked if I would ever look back and remember what he said? After reading it again, I was more confused than ever so I grabbed the phone to ask him myself.

"Steven."

"Hey, Love."

"I got your letter, well, the poem."

"Good, did you like it?"

"Yes, but it's got me a little confused."

"Don't over analyze it, Tiffany. I just miss you…like crazy miss you."

"What did you mean by me looking back and remembering what you said and wishing we had truly become one?"

"Just writing you a poem, baby," he said, his voice straining.

"Okay."

"So, how is work?"

"It's work. How's the writing?"

"Getting closer every day. About twenty-five thousand words to go, more or less."

"We should be wrapping everything up here in about three weeks or so."

"Then we'll get done about the same time," he replied, sounding a little pre-occupied.

"What's wrong, Steven?"

"Nothing."

"How's your mom?"

"They think its cancer."

"I'm so sorry, darling."

"We'll find out in a few days."

"Let me know if there's anything I can do?"

"Sure. But what can you do from half way around the world?"

"I can't just drop everything and come running to Natchez just because your momma is not feeling good, Steven."

"I never ask you to."

"Look, I'm sorry. I didn't call to argue."

"We're not arguing," he said, softly.

"I do love you and I miss you very much."

"You are my world, Tiffany. And when we are this far apart..."

"I asked you to stay."

"I had to come back, and you know why."

"Yes but I don't understand it. We are married now. If I'm your world shouldn't I come first?"

"I don't know what to say," he said, his voice deepening with pain.

"Oh my gosh, I'm sorry again. Let's just say goodbye before I screw everything up."

"Good-bye," he said sadly, with a rasp in his voice.

"Bye, darling. I love you," I said, trying not to let my emotions come through my voice.

"Love you too," he said before hanging up.

Once I had tossed the poem onto the night stand, I rolled over and pulled the covers over my head. Each tear pushed its way over the brink of my eyelid even though I fought to keep them held inside. My words had only hurt the man I loved and in turn they had hurt me. Why did my big mouth always get me in trouble? It had been the same way all of my life. When was I going to become a mature woman, able to control my fear and anger? If only I hadn't called him or at least calmed myself down before speaking to him.

It was turning over in the bed and reaching out for a tissue that made me feel better. When I turned and reached out, my eyes caught a glimmer of hope from the words I read, *the fire we've created within our souls,* from the poem. Steven and I had done that. It began a long, long time ago when we were only teenagers. Each of us had fueled the fire for many years in one way or another. I was being foolish to think a few weeks apart, a sick mother or an old girlfriend would ever be able to put out that flame.

With my mind set to let go of the worry and anxiety that had my stomach in a perpetual knot, I sat up to look at the menu for room service. Over the past few weeks I had sampled nearly everything they had to offer and was becoming bored with the few choices that suited my taste. When the phone rang, I grabbed it, saying, "I love you, I love you, I love you."

"Well, I thought you did but it sure is nice to hear it."

"Who is this?"

"It's Michael. You don't recognize my voice?"

"Michael! I thought you were Steven."

"Nope, it's me."

"What do you want?"

He laughed, making me realize how blunt I sounded, then sang, "I just called...to say...I love you. I just called...to say how much I care...I do"

"Alright, that's enough. Really, why did you call?

"To see if you wanted to go grab a bite to eat. I'm hungry and I don't want

room-service again. I hate to eat alone."

"You...alone?"

"Yes, even Prince Charming finds himself alone from time to time."

"Okay. Where do you want to go?"

"There's this little place right up the street. We can walk. I'll meet you in the lobby in fifteen?"

"Make it ten and you got a deal."

"See you in ten," he answered, hanging up without saying goodbye.

In a flash, I jumped out of bed and put on a dress. Then with a dab of perfume and blush I was almost ready. I looked in the mirror to smear on some lipstick before slipping on my shoes and I was out the door.

Michael stood in the lobby near the elevator door, waiting with his arm folded which I gladly took after saying hello. A bellboy opened the lobby door which led to the street and we walked arm and arm toward the restaurant. We made small talk about the weather, New Zealand and our hunger. Even though it wasn't easy, I did my best to hide my feelings about Steven, his poem, and our upsetting phone call.

After we finished dinner, I noticed more and more people coming in to have dinner. It was odd to me, considering the time so I asked our waitress if it was normal to eat this late in New Zealand. She laughed very loud then leaned over, whispering in my ear.

"What was that all about?" Michael asked, when the young girl walked away.

"It was about you and me."

"What about you and me?"

"She said we're the reason so many people are here this late."

He moved a little closer, putting his arm around my shoulder, saying, "Let's give em' something to talk about."

I picked his hand up, removing it from my body and said, "Michael, have you forgot? I'm a newlywed."

"No, I haven't forgotten," he replied, scooting away.

"Sorry, I didn't mean to…"

"Listen, it's late. Let's just call it a night."

"Sounds good," I said, slipping out of the booth.

Deep within my mind I wondered what was going on with me. It seemed like everyone I talked to today had taken what I said the wrong way. Or maybe it was me taking what they said the wrong way. Either way, I thought it would be best to get back to the hotel and get some sleep. Then I could start over again tomorrow and maybe it would be a better day.

When Michael opened the door for me he held out his hand. As soon as I took it, I could hear the crowd moving our way and the cameras starting to flash. Michael and I made eye contact and in an instant I knew what to do. We both straightened our posture and smiled our happy smiles knowing that it was part of the job.

Once we ducked into the safety of the hotel, we both went our separate ways. I went to the elevator and Michael went toward the bar. Alone on the ride up to my room, I wondered if the photographers were a set up. If so, was it the studio or Michael who had sent them there? The thought turned me around in a blaze of fury. As I made my way down to the bar, I rehearsed the words I would say.

When I spotted him sitting on a bar stool, my fury changed to extreme irritation. The frustration of Michael and his motives had a grip on me. With each step, I prepared for confrontation knowing he could be very sly when it came to something he wanted. He smiled, waved me over and that was when I noticed he was completely alone.

"Tell me you couldn't go to sleep without having one little night cap with me," he said, trying to sound debonair.

"You wouldn't want me to lie, now would you?"

"Lying never hurt no one," he replied, raising his hand to get the bar tenders attention. "What will it be?"

"Vodka on the rocks," I said, sitting down on the stool beside him.

"So…if you weren't having trouble going to sleep without me, then let me guess," he said, hand stroking the imaginary beard on his chin. "You came down to the bar to drown your troubles in alcohol?"

"Not even close, mister."

"Here, this should help cool that attitude," Michael said, picking up my drink and putting it in my hand.

After taking a small sip, I said, "I've got one question for you, Michael."

"Yes, I would love to come back to your room."

"Married….see!" I exclaimed, putting my wedding ring about an inch from his eyes.

"You can take that ring off and put it on the night stand and it won't come anywhere between us tonight."

"Look Michael, all I want to know is did the studio send the photographers tonight or was it you?"

"Lady, you should know by now those people follow you whenever they can. They got to make a living just like you and me," he said, motioning the bar tender over again.

"We're in New Zealand. Or have you forgotten?"

"They have magazines and newspapers here too, Tiffany," he replied, after ordering another round.

"Michael, why do you always act so innocent?"

"Are you one of those women who hate men? What are they called?"

"No! I am not like that."

"Then why are you so bitchy all the time?"

"Now you're calling me names?"

"I never called you a name. Look, you came here to ask if I had ordered up the photographers, I guess to promote my career…and I told you the truth. No, I didn't. So why are you still here?"

"Because, I'm finishing my drink. Morning will come all too soon and I need my beauty sleep."

"I have a feeling you would still look beautiful without a wink of sleep," he said, winking at me.

"Really? Don't you think you might overdo it sometimes?"

"It's always worked for me before."

"No need to use all your smooth moves on me. I'm leaving."

"Come on! You've only had a couple of drinks. Let's have one more for the road."

"No, I've really had more than I need. I hardly ever drink," I replied, while Michael ordered another round, ignoring me completely.

"Then this is your chance," he whispered, setting the drink down in front of the old one. "Besides, we haven't even had a chance to dance yet."

"I love to dance," I replied, suddenly noticing the effects of the vodka.

"Finish your drink first, then we'll dance."

In three gulps the glass was empty. I held out my hand for Michael to help me off the bar stool, saying, "Let's do it."

"I thought you'd never ask," he answered, leading me to the dance floor.

There were several other couples, so Michael held me close as we worked our way around the floor. Sometimes he could seem like such an underhanded thief that someone, somewhere had scraped out of the bottom of the barrel from New York City. At others, he appeared more prince-like, with enormous grace and charm. His dance skills certainly put him somewhere between prince and thief because I definitely could feel the magnetism from his moves and knew without a doubt he was simple a bandit in disguise. If the alcohol had not coursed through my veins so quickly I would have left him standing all alone. And if I hadn't been so intoxicated I would have refused his help back to my room but I didn't.

The next day came and went without much fanfare at all. Other than making it to work late, no one knew about mine and Michael's night at the bar together. Neither of us discussed it either, other than an occasional smile with a know-it-all-look we kept it hush-hush. It had been our moment, our secret time to get to know each other and now it was time to focus on work and getting this film wrapped up. In fact, the next few days went by pretty smoothly and I was feeling better after having a couple of good conversations with Steven.

His mother had been diagnosed with brain cancer but it was in the first stage so it was treatable. Steven seemed to be optimistic about the outcome and spoke a lot about prayer and positive thinking. As usual he tried to keep the subject on me and my life but I managed to get him to talk about his mother enough to realize he was concerned.

Michael and I were becoming more than co-stars, we were becoming fast friends. With each passing day I realized he was not much different than I was when I first started acting. We really had more in common than I had initially thought when we first started this film. Our friendship was growing stronger day after day and instead of being overly protective about what his hidden motives might be I decided to embrace Michael and help him. So whenever we happened to be out I smiled for the photographers knowing in the end, it would only help both of our careers.

More very busy days passed before I received another letter from Steven. I did what I had always done, I prepared to read it then sat down on the bed. This time, I took a deep breath, hoping I would find his words soothing instead of confusing. Regardless of how much we tried to prepare ourselves for this initial separation, it had hit us harder than we could have imagined. Perhaps him even more than me because I was so busy working long hours with very little time to think. But in his chosen field of work, thinking was all he did. Sure, I guess he might get lost in the story some of the time but writing certainly is very different from acting.

As I unfolded the pages, to see only a poem, my heart sank. It wasn't enough. I needed more. I needed more words to explain exactly what was going on in his heart and mind. At least a letter with paragraphs that might give me clues as to how he was feeling and what was happening back in Mississippi. But all he had enclosed was a poem so I sat up straight and read it aloud.

Where can I go
to see your face?
How can I gather
the energy and strength
that being in your presence
gives to me?
I feel hopeless
like a bird
with clipped wings.
Only the promise
of loving you…
no matter what
keeps me afloat.
Without you, my love
I grasp
at this harsh reality
and face the future
staring back at me
only clinging to the love
that is surely ours.
Where can I go
to see you now?
Only in my dreams…
only…
        in my dreams.
So let sleep come…
come sweet slumber; come.

Again, there was no signature but this time he had written a short note on another sheet of paper. I read the poem again aloud before reading the note. It said, *Tiffany, You are my world. Please come to me. I need you. I want you. I love you. Steven,* which made me very upset. When we spoke on the phone, he seemed a little bothered but handling everything okay. His poetry told me another story. After all these years, I knew that these words came straight from his heart.

Without hesitation I knew what had to be done. First I would call dad to ask him to check on Steven. Also, I would see if he knew how I could get in touch with Victoria. If there was anything I remembered about her, it was she knew everything about everyone within a five to ten mile radius of her. If I wanted to know the truth about what was going on in Natchez she was the one to ask.

Dad gave me the usual barrage of questions. Why had it taken so long for me to call? Didn't I know he wondered if I was okay? Then the subject changed to, how's work? Last but not least, one of my favorite subjects, Steven.

He promised to make a special trip over tomorrow afternoon to see Steven in person. Then we talked about the last time they had talked. It was right after Steven had gotten back from New Zealand. Dad said he had clearly seemed fine, only eager to finish writing his new novel.

When I brought up the subject of his mother's illness he was absolutely shocked. Steven had barely mentioned it other than saying she had not been feeling well. This made it much easier to ask him about Victoria, which he told me would not be a problem since she and Blake only lived a few blocks away.

The next day after work I had a message from my old friend with a number. After washing off the long day on set off my skin, I sat down at the desk debating what I would say to Victoria. It had been a long time since we had talked on the phone and for some strange reason I was a little nervous.

"Hello, is this Victoria?"

"Hey, girl. What's up?"

"Well, not too much. How are you?"

"Getting as big as the side of a house," she said in her deep southern twang, laughing loudly.

"Steven told me you were getting bigger."

"What a nice thing for him to say."

"He wasn't being mean, he was…"

"Oh, I know, girl. He was just being a man. Sometimes I wonder if they even think before opening their big mouths."

"I think we all make that mistake sometimes."

"So when you coming back to Natchez? Did you know Amber is back?"

"Yes, Steven told me she was back."

"Did you know she's taking care of his momma?"

"She is?"

"Yep! Steven and his daddy decided it would be better to hire her instead of me. They think I can't do the job just because I'm preggers. Can you believe that?"

I swallowed hard, trying to keep my composure, saying, "That is hard to believe."

"You know that poor, poor pitiful me act she is playing may have worked on everybody in this town but it ain't worked on me. She ain't fooling me with that crap."

"Are you talking about her husband?"

"I guess Steven told you about that, too?"

"He said she's a widow."

"Did he tell you it was because he was drunk? In fact, they had both been out drinking and got into a fight at the bar. He left and she stayed with a friend of his and that was it. He was gone forever."

"No, he didn't tell me that."

"You know she's still in love with him. I think that's why she's here. That and the fact that ya'll got married. It's driving the old witch crazy," she said, laughing again.

"That's why I called you."

"I figured that. I was kinda hoping you might have been checking on me seeing as though I am about to have this baby."

"I do think about you."

"We are practically sister-in-laws."

"That's true, isn't it?"

"Duh! So I've told you what's going on around here, now it's your turn. What's up with you and that guy… Michael McFarland?"

"Nothing. We're working together. He's a nice guy."

"Well honey, that's not the picture most of these magazines around here are painting."

"What do you mean?"

"You know what I mean," she said in a weird tone of voice.

"Victoria, I am half-way around the world working my butt off. I don't know what you mean."

"They have pictures of ya'll together and the rumor is…come on Tiffany."

"I get it. You know it's not true?"

"Sure," she answered, not sounding so sure.

"Listen, I know this is a lot to ask of you but I really need a favor."

"I knew this was coming."

"Will you keep an eye out and let me know what's going on. I'd be more than happy to compensate you for your trouble."

"It's no trouble, no trouble at all."

"Also, will you promise not to say anything? Steven would kill me if he knew what I was doing."

"I promise. You know he's still just being Steven."

"What do you mean?"

"He's just trying to help everybody."

"But why wouldn't he tell me?"

"I don't know. Guess it's not right for him to hide something from you, especially Amber. Ya'll just got married."

"Has he said anything about Michael?"

"Not a word but just about everyone else in town is talking," she said, sounding uneasy.

"Oh, my… there's really nothing to talk about. Look, will you give me a call in a couple of days? When I get home, I mean when I come to Mississippi I'll catch up with you."

"Sounds good, girl."

After giving her my numbers and saying goodbye I sat holding the receiver long after she hung up. It felt like I had no control over what was happening and I didn't like it. Before we were married, I never worried about where he was or what he was doing. I thought about him every day and hoped he was happy and healthy. In my thoughts I assumed he thought about me too. There were times when I longed to see him, to hear his voice or to touch him. Then there he would be, in a letter or a poem or in the flesh and I was happy just to spend a little time with him. It was never a question of truth or lies. Nor about what he was doing or who he was spending his time with. For that moment, he was with me and what else was happening in his life was neither here or there. But now everything had changed. The moment I said I will, the moment I said I do his business became mine. And I would go to the ends of the earth to make sure my business was in good shape.

With all of this new found energy so late in the night, I found myself pacing the room. After half an hour of debating what move to make next I dug through the desk and found the letters Steven had sent. After reading the poems again I knew there was only one weapon of defense against a distressed marriage I could use this late at night. So I found pen and paper and got to work.

My beloved Steven,

Each day I pray that our love is strong enough to outlast any storm life throws our way. When I lay down in bed at night, you are the only thing on my mind. I wonder how you are doing and what you are thinking about and I hope it's me. Every morning when I wake up, you are the first thing on my mind. You know there is not one day that I don't wish you were with me, to hold me and kiss me good morning.

Steven, you and I have something very rare and special that only the two of us share. We cannot let other people or their problems contaminate our lives. If we let lies and gossip ruin what we share then we are fools and deserve the future that will certainly be ours. I don't want to live in regret. I don't want to fail at something as simple as loving you. You know it is simple. I love you and that's all. It may have taken me a long time to wrap my brain around it but without any doubt I can say that I have always loved you and I always will.

Darling, please remember the months we spent together, the months we spent every night and day together before we were married. We made love to each other in every possible way imaginable and never worried or doubted who we were or what we wanted. When you finish thinking about those precious moments we spent together then turn your thoughts toward Italy. To me...those were some of the best days of my life. It truly felt like we were the only two people in the world. We didn't need anyone or anything, just each other. How I wish that that was the way we could feel today.

The miles separate us but my heart is one with yours. We have a bright future together, this I am certain of because of who you are and who I am with you in my life. Please know that I appreciate everything about you and truly love you with all of my heart. Until I am in your arms again I am incomplete.

Love,
Tiffany

14
Chapter

The plane landed in Mississippi two hours after the scheduled time without any problems; other than making me late. It felt like I had not seen Steven in a year or longer but in reality it had only been five weeks. As usual, filming had ran longer with retakes and stupid mistakes that cost everyone time. I suspected it was a cruel fate that had been delivered especially to me. Certainly it was beyond my comprehension why in the world I had to wait longer to see my husband. My fear of Amber and why she had come back to Natchez almost caused me to walk away. But the lawsuit that would have ensued made me stay in New Zealand for two grueling extra-long weeks.

Victoria had been my only link to what was really going on around here. Now more than ever I was glad to have her as a friend. It was strange how we had gone so many years without communicating and now we were back to talking every day. She had even befriended Amber to the best of her ability so we could get the scoop from the source.

Now it was my turn to find out the truth behind her and Steven's so called friendship and where I stood with him. If that girl wanted a fight, she certainly had one coming. Too many years and too many opportunities had passed for her to be looking back now. She could have tried to have a relationship with Steven hundreds if not thousands of times without me even knowing about it. So priority number one was to find out why she waited until we were married to try and hook up with him. That and to make sure she saw how happy we are together.

As I got off the plane, I could see Steven waiting for me with flowers in his hand. He was alone, looking so happy and even though I wanted to run to him, I walked toward him with poise and dignity, trying not to let my suspicions show. He locked eyes with me and stared for a moment, like he wasn't sure what to do next. I never looked away, keeping my same steady pace, walking to where he stood.

We embraced, not letting go for a long, long time. Steven finally pulled back, telling me how beautiful I looked, handing me the flowers. I put them up to my nose, pretending to smell them but really only hiding my face. Tears filled my eyes, tears of fear that I would lose Steven before we had even begun our lives together.

"Will you hold these," I asked, handing the flowers back to him.

"Sure," he said, turning his face to look at me.

I lowered my eyes, avoiding his, saying, "I'll be right back. I need to go to the restroom."

"Be right here," Steven answered, reaching out to squeeze my hand.

As soon as I pushed the door open, tears began to fall. Try as I might, they would not stop. I went into the stall, pulling off a piece of toilet paper to dry my eyes. My emotions were running wild. I still had so many unanswered questions. Victoria had been my saving grace in this situation but she had also given me information that I shouldn't have known. Now, that I am here what good does it do me to know what I know when I can't ask the questions I need answers to?

Finally I walked out of the stall and looked at myself in the mirror. It didn't take too much of my reflection to stop the tears from falling. Besides, there was a man out there that was anxious to see me and I had to get it together. He had no idea how upset I had become over the past few weeks because of his deception about his mother's illness and Amber's involvement. For all he knew, I was thrilled to see him and couldn't wait to make love. When he knocked on the door calling out my name, I realized I was about to play the biggest acting role of my life.

He stopped me as I walked out of the bathroom, taking me into his arms. Without a word, he led me over to the seating area and we sat down. He gave me a sideways look with concern all over his face. I returned an expression of happiness which only made him stare at me with sadness.

"What's wrong, Love?"

"I'm just happy to see you," I said, trying to control the quiver in my voice.

"Something's wrong. I can tell."

"It's nothing, baby. You know how long that flight is. I'm tired, that's all."

"Being tired doesn't usually make you cry."

"I've been feeling very lonely since you left," I said, fighting back the tears, wanting so bad just to break down and tell him the truth and ask all the questions I had bottled up so deep inside.

"I've been missing you, too. Hey, let's get out of here. You'll feel better after a good nights' sleep."

After standing up, turning away to wipe a tear from my check, I said, "I think you're right."

It wasn't until we got to Steven's house that I realized he had called this home. It was a house but most of my memories of this place kept it from feeling like a home to me. He had gone out of his way to welcome me back. The flowers at the airport, a card sitting on the coffee table and a small present wrapped in white paper with a gold bow sitting beside it. After I opened the card and read it aloud, he went to put the flowers in a vase.

It was strange how my mind was so divided that I could barely think straight. Part of me felt true happiness and bliss to be here with him, enjoying the flowers, the gift and the card. Then the other part, the part with too much information about what he had been doing wanted to rip the card up and throw it at him. That part of me wanted to pull the flowers out of the vase and cast them on the floor, crushing them beneath my feet. That part wanted to throw his 'I'm guilty as sin' gift in his face, while screaming go give it to Amber. But instead, I smiled like any professional actress would do and gave him a facade of my true feelings. All the time remembering, I know what I know and the truth would be revealed soon enough.

Inside the box was an Aquamarine gemstone that looked to be around two carrots. When I picked it up I wondered why in the world he would have bought such a large stone without having it set in anything. He got down on his knees in front of me, watching me look at it.

"It reminded me of the water in Italy."

"Yes, it is about the same color," I said, holding it up to the light.

"I wasn't sure how you would want to wear it so I bought the stone and thought I would let you choose."

"I was wondering what you expected me to do with it," I said, setting it back in the box.

"I thought maybe we could have it put in a ring, or a necklace," he suggested, putting the top back on the box.

"Thank you. It's gorgeous."

"Just like you, Love," he said, calling me by my middle name, putting his arms around me, pulling me close.

At first, I resisted his touch, trying not to be too obvious. Then as he continued to caress my skin, I yielded, letting my mind go blank. For the moment, nothing mattered about him, me, Amber or Victoria's constant news updates. His lips on my skin and his hands pushing and pulling at my clothes were the only things I could feel.

We were both starving for gratification that we could only receive from each other. Giving pleasure was an unspoken agreement between us. It had begun when we were teenagers and as far as I could see it would never end. Besides, who could argue with this type of fulfilment that brought such utter joy and contentment? It certainly wasn't me, not even when something deep inside me was filled with rage. That rage only turned into energy for passion and possibilities for a great release of tension.

Steven did not fail to impress me with his appetite for affection or his desire for my flesh. His attempt to pace his self or to govern his self-control over this craving was wasted. Instead, like a child he plundered every inch of my body with a yearning that I had never felt from him before. It was the same man I had shared so many intimate moments with but yet his longing for satisfaction left me lying in a muddled heap.

With each deep breath my mind wandered in no particular direc-tion. I was high as a kite from enjoying his passionate love and at the same time it felt like I had been pillaged and left ransacked. Then my mind suddenly felt clearer than it had in a long time. What had just happened, what we had just shared made me smile because I couldn't remember the last time I had felt this exhausted or this good. Then I felt so calm because I knew there was little chance that Amber had broken the bonds of our marriage.

It crossed my mind to begin questioning his every move and motive for keeping me in the dark about his mother and the hired help. Steven moved closer, gathering me into his arms and sighing in relief. Never had I felt such a deep sense of peace or comfort from him. He obviously had been through a lot since the last time we had been together and if I were to break the silence I wasn't sure I would ever feel this from him again. So I closed my eyes, living in the moment and let sleep overtake me. Whatever needed to be said, the questions that weighed so heavy on my mind would have to wait for mornings light.

We awoke to the chirping of birds outside the window, in each other's arms. His lips pressed against my forehead as his arms pulled me closer to his warm body. When I loosened my grasp on him, he turned slightly to look into my eyes. In that instance, everything came flooding back and I turned away trying not to let my eyes give away the pain.

"What's the matter, Love?"

"I don't feel well."

"Probably just jet lag," he said, letting me lay back on the pillow.

"No, I think I'm going to be sick," I said, jumping up and running to the bathroom. Before I could make it to the toilet, I was throwing up. I flung the toilet seat up and fell to my knees. Then I felt Steven standing behind me, gathering my hair into his hands and holding it away from my face.

"Can I get you anything," he asked.

"Yes, a wet wash cloth."

He turned on the water as my stomach finally stopped heaving and I slumped down sitting on the floor. Steven kneeled beside me handing me the wash cloth and flushing the toilet. He pulled my hair back as I wiped my face and then handed the cloth back to him. He laid it on the side of the tub and put his arm around me.

"I'm okay," I said, pushing him back.

"Can I help you up?"

"I got it. Just give me a minute, I'll be out."

He sat still for a moment, then stood back up and walked out, closing the door behind him. I got up to my feet and walked to the sink, looking in the mirror. I looked a mess; pale, grey, tired, even ghostly. After splashing my face, I brushed my teeth until my arm was tired and the bad taste was finally gone. After looking in the mirror again I saw a reflection that looked like death warmed over. Now I knew I had to ask him what in the world was going on. If all of these questions had me looking this way then it was time to confront the one who had the answers.

"Are you okay, Tiffany?"

"No, I'm not."

"Come here and let me hold you, baby."

"I'd rather go sit on the couch."

"Okay, let's get some clothes on," he said, making me remember I was naked.

We dressed in silence and then I followed him into the living room. After sitting down, Steven reached for my hand. So many times I had rehearsed in my mind how this conversation would start but it never involved me feeling so sick. His hazel eyes appeared dimmer than I remembered and I could tell he had a lot on his mind too.

"What do you want to talk about?"

"How did you know I wanted to talk?"

He let go of my hand and leaned back against a pillow, saying, "Because I can tell that something is bothering you."

"I want to talk about Amber."

"What about Amber?"

"I want to know what's been going on since she's been back in town."

"Nothing's been going on," he said, looking straight into my eyes.

"Have you seen her?"

"Yes, I've seen her, almost every day."

"That's what I thought," I said, looking down at my hands, staring at my wedding rings.

"Listen, somebody must have already told you she's taking care of my mom. I didn't tell you because I didn't want you to worry."

"You should have told me."

"Maybe I should've but I thought you knew me well enough to trust me."

"That's beside the point, Steven. If your mother needs someone to take care of her why in the world would you get Amber to do it? You have the money to hire the best of the best, even a registered nurse and pay her a year in advance. It feels like a slap in the face for you to get your ex-girlfriend who was such an evil bitch to me, to babysit your mom."

"That's who mom wanted. What else was I supposed to do, Tiffany?"

"Tell her no. You should have told your mom that you would not hire that girl to take care of her."

"I guess you're right."

"You're damn straight I'm right. What in the hell were you thinking? Don't you realize this girl is still after you? I wouldn't doubt it for a second that your mom isn't trying to get you two back together. That's all she ever wanted."

"I don't think you realize how sick my mom is, Tiffany. I know you're upset but damn it! I was just trying to give her what she wanted."

"What about me, Steven? Do you even care about me or what I want?"

"I do care about you, very much. But while we're asking questions, just what in the hell is going on between you and Michael McFarland?"

"Nothing, Steven. We were merely co-workers. I know what you're going to say…"

"And what's that?"

"Why is there so many pictures of us together?"

"That's one of the questions. Another one is why is everybody in town saying I'm the biggest fool around here?"

"Steven you know that gossip is a part of my business. You should know by now that I would never have anything to do with someone like Michael, especially since I'm a married woman."

"Well, I thought I did, until magazine after magazine was brought to my attention. Did you go out to eat with him?"

"Yes, we went out to eat," I said, starting to feel nauseous again.

"Did you have a drink with him at a bar?"

"Yes, Steven. I even had a drink with him. Believe it or not all I talked about was you. People over there were sick of hearing about you and our wedding and our honeymoon."

"Did you sleep with him, Tiffany?"

"How dare you even say that, I can't believe you!" I yelled, standing up, running back to the bathroom.

This time I was alone, holding my own hair the best I could. When the illness passed, I made a fresh wash cloth and cleaned my face. This time when I looked into the mirror, I began to cry. I looked old and ugly, nothing like the beautiful actress that I saw on the big screen. Suddenly, I wanted out of this house. I wanted to be at my beach house in L. A. with someone there to do my hair and make-up. But I knew he was waiting for me out in the living room. So I washed my face again, then brushed my hair before walking out of the bathroom.

"Sorry, I'm sick but that's how I get when I think about you and Amber."

"I can tell."

"Steven, the only damn thing you can tell, is I'm mad as hell. I'll tell you another thing, I'm not going to take this crap from Amber anymore! She may have the rest of you fooled but I'm not buying it."

"What do you want me to say?"

"I'm going to ask you one time and one time only. Why? Why in the hell didn't you tell me about hiring your precious Amber to be your mother's nursemaid?"

"I already told you, I didn't want you to worry."

"Is that the truth or just another way for you to spare my feelings?"

"Good God, don't you trust me, Tiffany? Haven't I loved you long enough for you to know that I would never do anything to hurt you?"

"I did trust you, Steven. But your deception has filled me with fear."

"What are you scared of?"

"Of losing you."

"Is that why you recruited Victoria to be your little spy?" He asked, his voice filled with resentment, anger and sarcasm.

My eyes closed as my chin dropped and my head started moving side to side. Words were trapped in my throat giving the disguise of speechlessness. The walls of his little house felt like they were closing in as his words uncovered what I thought he didn't know.

"Are you telling me you didn't do that, Tiffany?"

"No, I'm not going to lie or conceal the truth like you have. But I will tell you, don't ever take that tone of voice with me ever again."

"So you just answered my question. You did get Victoria to watch me, didn't you?"

"Yes," I said lifting my head to look into the angry eyes of my husband.

"How dare you?"

Tears fell from my cheeks in a rush of emotion as I whispered, "I'm sorry."

"How could you do that to me? And in my own town," Steven said, in raging anger.

"I thought Amber…"

"How much did you pay her?"

"Who?"

"Victoria! H-o-w m-u-c-h d-i-d y-o-u p-a-y h-e-r?"

"I haven't paid her anything."

"Why don't you let me pay her? In fact, I think I'll go pay up right now. How much?"

"Steven, you're twisting this around."

"Well you had to have an agreement with her, right?"

"Why are you making me out to be the bad guy?"

"Did she do a good job, being a spy?"

"She told me the truth about Amber. You should try it sometime."

"She told you what you think is the truth but what lies did she tell you, Tiffany? Have you forgot that your old pal Victoria is not the most honest person in the world?"

"I'm sorry, Steven. I guess when I married you I should have left my brain, along with my emotions at the altar. Then I should have taken on the mentality of simply being grateful to be your wife, regardless of how you treat me."

"Whatever you think, Tiffany. I'll just ask her what you owe when I get there," he said, storming out the door.

I rushed to the door, saying, "Please don't go. I don't want you to leave here mad."

"It's a little too late for that," he said, slamming the truck door and starting the engine.

My first instinct was to run after him but when I walked outside I felt dizzy and sat down on the steps. He never looked back at me, just kept his eyes focused on the road before speeding down the street. My next thought was to call Victoria and warn her that Steven was on his way. But I didn't want to betray his trust again. Somehow my justification for Victoria keeping me in the know had been blurred by Steven's rage. It made me feel like I had made such a mess of everything. I wanted to make wise decisions from here on out so I sat there contemplating my next move.

For a moment, I felt like we were back in high school, surrounded by controversy and drama. It was a feeling that I didn't like, didn't want and I wasn't sure what I could do to make things better. Steven was wrong to hire Amber to care for his mother but he didn't see it that way. To him he had only done what his mother had asked, his mother suffering from cancer and perhaps living the last days of her life. The only thing I could think to do, maybe the one thing that would make things better was to go and see his mom.

After a shower and clean clothes, I wrote Steven a note, leaving it on the coffee table. When I walked outside, I realized there wasn't a car waiting for me and I had no way to go. So I started walking towards dad's house, hoping he might be home.

Winter was almost here but you could barely tell with the warm Mississippi sun beating down. After only a few blocks I took off my jacket and draped it over my arm. That's when I realized how weak I felt and remembered that I hadn't eaten or drank anything yet. With a couple of deep breaths, I decided I would not walk back to Steven's, I would make it to dad's house no matter what.

When I turned the corner, a car slowed down behind me and beeped the horn. I turned to see Victoria waving me over as she rolled down the window. A part of me shuddered to think about what was about to happen and another part knew I had to be a woman and not a child and face the music.

"Come on girl, get your ass in the car," Victoria said, stopping beside me.

"I was walking to dad's house," I said, opening the door, sitting down.

"What in the sam-hell did you do this morning?" She demanded in a tone of voice that was between frustration and anger.

"I got up, got very sick then asked Steven why Amber is at his mom's house every day."

"Girl...he came storming in over there, raising-cain and threw this at me before walking out," she said, handing me an envelope.

"How much," I asked, opening the envelope.

"I don't know. I didn't stop to count it. I came to find you."

"Looks like a lot of money," I said, handing the envelope back.

"Well, I can certainly use it but I didn't want it that way. Do you realize he is practically my brother-in-law?"

"Yes, and I'm sorry. I've messed everything up."

"No you haven't. But damn! Couldn't you tell a little lie or at least skirt around the truth?"

"He already knew. I don't know how?"

"Most likely it was his stupid brother, Blakerd."

"You mean your future husband?"

"Yes, my baby's daddy. The dumbass," she said laughing.

"Victoria, you're such a trip," I said, laughing with her.

"You're just now figuring that out?" She asked, completely puzzled by my comment.

"No, but thanks for making me laugh. I thought I was about to throw up again."

"How many times this morning?"

"Twice."

"You look a little putrid. Have you eaten?"

"No."

She laughed again, picking up the cash filled envelope, saying, "Let me take you to brunch. A pregnant woman is always ready to eat."

"Sounds good, I'm starving."

"Do you think you could be pregnant?"

"No, not really. But I guess I could be. I am married."

"You don't have to be married to be pregnant," she said, flashing her finger.

"Oh, I'm sorry. I know you don't. Boy, I wish I could start this day all over again. Then I would keep my big foot out of my mouth."

"I think we better stop by the store and pick you up a test. You can pee on the stick before we eat."

"You don't think I should do that at home?"

"Heck no, girl. Don't you want to know as soon as possible? So you won't drink or take anything?"

"I guess you're right. Besides, we just got married and I don't think I can be pregnant this soon."

"Do I have to keep reminding you? You don't have to be married to get pregnant. You just have to do the deed," Victoria said, pulling into the parking lot.

As we walked into the store I told her about my plans to go and see Mrs. Cross. She looked at me like I was crazy and said that was the worst idea I had had so far. Slightly above a whisper, she reminded me of his mother's hatred toward me and now with Amber there it had only gotten worse. Plus she was certain that lovely Amber had made sure to bring as many gossip rags in the house as possible so mother Cross would know about her daughter-in-law and her new lover, Michael Mc-Farland.

Victoria insisted on paying for the pregnancy test and bought herself a new pair of shades which she asked the cashier to cut the tags off. After putting them on we walked across the parking lot to the little restaurant next door. She said hey to the girl at the counter and we walked straight to the bathroom.

"Have you ever done one of these before?"

"Yes, but it's been awhile," I said, taking the stick from her hand.

"Well do your business and let's see. Man, it would be awesome if we both had babies at the same time, wouldn't it?"

"I guess, Victoria."

"Well you don't have to sound so happy about it."

"I...I...I,"

"What?"

"I don't know."

"Are you going to pee?"

"I can't do it with you in here," I said opening the door slightly, looking out.

"Alright, I'll walk outside, call me when you're done."

She walked out and I put the stick between my legs. Then I sat on the toilet watching the lines turn pink. First it was the test line and then as the liquid absorbed further down the stick was the line that indicated pregnant or not pregnant.

"Well?"

"You can come back in," I said, flushing the toilet and buttoning my pants.

"Are you going to come out of that stall or am I going to have to bring this big pregnant belly in there with you?"

I opened the door, looking her in the face and held out the stick, saying, "Here."

"Oh, my gosh. Oh, my gosh!" She shouted, hugging my neck.

"I can't believe it."

"It's perfect timing, Tiffany. Now Steven won't be mad anymore. I'll put ole' Momma Cross in her place and possibly ship Amber back off to wherever she came from."

"I'm going to have a baby."

"Yes, we're going to have babies together. Isn't that awesome?"

"I have to find Steven. He has to be the first to know."

"It's a little too late for that. Besides the fact that you said you would eat with me. Can't you smell that food, girl? It's calling my name."

We ate our meal with Victoria's constant chatter about the future that lay ahead for our children. Before we left the restaurant, she had told me that she was having a girl and the names she and Blake had picked out. She then decided it would be perfect if I was having a girl too so they could grow up together and be best friends. She said it would be great if Steven and I would move back home so we could all be closer. I never agreed with what she said but I didn't disagree either. All I could think about was finding Steven and giving him the news.

Victoria drove me back to his house and his truck was sitting in the driveway. She offered to go inside with me but I refused her help, deciding to go in alone. After a giving her a hug goodbye, I opened the door and walked up the sidewalk to the front door.

"Steven."

"In here," he called out from the kitchen.

I walked into the entry way and saw that he was cooking and said, "I'm glad you're here."

"Where else would I be?"

"I don't know."

"Hungry?"

"No."

"I'm cooking some eggs."

"I see."

"Where you been," he asked, turning to look at me for the first time.

"I have something to show you," I said, digging in my purse and handing him the pregnancy test.

"Does this mean you're pregnant?" He asked studying the stick with two pink lines.

"Yes. That's what it means. I hoped you would be happy."

"Is it mine, Tiffany?" He asked turning to look me straight in the eyes.

"Yes, it's yours."

"Without a doubt?"

"You are the only man I've been with since the day we kissed under the old oak tree at the park," I replied, with tears trying to force the boundaries of my eyes.

"I knew that, I just had to ask," he said, turning the stove off and walking toward me.

"I'm having your baby."

"No wonder you were sick this morning."

"I know."

"And probably the reason you've been acting so crazy lately," he said, putting his arms around me, hugging me close.

"No, that's because of that little green monster."

"You need to tell that little green monster to get lost. Tell him I'm not going anywhere. I've waited too long to share my life with you."

"I'm sorry I made you wait so long."

"You were worth it. I would have waited two lifetimes to hear you say that you're having my baby."

He leaned back, wiped the tears from my eyes and kissed my lips. Over and over he kissed me until I felt dizzy and lightheaded. He swooped me off my feet and carried me to the bedroom. We tore at each other's clothes in a hurried fury while fighting to keep our lips pressed together.

It was strange how just a few hours ago I thought that we may never make love again. How was he going to get over what I had done or how I was going to get over what he had done was beyond my comprehension just moments ago. We had both gone too far and hurt each other unknowingly. He, by trying to protect me and me, by trying to find out the truth. Now, everything had changed and Victoria was right. It was perfect timing and by the way Steven touched my belly, kissing it softly, I knew he was not angry at me anymore.

15
Chapter

The California sunshine was exhilarating, exactly what the doctor ordered. It fell on our shoulders, soaking into our skin and rekindling the passion in our hearts and souls. It allowed both of us to free ourselves of New Zealand and Mississippi, with its unwanted drama. The beach had a way of slowing the pace of life and bringing the here and now front and center. We didn't have to make-believe that we were okay and our marriage was strong. With each passing day the genuine love and affection we had for each other was growing just as my belly was growing with our child.

It was strange when I thought of those last few days in Mississippi. It was almost like I was thinking about someone else, somebody else's life. Those hours felt similar to a roller coaster ride or a high speed race. Victoria and Blake acted like they were the welcoming party for first time parents as if they had been the winners of a parent's of the year award. Steven's parents treated us like we had head lice or had contracted the plague. With that being my one and only visit, unfortunately, extreme rejection and dread was all I felt after leaving their home.

Amber had the look of shock, anger, hate and surprise as she left Steven's mother's bedroom without a word. It was one of those awkward moments that brought up the same old feelings from our past. If it would have been up to me, I would have chased after her and put her in her place. However, Steven, being Steven went to check on her while I sat quietly by his mother's bed. Mrs. Cross never spoke a word while he was out of the room but as soon as Amber and Steven walked back in she began to coddle poor little Amber. For the life of me I still couldn't figure out why this woman hated me with a passion. In reality, I had never done anything to deserve the way she treated me, so I excused myself with good-bye and never looked back.

It was one person who brought the roller coaster ride around the biggest upside down loop filling me with the delight any pregnant woman wants to feel when she announces her pregnancy. He was happier than Steven and I combined, talking about the future and what it would hold for us and for him. So the memory of my dad's joy was the one I clung to now as my whole world was changing before my eyes.

The studio was not too excited about my condition. They were counting on me to start shooting my next film in a few months. There was talk of shooting around my growing belly and possibly extending the beginning of production. After a whole lot of negotiations, we settled on a solution. They would find a new actress to replace me and I would have my baby in peace. Sometimes things go your way and sometimes they don't. This time I won the battle.

Steven had been fighting his own battles while I fought mine. He was very late with his new novel and everyone was rushing him to finish. So we would wake up in the morning and have breakfast then he would go over to his house to write. But it never failed that in a few hours he would be back at the beach house wanting to take care of me. I tried and tried to tell him I was okay and he needed to finish the book but it was like he didn't want to be away from me. When I suggested he go to Mississippi to get it done he looked like I had stabbed him in the heart. As a result of his reaction, I kept my nose out of his business and let him handle it.

As the seasons changed my belly grew larger and larger. Our son was the only thing Steven and I talked about. We discussed names and bought furniture and clothes and tiny shoes. We decided what rooms in our houses would be turned into nurseries and made arrangements to have the work done.

His long awaited book finally was in print and on sale. He seemed hesitant to bring me a copy but I didn't give up until I had one in my hands. Whenever he would go out for a little while I would read a chapter or two. Sales had been disappointing and as I read the book I understood what no one else in the world knew. He had changed as a person after becoming my husband and it showed in his writing. All of his loyal readers were expecting the same material he had delivered over the years but he had gone in a new direction. It wasn't that the work was bad, it just wasn't what his readers wanted or expected from him.

Steven never talked about it or the bad reviews he just focused on me and the baby. He reminded me of a bird. All day he was checking the nest and trying to make sure the eggs stayed warm and dry. The situation was perfect; I had the man I loved at my beckon call, and Steven had found his new focus in life. We were happier than two roosters in a room full of hens.

With both houses ready to receive our newborn baby and my belly about to pop we did what any expecting parents do. We slept. A lot. Steven would rub my feet and cook anything I craved in-between naps and movies. We were both waiting for time to pass and for our son to finally be in our arms.

One morning Steven called me to the phone, covering the mouth piece to say it was my mother. She had been happy about the baby but didn't look forward to becoming a grandmother. She said it made her feel old and she was certainly not old. She had also decided that 'the child' could not call her grandma. He must refer to her as Me-Me which

Steven and I both thought was strange but we agreed, just to make her happy.

"Good morning."

"Hello, Tiffany. How are you feeling?"

"I feel good, Mom. Big but good."

"How much have you gained?"

"Twenty-seven."

"Is Steven giving you everything you want to eat? Doesn't he realize that every pound you put on you'll have to lose?"

"Not every pound, Mother," I said, trying to sound optimistic.

"You always try to find the positive in everything."

"I try."

"Okay…well, I know you will be needing some help so I've arranged to move out to L.A. for a few months. Cheryl will be coming too and that boyfriend of hers."

"You mean Kenny?"

"Yes, Kenny."

"Mom, I really appreciate the thought but I think Steven and I will be okay."

"It's not a thought darling. It's what I'm doing. You can expect us to be there next weekend. I found a little place not too far from you. You can show me where Steven's house is so I can help you there too."

"Really, you don't…"

"This is hard enough for me, Tiffany. Would you please just be nice and accept my help. You're going to need it."

I swallowed my pride and said, "I can't wait to see you."

Stevens' eyes told the story. He had understood exactly what was about to happen just from listening to my end of the conversation. I think he could tell I was worried about how things would go with my mom, sister and her boyfriend living so close. He wrapped his arms around me, hugging me and never said a word until I broke the silence.

"Why now?"

"It's the baby, Tiffany. He will bring us all closer."

"Including your mom and dad, Steven?"

"Yes, he will even melt their hearts and bring them closer to you."

"That's good. All I ever wanted was for them to like me. They don't have to love me or think I'm the best daughter-in-law in the world but it would be nice if they liked me a little."

"They certainly like Victoria a lot more since she gave them a granddaughter."

"You're right. So I stand a chance," I said, remembering how his mother had spoken to me on our wedding day.

"Yes you do. It won't be bad having your Mom nearby."

"I guess you're right."

"Yes, I am. It'll do both of you some good to spend a little time together. Family is priority number one, right?"

"Right."

He led me back to the couch and made sure I was comfortable. I laid my head back on the pillow and closed my eyes. Everyone in the world seemed to be waiting for this baby to be born. There were hardly any magazines that covered Hollywood news that weren't talking about this child and hoping to be the first to get a picture. Even mom and my sister were coming for the birth. I guess next it would be Dad, Victoria, Blake, and Diane. At this point I didn't know who else might be coming to our door. It was strange because on one hand I wanted to share our joy with the world. On the other hand, I wanted to protect him and his innocence as long as possible.

Steven brought me out of my deep thoughts with a whisper and I struggled to sit up straight. He sat across from me with a piece of paper in his hand looking very happy. I shook my head, trying to make myself alert and fixed my eyes on him.

"I have something for you."

"Okay," I said, reaching out for him to hand it to me.

"Will it be okay if I read it to you?"

"Sure," I said, sinking back into the couch and putting my hand on my belly.

"It's just a little something I wrote for you," he said clearing his throat.

"Wait. Come here," I said, putting his hand on my belly.

"He sure is strong," he replied, smiling.

"Just like you," I said, looking up into his eyes. He left his hand on my skin and leaned down to kiss me softly.

"I love you, Tiffany."

"I love you, too, Steven."

He lingered, waiting to see if the baby would kick his hand again. After a few moments he sat back in the chair and looked at me with admiration. It was in that very moment that I knew marrying him had been the best decision of my life. I no longer had to seek approval from another living human being. This man loved me more than I would ever understand and I felt so grateful to have him as my husband.

"You show me the world
    through brand new eyes
I watch as it grows
        so completely mesmerized
With the glory to come
        to see what we've made
such a precious little one
        a gift from above.
Time and time again…
I would journey through the desert
to find you my friend
and gather you up
to make you mine
where wedding bells ring
and wedding rings shine.
These words do tell
a love story of the ages
boy meets girl

their lives move through stages
but once in awhile
the boy wins the heart of his girl
to live the fairy tale
coveted by the world.
So it will be… with you and me
the prince and the princess
the king and the queen
with a baby to tie us together
for all eternity."

"You never cease to amaze me, Steven."

"I hope that's good," he said, sitting the piece of paper down on the end table.

"It's better than good. Come here," I pleaded with my arms stretched out toward him.

He kneeled down in front of me and put his arms around my neck, pulling me toward his mouth. His kiss woke me up and I returned it with enthusiasm. His hand wandered down to my swollen breasts which he touched gently. I tugged at the bottom of his shirt, urging him to take it off. When my hands touched the skin of his bare chest, I knew it was time for us to make love.

Slowly he took my gown over my head to expose my new body to his touch. He kissed my neck, working his way down to my ever grow-ing baby bump which he kissed ever so softly. We worked our way into a position that was comfortable and he held me close as we became one. In my mind I wanted more. My body was raging with desire but I knew we were limited due to my condition. It was the closeness of his body against mine that gave me the pleasure I so desperately needed. With every passing moment, Steven brought me closer and closer to the point of no return.

We lay recovering in the bright California afternoon sunshine that flooded the living room beckoning us to come outside. He helped me up and then helped me get dressed so we could walk out to the beach. As soon as the salty air blew through my hair, he asked me to wait on the porch so he could get me a hat and glasses. I sat down, holding my belly and looked out across the horizon. For the first time in a very long time, I talked to God.

First, I asked him to forgive me for not praying as much as I should. Then I thanked him for my life. It had been good and I knew that He was the reason I was so blessed. Then I thanked him for Steven and having such a good husband who loved me so much. Then I promised him that if he would let this baby be born healthy that I would do better, I would be better. If He would let me know what I could do to be a better wife, mother and person in general, that would help the world be a better place; I would do it to the best of my ability.

Steven placed the sun hat on my head and put the glasses over my eyes. Then he took my hand, helping me down the steps and held onto me tightly as we walked toward the water's edge. We let the waves wet our feet as we stood hand in hand. Soon our whole world would change. We would have a son. A precious son who we would call, Tristian Henry Cross.

16 Chapter

Someone once told me that I had never experienced true love. They said there was only one way for me to ever have a taste of its pure meaning. It was not to be bought because it could not be sold. There was no place on earth that you could travel to in order to find it or feel its warmth. No in fact, they told me, there was only one way to encounter the authentic significance of love. It happened during the very moment that you hold your first child in your arms.

At the time these words of wisdom were spoken, I found this person to be a little over zealous about babies. With even more thought, I realized they most likely had been burned by love and that is what had shaped their opinion. Now, the same words, the same feelings poured from my soul. As I looked down onto the face of this little baby I held in my arms I learned that no words could be truer. In my life, I felt that I had loved and been loved but never had I experienced love this deep.

In the next moment, as tears wet my eyes, I had a question that shook me to the core. Could there be any way that this is how my mom and dad loved me? Then I ran more questions through my mind…had I been a good daughter? Had I made them proud of me? Did I treat them with respect? Did I make sure that they knew that I love them?

Steven reached out, asking, "Can I?"

"Sure," I said, helping to move Tristian from my arms into his.

My breath quickened as I looked at the scene before my eyes. The man I loved, holding our tiny baby in his strong arms was almost more than I could take. My joy was overflowing as tears fell gently down my face.

"Don't cry, Love."

"I can't stop. The two of you together, it just makes me emotional."

"Your mom is waiting to come in," he said, handing me a tissue.

"Okay, give me a minute."

"Your dad is here too."

"Good, I can't wait for him to meet his grandson."

"He's perfect, Tiffany. I love you so much. Thank you," he said, leaning over, kissing my cheek.

"No need to thank me, we did this together."

A knock at the door ended our loving gaze. Steven placed the baby back in my arms while saying just a minute to whoever was knocking. He walked backwards, toward the door, checking to see if I was ready. When I gave him a big smile he gave me the thumbs up before opening the door.

"My goodness! I thought they would never let me come back here to see you."

"Sorry, mom…"

"Let me see this little man. He is so precious, Tiffany."

"Do you want to hold him?"

"Yes. Do you think now is the right time? I mean he was just born."

"It's the perfect time," Steven answered, taking Tristian from my arms to hand him to my mother.

"Now wait just a second," mom said, sitting down in a chair.

"Are you ready?" Steven asked.

"It's been a long, long time but yes, I'm ready," mom answered, in a trembling voice.

There they were. Three of the most important people in my life huddled so close together. Steven looked so happy and proud while mother appeared healthy and younger looking than I had seen her in many years. Tristian lay comfortably sleeping, safe in the arms of his Me-Me, without a care in the world. It had taken a lifetime for me to see the world through new eyes but how thankful I was to finally see it.

With another knock at the door, Steven turned his attention to me. I struggled to sit up straighter and he rushed to help me. Once the covers were nice and neat he nodded his head yes and I nodded back. He left me with another kiss on the cheek and then happily opened the door.

"Henry," Steven said, shaking my dad's hand.

"Steven, so good to see you."

"Come in and meet your namesake," he said, opening the door wider.

"Not before I kiss my girl hello," dad answered, making me well up with tears again.

Dad walked to my bedside, leaned over and kissed my forehead, letting his lips linger a moment or two longer than usual. I took his hand, unable to speak and squeezed it hard. He stood beside me as I looked up and smiled.

"Are you okay?" Dad asked.

"Yes, I'm alright," I said, choking back my emotions.

"Oh, she's fine. Come here and look at your grandson, Henry," Mom said.

"He's a good looking boy, Steven," Dad said.

"Do you want to hold him?" Steven asked.

"That would be great," Dad answered, taking a seat on the other side of the room.

Steven took the baby from mom's arms and placed him in dad's. When he started to talk to his new grandson, Tristian woke up. He started to fuse a little and Mom walked over to take him from dad but before she did dad started to sing. Tristian looked up at him, stopped making any type of noise and watched as my dad whispered a nursery rhyme.

Now where there had been three, there were four. Four of the most important people in the world all hunched together within a few feet of my hospital bed. Suddenly a pain shot through my body that made me moan which caused Steven to run to my side.

"Are you okay?"

"I don't know."

"What is it?"

"Pain, really bad pain."

"I'll get your nurse," he said, running to the door.

"I think I'll be alright."

Then everything went black. Somewhere, out in the far distance I could see a bright light. Hour after hour of walking until I couldn't walk any more barely seemed to bring me closer. It was only the knowledge that someone was in the light, waiting for me that kept me going. Sometimes, I thought it was Tristian. At other times, I thought it was Steven. Whenever I would call out their names they would never answer. The only reply I ever heard was, 'it's not time yet.' I knew this was the truth but I couldn't help but walk out of the darkness toward the light.

With a startle I woke up again, saying, "I'm alright. Stop it, I'm alright."

"Tiffany, I'm right here," Steven said, squeezing my hand.

"Where's Tristian?"

"He's at home, Love."

"What do you mean?" I asked struggling to sit up.

"Take it easy," he replied, holding my shoulder down.

As my eyes began to focus, I could see I was still in the hospital. There were more machines around my bed and the room looked different. Steven looked like hell warmed over, his hair was dirty and he had dark circles under his eyes.

"Where am I?"

"You're in the ICU?"

"Why?"

"You had to have surgery, Tiffany. They couldn't stop the bleeding."

"How long have I been here?"

"Four days," he replied, looking over his shoulder.

"Mr. Cross, we need you to leave the room," a man said, ushering him out.

"But I...," Steven said.

"We'll let you know when you can come back," he said opening the door.

"I love you, Tiffany," Steven said loudly, before being forced out while other people in scrubs walked into the room.

After the medical team ran a series of tests they finally left my room allowing Steven to come back. Standing beside the bed he took my hand, and pressed his forehead against it. My head was swimming with questions but none of them came out of my mouth.

"Thank God, you're alive. I wouldn't want to live without you," Steven said, breaking the silence.

"I'm alright," I said, feeling myself drifting off to sleep.

A bright light shined into my eyes, bringing me out of the nicest dream. We were sailing on the clearest blue-green ocean I had ever seen. You could see all the way to the bottom even in a hundred feet of water. The fish and other wildlife were totally visible as if you were seeing them from a few feet away. Tristian was older, perhaps seven or eight and he and Steven were like two peas in a pod. The only strange thing about the dream was sometimes I was on the boat with them and sometimes it felt like I was looking down at them or watching them on a movie screen.

When my eyes focused, I recognized the same hospital room that I had seen before. This time Steven was nowhere in sight and there was a woman in a white uniform doing something to one of the machines near my bed.

"Where's my husband?"

"Mr. Cross stepped out for a moment."

"I want to see him," I pleaded.

"I'll see if I can find him," she answered, writing something on a chart.

"How long?"

"Well, I'm not sure where he is."

"No, how long have I been here?"

"Six days."

She walked out the door without another word. My eyelids felt so heavy that I had to close them again. As my mind searched for information about why I was here, I vaguely remembered Steven saying something about me bleeding. I forced my eyes to open and looked around the dimly lit tiny room. I wanted my baby. My arms ached to hold him. My lips ached to kiss his soft skin. There was only one way that was going to happen and I knew it. So before I fell back to sleep, I found the buttons to raise the back of my bed so I could sit up.

It felt as if my world was spinning, but somehow I found the button to call for a nurse. Then I did my best to focus and figure out what I was going to say. My heart and soul cried out for Steven. This would be so much easier if he were here to speak for me. Then I said his name aloud as the nurse walked into my room.

"What can I get for you, Mrs. Cross?"

"I want you to stop giving me these drugs to make me sleep."

"I can't do that. The order has to come from your doctor."

"Then get him in here. Now!"

"I can put a call in for him to come by to see you."

"I don't think you understand what I'm telling you."

"Mrs. Cross, if you stop taking the medicine you won't be able to handle the pain right now."

"What I can't handle is being away from my son any longer."

"I understand. Maybe we can make arrangements to have your mother bring him for a visit."

"I don't want to visit him! I want to go home."

Steven rushed in the door, giving the nurse a sideways glance before taking my hand to say, "We are going home. Are you ready?"

"Yes, Steven. I want to see Tristian."

"Okay, Love. Let me get the doctor and we'll…."

"I don't want to see the doctor! I want this shit out of my arm and I want my clothes."

"Tiffany, you are in the Intensive Care Unit. You have been here for six days. We almost lost you, baby. I know you want to see Tristian. I'll call Me-Me and get her to bring him."

"Why in the hell can't anyone understand that I am leaving, today, right now! Either you can help me or you can get out of my way."

"Mr. Cross, the doctor will be here in a few minutes. I'm afraid I'm going to have to ask you to leave," the nurse said, calmly.

"I am not leaving her."

"Then you must understand that what is about to happen is the best thing for your wife," she replied, injecting a needle into the I.V.

Anger rushed through my veins when I saw what the nurse had done. Then in rushed a group of people, all dressed in scrubs trying to keep me from taking the I.V. out of my arm. Try as they might, Steven would not be pushed aside. His face was the last thing I saw before drifting off into the oblivion of darkness.

Then I was falling. It felt like forever I was falling, flipping head over heels, tumbling through the darkness into an even deeper darkness. I wasn't afraid. Nor was I happy. It felt almost like nothingness, just falling, falling, and falling. Until I jerked myself awake and out of the dream.

"Tiffany, my darling. I'm so glad to see your eyes open," Dad said, leaning over my bed.

"Is it really you, Daddy or am I still dreaming?"

"No, baby it's really me."

"I was falling and I couldn't stop."

"I have good news. The doctor is moving you to a regular room today and if all goes well, you'll be home in a day or two."

"How long have I been here?"

"This is the seventh day, sweetheart."

"Thank God."

Dad chuckled, asking, "Why do you say that?"

"Because it seems like every time I wake up a few days have gone by."

"They are lowering your pain medicine so you probably won't sleep as much. The first few days you were in a coma."

"What?"

"We were afraid you might never wake up, baby," he said, fighting back tears.

"Nobody told me that."

"Well, you're getting better now. Don't worry about Tristian. Your Mom, Cheryl and Diane have things under control. He is being spoiled rotten properly."

"Diane is here?"

"Yes. She's come to see you a few times."

"Dad, am I going to be okay?"

"Yes, yes you are. But they say you don't need to have any more babies. They wanted to fix that when you had surgery but I told Steven not to let them do it."

"What did he want to do?"

"He wasn't sure what to do. He didn't want to lose you, that's all."

My head turned away from his face and I stared at the wall. It was hard to take all this information in because my mind was so foggy. So many hours had passed since I had seen Tristian's face that I barely remembered what he looked like. Tears slid silently down my cheeks as I did my best to process the words my dad had spoken.

Ultimately, the days ahead would be my choice. I could choose to stay sick or I could choose to be healed. There was the possibility of wallowing in self-pity or I could hold my head up high and know that tomorrow things could always get better. Sure, I had lost a lot of precious time with my son but I had a whole lifetime ahead to enjoy with him. Maybe I would never give him a brother or sister from his own blood but I could always find a child who needed a home to be his sibling.

When they took me to a regular room, in no time the room was overflowing with flowers, balloons and gifts. It felt like the whole world was saying 'I love you' with every glance around the room. Before long, the hospital had to refuse anymore deliveries, so I asked if they could send them to the children's hospital. It took a few hours of deliberation but finally they approved my request.

It was only one more day until Steven was finally allowed to take me home. When we got there everything was so familiar but yet unfamiliar. Things had changed a lot since the last time I had been here and with it new faces that had made themselves right at home. Not that I wasn't grateful. Without them what would Tristian, Steven and I have done?

Still, it was strange to have Mom, Cheryl and Diane basically living under the same roof with us. Especially when all I wanted to do was be alone with Tristian. So much time had passed since he had been born and it seemed almost every time I held him he would start to cry. Then someone would swoop him up and someone else would take his place trying to occupy my mind with some unimportant task or question.

As the days passed by slowly, the first to leave was Diane. Then it was my sister Cheryl that started dropping by for a few hours each day. Steven and Mom rarely left the house and were always busy with the chore of taking care of a newborn and me. Each day I was recovering and becoming stronger. Tristian was the only thing that pulled me along and kept me from falling into despair.

When the movie I'd made in New Zealand hit theaters, it hit with a big bang. This gave me even more strength to recover and jump back into life with zeal. But when the Oscar buzz started floating around Hollywood, I felt like a new woman. Yes, I may have come as close to death as I had ever been but I was still here. Still breathing. It was time to get up and get moving. Besides, I had to get my body back in shape for my Oscar's gown.

As soon as I started leaving the house, picture after picture appeared on multiple magazines. Some claimed I had risen from the dead. Others were merely focused on my weight and body, reporting that I still looked pregnant. But there were a few that speculated whether or not my son was alive. They said I was going crazy, working out relentlessly because of the agonizing depression I was experiencing since the loss of my son. There were even a few that said Steven had left me because I secretly gave Tristian up for adoption and told my family he was dead.

It made me laugh, all the lies. It also made me cry. Why would people want to write such horrible words just to make a few dollars? Didn't they realize that Steven and I were real people exactly like them and their families?

Their lies are what made me decide to accept an offer from a respectable magazine and do an interview. Plus there would be family portraits for the whole world to see. In fact, Steven, Tristian and I would be on the front cover and then no one could deny the truth. We were still together, still in love and happy to have our healthy son in our lives.

Two days before the photo shoot, news came through the grapevine that I would be getting an Oscar nod for my role in Fly Higher. Against all odds, the newcomer Michael McFarland would most likely get one too. Since I was unable to appear at any of the premieres, Michael and I had not seen each other since the day we had said good-bye in New Zealand. With all the fuss over the movie, I knew it wouldn't be much longer before our paths crossed again.

The night before the photo shoot I wrote Steven a letter because I wanted him to know my feelings. He had been so good to me and Tristian, attending to our every need. When I handed him the envelope, he handed it back to me. Then he took my hands in his and looked into my eyes.

"What's this?"

"I wrote you a letter," I said, wondering why he sounded so sad.

"What does it say?"

Pulling my hands out of his, I held the letter up with both hands toward him saying, "Only good things."

"Then why don't you read it to me. The words would be so much sweeter spoken in your voice," he spoke, softly.

"Where do you want to go?"

"Your mom is with Tristian, let's go to our bedroom," he replied, taking my hand.

When we reached our room, he turned on the lamp which cast a shimmering glow across the large space. He fell back against the bed, scrunching up the pillow under his head to be comfortable. Instead of crawling over him, I walked around the foot of the bed to the other side. Then I propped some pillows up to support my back before I sat down beside him. He stretched out, closing his eyes and put his hand on my thigh.

Dearest Steven,

You will never know how much these past few months have meant to me. This is my attempt to help you understand how thankful I am for you. You didn't have to stay with me in the hospital, but you did and that means the world to me.

When I couldn't take care of our son, you made sure he was taken care of by people who love him. What mother would not be grateful in the same situation? It is always amazing to watch the way you care for me and Tristian. Although, I never feel truly worthy of this compassion from you, you still deliver, time and time again.

It was a revelation to me, those days after you brought me home from the hospital. My bad attitude did not deter you from holding me. My anger never sent you running out the door to leave the burden of our care on my family. Even when depression began to try and get a grip on me, you never left my side. It was a real shock. I'm not sure I would have returned the same kindness to you. But it filled me with wonder at the depths of your love for me and our son.

Steven, what I am trying to say is I don't deserve your love. I have never done anything to deserve your devotion. And the truth be told, I will prob-

ably never do anything that is worthy of your dedication and loyalty to me and our family. In spite of everything I lack, regardless of everything I am not, there is one thing you can be sure of…and that is…

I really love you.

Forever yours,
Tiffany

"I needed that. Thank you," he said, reaching out for me.

I sat the letter down on the night stand and curled up beside him, kissing his cheek, saying, "I know you have been working so hard, day and night for a long time to take care of us. You could have hired people…"

"I was trying to protect you."

"That's why I'm even more grateful. Not many men would have done what you have done."

"I'm just a country boy from Mississippi, but I'm doing my best."

Leaning up on one elbow, I looked at him to say, "Your best is perfect to me."

"I wish I could take you home and shelter you from this craziness," he said slowly, putting his hand on my waist.

"We are home. When we do the photo shoot in the morning a lot of it will stop."

"Yes, until the next guy comes up with another screwed-up lie about me and you," he said, sullenly, rolling onto his back and closing his eyes.

"Hey. What you have to remember is that it is all lies. We know who we are and we know what we have. Don't let these people full of hate destroy our peace."

"I don't know how you have done it all these years."

"This is what I wanted. I wanted to be an actress so I have to take the good with the bad."

When he opened his eyes, I could see how tired he looked. I moved closer right before he said, "I wanted you, I wanted us, so I will take the good with the bad."

We kissed a deep, slow, long kiss. It felt like it had been years since we had kissed this way when it had only been weeks. My heart began to race exactly the way it had so many times before. I slipped my hand under his shirt to feel his heartbeat. Then as my hand caressed his skin I closed my eyes, hoping he would kiss my lips again. Instead, he pulled my hand out from under his shirt and intertwined his fingers in mine.

"Is something wrong, Steven?"

"No, nothing's wrong, Love."

"Kiss me…"

"Kissing you starts a fire in me that's rather hard to put out."

"I know how to put it out," I said, leaning up, pressing my lips against his.

He returned my kiss with eager anticipation, then lay back, sighing. My mind was racing as my body twitched with desire. Why was he rejecting me? Maybe he was mad about what had happened? I couldn't control the press. I certainly couldn't control my health. What had I done wrong?

"Tiffany," he whispered, trying to pull me closer.

"What?"

"It's too soon. I will have to make love to you in another way."

My mind rushed with the relief his words brought. How stupid could I be? Of course, it was too soon. In the heat of the moment, I had forgotten what the doctors had said. Now I felt even worse because of what I must be putting Steven through. He had not been damaged. He had not been in the hospital. No, he was completely healthy. In fact, he most likely needed to make love more than ever after all he had been through in the past few weeks. But ever the gentleman, he laid silently beside me, doing his best to hold me close.

After a couple of deep breaths, I snuggled up beside him and held him too. I didn't refrain from touching his body or kissing his skin. It was more carefully placed kisses and more modest touching than usual. Still, there was something happening between the two of us. Some type of exchange that did not involve taking our clothes off. It brought me great pleasure to lay in his arms and feel his warm body close to mine. As we lay together in the twilight of dusk we were making love in a different way. It was a deeper love, a richer love, a love that I could feel more fully than any other time I had ever made love in my life.

17
Chapter

Tristian had begun to speak his first words, walking anywhere and everywhere before I saw Michael McFarland's face again. The studio had prearranged our meeting on the red carpet before the Oscars so there would be pictures. He was cordial as usual with his large entourage waiting in the shadows. We exchanged greetings then went right to work. We posed as the cameras flashed, wishing each other luck loud enough for the reporters and bystanders to hear.

"Tiffany, you are absolutely glowing. What's your secret?"

"It's the glow you get when you fall in love," I said, looking over at Steven.

"I just figured you were hamming it up for the cameras," he said sneeringly, putting his hand on my waist.

"Thank God you're not a comedian, Michael. You'd starve to death," I prodded, pulling away from his grasp, walking forward.

"It was just a guess. I have others," he replied, directly in my ear with seduction in his voice.

I turned away from the crowd and whispered, "Either you quit or I quit smiling and posing. It's your choice."

"Well, well, well. Aren't we the Michael hater tonight?"

"Get over yourself."

"I'm trying but it's so hard," he said, with too much emphasis on the word hard.

"Give it a rest, Romeo," I replied, walking ahead.

Michael stopped me, moving me to pose again for the cameras, then asked, "How is our son?"

"What the hell are you talking about?"

"Do you think I could see him?"

"What are you doing, Michael?"

He turned, stood in front of me, saying, "You know what I'm doing, Tiffany."

"No, I don't."

"I want to see what he looks like," He answered, taking my hand and walking down the carpet.

I kept my silence for a few moments then I grabbed his arm making him stop. "You are completely insane."

"You can call me whatever you want but I have one question for you. Have you forgotten the night we shut down the bar in New Zealand?"

"Do you think this is the time or place to discuss this," I answered, looking back over my shoulder at Steven.

"No one has allowed me to get anywhere near you to discuss anything, Princess."

"Well, we damn sure are not doing it here or now," I said, pulling my hand from his grasp and walking back to Steven.

After I took Steven's hand we both turned and watch Michael walk back into his crowd of friends. Cameras were flashing and so much energy was in the air. When Steven squeezed my hand forcing me to grimace and look at him, I knew I had not hidden my anger well enough.

"What happened, Tiffany?"

"Nothing. We can talk about it later."

"What does that mean?

"What?"

"Either it's nothing or it's something. Which is it?

"He's crazy, Steven. Certifiably crazy."

"You mean crazy about you? Is this guy trying to piss me off?"

"No, he was asking about Tristian. I think he's trying to upset me so he gets more press. I'm not going to let him win this time."

"What do you mean?"

"Steven, he gets so drunk and messed up that he must think…"

"That Tristian could be his?"

"Yes, that's what it sounded like," I answered, looking around to see where Michael was standing.

"I got a word or two for that son-of-a…."

"Wait Steven, don't make a scene," I pleaded, taking his hand.

Steven, pulled his hand out of mine, making a fist, through clenched teeth he said, "That low-life piece of shit is going to regret coming here because if he as much as says one more word to you tonight I will beat the ever-living hell out of him. You better get the word to his cronies that unless he wants to go home on a stretcher, he better stay the hell away from my wife."

"I'll do it, I'll do it…just calm down."

"I'll calm down after we leave this circus."

"If you want to leave now, we can go."

"I don't want you to miss this, Tiffany. I know how important it is to you."

"It's not more important than you. It's not more important than my family."

"Then let's get the hell out of here," he said, in his country slang, taking my hand in his, escorting me back down the red carpet toward the car.

As we crawled in and Steven told the driver to take us home I felt sick. It felt like my whole life was flashing before my eyes. I could see me working hard to be in every play in school and doing my best to be a good actress. Then moving to Mississippi, where the opportunity to grow in acting was limited but I still kept my dream alive. Then being discovered in Florida which was how I knew this was exactly what I was meant to do with my life, acting. Then year after year of putting up with assholes and idiots to climb higher and higher on the Hollywood ladder to fame. All of this had been done to hopefully receive the highest honor anyone in my field could receive, an Oscar.

It was the sound of the tires rolling over the pavement that made me sick. That and the miles that were separating me and the stage that I was supposed to be on tonight. It was my destiny to be on that stage. When you are robbed of your destiny everything else seems to grow darker as the moments pass by.

Was it Michaels fault that I was not where I needed to be? Was it Steven's fault by not being able to control his anger? Or did the fault lie squarely on me? Maybe I was the reason that I was about to miss the biggest night in my career? Somewhere in the distance, I could hear a voice but I was unable to understand what it was saying. I was deep in thought, trying to figure out how to have what I wanted so badly but keep everyone concerned happy and in one piece.

"Can you hear me talking to you?"

"What, Steven?"

"We're home," he said, scooting toward the door.

"Okay," I said, looking away.

The driver opened the door and Steven looked back, asking, "Are you coming?"

My head moved from side to side as my body felt like it was full of concrete. Then I mustered, "I can't."

He moved back beside me in the seat, saying, "You can't. You shouldn't miss it," then patted me on the knee.

"I shouldn't."

"Are you going to be disappointed if I sit this one out?"

"Of course I will," I replied, looking up into his eyes.

"Then I'll go. Driver," he said, before I touched his hand.

"You can stay, I'll be alright."

"Are you sure?"

"Sure, I'm sure."

"Please take Mrs. Cross back," he said, then kissed my lips briefly before getting out of the car.

I watched him walking toward the house until we pulled away from the curb. Steven never looked back and as my mind wandered through the last few minutes, I wasn't sure if he was mad or not. If I was being selfish, then I would have to make it up to him later. If I was being stubborn then he had to know that was the way I had been since we met. If I was being stupid, unfortunately it would be something I would pay for.

Deep in my mind the debate continued. Michael was such an ass and if I could get my hands on his dirty neck I would wring it until he choked. Human nature caused me to rehearse the lines I should have said to him instead of the words I spoke. Then maybe this night would not have been such a train wreck. After all, I was the one who could have handled everything in a more lady like fashion. I had nothing to hide or to fear. Then there was Steven. What kind of a man, no, a husband abandons his wife on Oscar night? No matter who said what or who did what…he should have stuck beside me. Whose team is he on, anyway?

When the car stopped this time it was in a dark alley, not the bright lights of the red carpet. After he talked to a couple of guys, the driver opened my door and another very tall man escorted me inside. Then he handed me off to a young girl who seemed very excited to bring me to my seat. It wasn't long after I sat down that they made the announcement for best female in a leading role. All of the other women who were nominated deserved to win. Each of us had paid our dues in this rat race they called stardom. All of us except for Daphne Mixon. This was her second film and the only reason she had been nominated, according to the grape-vine, was because she was dating the son of one of the men who ran the underground of Hollywood. Seemed like everyone had some way of pulling strings in this town.

After all of these years of waiting and dreaming of this moment, here I was sitting alone, not a friend in sight as my name was announced. It felt like three minutes, the time I held my breath until they finally called out the winner's name. Then it must have taken ten or twenty seconds before it dawned on me it was my name they had called. Everyone stood to their feet as a spotlight fell upon my face. Then the people around me urged me to my feet and toward the stage.

It must have been shock or the mixture of adrenaline and anger that made me feel like I was floating. They handed me the award amongst hugs and congratulations. I stood before the microphone, searching for anything intelligent to say. It had never occurred to me to prepare a speech; I figured I would just wing it if I actually won.

"First of all, I would like to thank my fans. Without them, I wouldn't be standing here today. Then I would like to thank everyone involved with the movie business, from the writers, directors, producers all the way down to the make-up artists. It takes a village to raise an actress," I said, which got a good laugh from the audience.

"Most of all, I would like to thank my family. My mom and dad, for believing in me and my husband and son, their love makes me get up every day and face the world with a smile."

With both hands I held the heavy award up in the air as I was escorted off stage. It was very dreamlike, with so many people hugging and congratulating me as I was escorted deeper behind the stage into a large room with lots of other people. Before I realized what was happening, pictures were being snapped, then the award was out of my hand and replaced with a champagne glass. A lot of the who's who in L.A. filled the room with glitz and glamour that could only be witnessed on the night of the Oscars. It was exactly what I needed. Attention, more attention than I had received in such a long time.

When I found out I was pregnant with Tristian, I knew my life would change forever. Little did I know how much I would miss my old life. The lights, the cameras and all the people made me feel at home. All of it made me feel so right in a world that often felt so wrong. Surrounded by faces that lit up at the sight of me, faces that called out my name over and over until I gave them the time of day, made me know I was important. At least to somebody in this world I was important and tonight it was more people than usual.

It was at that moment, the moment I had begun to feel so important and not so alone that I spied the man who had ruined the red carpet for me. He was smugly nestled inside his entourage with at least an extra dozen or so people hanging onto his every word. We caught each other's eye then jerked our eyes back toward our endearing admirers. However, Michael couldn't help himself and before two minutes had passed he stood straight across from me with a crooked grin on his handsome face.

"Do you all mind if my beautiful co-star and I have a moment alone?"

I stretched forth my right hand for him to take amid the approval of the crowd, saying, "What on earth is so private? We're all friends here."

"Really, this won't take but a moment of your time," he replied, playing a perfect gentleman, raising my hand to his lips.

He led me out of the room and down a hallway into a changing room that was in disarray and dimly lit. I searched the room for more lighting and found a small lamp. He walked across the room, sitting down on the couch and patted the space beside him beckoning me to sit down.

I sat down in a chair on the other side of the room and asked, "What is it, Michael? Haven't you done enough damage for tonight?"

"Tiffany, if it wasn't for you wanting to get drunk and screw we wouldn't even need to have this conversation." "Look, I know we got drunk together, but that's all we did. Nothing else."

"That's not the way I remember it."

"I don't know why you are doing this to me. I am a happily married woman."

"You were not very happy in New Zealand. What was her name? Avery? Abbie? No, it was Amber, right?"

"What do you want from me, Michael?"

"I want to know if the kid's mine."

"There's no way he's yours because WE DIDN'T HAVE SEX!"

He stood up and walked over, standing right in front of me, saying, "I know that's what you want to believe but I want proof he's not mine. I want a DNA test."

I stared right into his eyes and said, "If you ever and I mean EVER, mention my son to me or another living soul, I will find out. And when I find out, your ass is toast in this town. You won't even be able to get a commercial after I'm finished with you. Do you understand the words coming out of my mouth, Michael McFarland?"

"I understand that you are threatening me. But your threats don't mean too much anymore, Tiffany Starr. You see, you're a has-been. Now you're washed up and being put out to dry. The proof is in the pudding...how many roles have you been offered lately?"

My mind went blank for a moment before I said, "I will squash you like a bug under my high heel shoe if you mess with me, my family or my career. Got it?"

"You are so hot when you're angry," he said, grossly, reaching out, grabbing my left breast.

"If I wasn't a lady, I would knock you to your knees right now with one kick," I hissed through clenched teeth.

"If you were a lady, you would have kept your legs closed and we wouldn't have to have this little conversation."

"For the last time, Michael, we never had sex. You must have me confused with one of your little whores."

"No, I think I can remember who I've slept with, especially when it's someone as hot as you."

"You haven't seen hot yet, buddy. Keep messing with me and you're going to find out how bad fire can burn," I said, turning to walk to the door.

He grabbed me by the arm, saying, "If you don't want a lawsuit, you better do what I ask."

"If you don't want to be ruined, you better leave me alone," I replied, shaking my arm loose from his grasp and running out the door and down the hallway.

The path ahead was littered with bodies and faces, most of which were propped up against the walls, talking and laughing about who knows what. With expert weaving and darting I hurried through the long hallway just wanting to escape. I was confused and angry. It was then that someone grabbed me into their arms, almost lifting me off the floor.

"Where are you going in such a hurry?"

"Steven?"

"Yes, who did you think it was?"

"I wasn't sure."

"Are you okay?"

"Yes, I'm fine," I replied, looking behind me to see if Michael was coming.

"Look, I'm so sorry about what happened. I was acting like an idiot," he said, hanging his head.

"It's alright, come on, let's get out of here."

"Okay. So you forgive me?"

"Yes! Now can we go?"

He took my hand as we weaved through the crowd together back into the main reception room, saying, "It took forever to get back here to you. I'm sorry…"

"It's alright, Steven, really. I just want to get my award and go home."

"Congratulations, I'm so proud of you," he said, slowing down to hug.

"Thanks."

The big room was beginning to look empty as couple after couple were exiting the back door which led out to the back alley. There was talk about this party and that party and who was going where and when they would be there. When anyone asked which one we were going to, I let Steven do the talking.

With the back door in sight, I looked over my shoulder to see if we might make it out of here before seeing Michael McFarland's face again. No such luck. He stared across the room with searing hatred and at least another dozen eyes from his entourage stared at me in the same way. Steven was too busy to notice, having struck up a conversation with some young girl named Sylvia who inspired to be a screen writer.

As soon as Steven had gotten her number and promised to see what he could do to help we turned to walk out the door. My mind was somewhere between panic and relief as I smelled the heaviness of the Los Angeles air. For some reason I had expected my car to be sitting right outside the door, waiting for us to jump in but it wasn't. Instead, there were other cars in front of ours which meant we had to wait.

Steven held out his arm for me which I gladly gave him. We walked down the dark alley toward our limo and the driver got out and opened the door. Sweet relief came the moment we sat down in the back seat of the limo and the door closed behind us.

"Tiffany, you are acting so strange."

"No, I'm not."

"Even your voice sounds strange."

"Why are you picking on me, Steven?"

"Because it's true. Are you mad at me?"

"No, not really. I mean, you did leave me alone and tonight was the Oscars."

"I already said I was sorry and I was wrong. What else do you want me to do?"

"Just drop it! I'm supposed to be happy right now. But between you and Michael I can't catch a break from the drama."

Steven turned away, looking out the window, softly saying, "I shouldn't have come back."

"You should have never left."

"Who is that?"

"Who?"

"The man standing beside your door."

When I turned to see who it was Michael's face staring down at me. He was motioning for me to roll down the window. The driver looked back as if to ask if I wanted him to do it. Before I had an opportunity to think it through Steven leaned over me, pushing the button to let the window down.

"Guess I should have known. A fool and his whore are never far apart," Michael rasped, leaning down into the window.

"Why don't you go home and sleep it off," I said, putting my hand on the button to roll up the window.

"Does he know about the baby?" Michael asked, in a loud voice.

"What the hell is going on, Tiffany?" Steven asked.

"I warned you, Michael. Remember that," I said, rolling up the window.

"We are free to go, if you are ready Mrs. Starr," the driver said.

"Go," I said, wishing he would punch the gas.

As we pulled away Michael banged on the window cursing and screaming as Steven asked, "Did you screw this asshole or not?"

"No! I didn't. He's a low-down, scum-bag, alcoholic wanna-be Casanova."

"I don't give a damn what he is," Steven said, looking out the window.

"Look, he's in it for the press."

"Are you kidding me?"

"Steven, in this business, any press is good press."

"Tiffany, another man is claiming to be the father of my son," he said slowly, his voice becoming louder with each word.

"You are Tristian's father. You are the only man I have been with in a long, long time. You are the only one I want to make love to. If it's up to me, you will be the only man I have sex with for the rest of my life."

"Damn it!"

"Not exactly the reaction I was expecting."

"Why does it always feel like no matter where you and I are in life, somebody is trying to rip us apart?"

"I don't know but don't let him. Don't let anyone do it anymore. It took me years to come to my senses. Now we have a beautiful family and a love that others dream about."

"You're right," he said, putting his arm around my shoulder.

"Of course, I'm right," I said as we pulled up to the house.

All of the lights were on and I noticed Cheryl's car was parked in the drive. At first I wondered what in the world would have her here so late. It was only after Steven reminded me it was Oscar night that I figured they were here to congratulate me for winning. Mom opened the front door at the same time the driver opened my door and I stepped out. Tristian wiggled to be set free from her embrace calling out daddy over and over again.

"I'm so glad you're here," Mom said, handing Tristian to Steven.

"What is it, Me-Me?" Steven asked, scooping the baby up into to his arms.

"It's your Mom. She's not doing well. Your Dad wants you to come home."

Steven looked at me then back at Mom, saying, "I can do that."

"We are so proud of you, Tiffany," Mom said, almost in a whisper.

"Thanks," I said, leaning over to give her a hug.

"Your Dad called. He got to see you too. He said he'd call you tomorrow."

"Okay," I said, kissing Tristian on the cheek.

Cheryl and Kenny walked into the entryway from the living room hand in hand. She took her time before, saying, "My little sister. She's made the big time."

"You're right. Now it's your turn," Kenny said, swinging her arm back and forth.

"Stop it, Kenny," Cheryl said, stepping forward to hug.

"I wasn't really expecting to win," I said, walking toward the living room.

"I'm going upstairs to pack," Steven said, handing Tristian back to Mom.

"Do you need any help?" I asked, looking over my shoulder.

"No, that's okay."

His voice made me turn back and take him from mom. He laid his beautiful head, full of brown wavy hair, on my shoulder. I began to softly sing a lullaby and mom turned to go to the kitchen, asking if she could get me anything. I shook my head no and kept on singing. Cheryl and her boyfriend crept back toward the living room like they didn't want to wake the baby. The minute everyone had gone their separate ways, Tristian leaned back, looked in my eyes then kissed me on the lips. It was the first time he had ever done it and it couldn't have been a more perfect moment.

He rested his head back on my shoulder and tucked his arms under his body on his chest. I wondered if the fabric of my gown bothered him but if it did he never showed it. As soon as he drifted off to sleep, Mom tip-toed back to us and offered to take him to bed with a whisper. Again, I shook my head no and carried him to bed myself.

After I walked into the hallway something made me stop. Leaning back on the wall, I took a deep breath and then another. So much had happened in the last few hours that my whole body felt like it was in a tail-spin. Now, with the news of Steven's mother we may not even get the chance to talk. My head pressed back on the wall as my eyes closed tight, forcing tears to stay within their boundary.

"Are you alright?" Mom asked.

"A little tired, that's all."

"You need to get it together, Tiffany. Don't screw up your marriage like I did."

"I don't intend on it."

"Do you think I intended to mess everything up for you girls and your dad?"

"Oh my gosh! What else is going to happen tonight? Look, I love you, Mom and I'm glad you're here. I know I need to get it together and that's exactly what I'm doing."

"I only want the best for you and my grandson. Tristian deserves to have a mom and a dad who love him and each other."

"I know that."

"Steven is not happy, Tiffany. If you can't see that you're blind."

"I'll make it better, Mom. I'll make everything better," I said, walking down the hallway, back to the living room.

"Are you going with him?" Cheryl asked.

"Who?" I asked, looking back over my shoulder.

"Steven. Are you going to Mississippi with him?"

I turned around, to face her, saying, "I don't know."

"Probably need to," Kenny said, shaking his head yes.

"It doesn't sound like she had much longer," Cheryl added.

"I'm going to talk to him. I appreciate you two being here. Sorry it's going to be such a short night. I thought we would be celebrating."

"I know. I thought we would be toasting champagne till dawn," Kenny said, sounding disappointed.

"There's plenty of champagne if you want some. Cheryl you know where it is?"

"Sure do."

"Help yourselves," I said, picking up the edge of my gown to walk to the bedroom.

Steven was sitting in a chair with his suitcase beside him watching T.V. when I walked in. He glanced in my direction then focused his attention back on the screen. It was an unusual reaction from a man who had always focused his attention on me. At that point, I knew it was circumstances beyond my control that caused him to react this way. So I stuffed my personal feelings down, deep inside my heart or maybe my soul, I wasn't sure.

After I undressed, washed off the heavy make-up and got ready for bed I came back from the bathroom and sat down on the edge of the bed. Steven looked over in my direction, smiled weakly and looked back at the T.V. As a consequence of his silence, I pulled back the covers and laid down without a word and covered myself up. Under their warmth,

I began to argue within my own mind about how Steven should be acting.

During this evening, I had been abandoned and left to face the world alone, by my husband. My co-star had attacked me with lies and threats. Then he attacked my husband, my son... my whole family causing me a great deal of pain and anguish. Then Steven was mad at me, almost accusing me of sleeping around on him and lying about it. Then there was my Mother and her great words of wisdom for me. Last but not least, the news of his Mom, the saint, taking her last breath, calling for her precious son.

"Enough is enough," I said, sitting up in bed, looking over at Steven.

"Just go to sleep, Love. It'll all be better in the morning," Steven replied, in a calm voice.

"Don't you think that after all that's happened to me tonight that I might need a hug or kiss?"

"There are other people to consider now," he said, in a dream-like state.

"Please come get in bed."

"I'll be gone in the morning; before you wake up."

"Do you want me to come?"

"No."

"Why don't you want me to come with you?"

"Take a day or two to get your priorities in order, then come."

My body fell back onto the bed as I jerked the covers up and turned over on my side. My emotions ran wild. Anger, hurt, frustration, self-pity and animosity filled my mind making me feel like I was going to explode. If I could have cried, it would have made me feel better but all I could do was lay there and curse.

With the morning's light streaming into the windows, I pulled back the covers to check the time. It was almost nine as I stretched out to feel for Steven. As I turned over, he wasn't there. In fact, he had not been in bed all night because his side was still partially made up. Then I remembered he was sitting in the chair so I sat up but he and his suitcase was gone.

That's when all the memories of last night came flooding back in waves. So much bad had happened in such a short amount of time that it almost seemed unreal, like a bad dream. On one of the biggest nights of my career, why did everything else have to turn out so bad?

Steven's advice for me to get my priorities in order was on continual replay in my mind. And after everything was said and done, he was right. It was time for me to make some changes and I was just in the right frame of mind to do it.

A long hot bath put everything in perspective. My family and my career was strong and nothing and nobody was going to change that. It was time for Michael McFarland to get his ass out of my business and go back to New York where he belonged. Nothing would stop me from making this happen, short of death. While people were heading back to the East Coast, I figured it was about time for Me-Me and my big sister to head back there too. But not before I went to Mississippi to bury my mother-in-law. The precious mother-in-law who had loved me since the first day she laid eyes on me. The same one who had treated me like the daughter she never had. Right?

Chapter
18

Tristian was safely buckled in the seat beside me, as the plane lifted into the air. The pilot announced that we were on time and he could not see any delays ahead. Weather was perfect for flying and he wished us all a good morning. If only he knew what was on my plate, he wouldn't have been so cheerful because it made me feel worse. As a matter of fact, Tristian seemed to be the only bright spot in my life these past few days. Steven had very little to talk about except his Mom and my Mom had very little to say except telling me what to do to keep Steven in my life.

With all of this happening, I wanted to see my Dad more than ever right now. It had been too long since he had seen Tristian and besides that I needed some wisdom from someone who cared. So after I had booked the flight, I asked him if he could come and pick us up at the airport. His yes came easier than Stevens. It was only after I insisted that he let Dad do it. If the truth be told, in a way I had hoped that I wouldn't be able to convince Steven and he would have come to get us.

Tristian's face lit up with excitement when he saw his Grandpa. I sat him down and he waddled straight over to Dad's waiting arms. He picked him up, turning him round and round with hugs and kisses. It was so beautiful to watch the two of them that I lingered for as long as they let me, just watching.

"Tiffany," Dad said, cheerfully, kissing my cheek and hugging me with one arm.

"Hey, Dad. Good to see you."

"You don't sound too good, baby. I better get the two of you home," he said, looking at Tristian, saying the last few words in a baby voice.

"That sounds good, I'm hungry."

"The driver's gone to get your luggage."

"What driver?"

"Steven arranged for a car to pick us up," he said, snuggling with the baby.

"Why did he do that? I told him you were coming."

"Let it go, baby. It's no big deal."

"You're right," I said, walking down the corridor with him.

Soon we were all sitting in the back seat of an older black limo that seriously needed some fine tooth cleaning. Truthfully, I was mad as hell because Steven had ignored what I had told him again. It almost felt like he was saying I don't care what you say or what you want. In reality, I knew he only hired the car because he did care and who knows, maybe he didn't even remember what I had told him.

When Tristian and I had settled into the comfort of Dad's house and had a bite to eat, I called Steven to let him know we had made it. He sounded somewhat happy but preoccupied with whatever was going on at his Mom's house. When I heard Amber's voice in the back ground, my heart felt like it jumped up in my throat. So I told him to give me a call when he was heading back to his house. Then I said goodbye as cheerfully as possible and placed the receiver back on the hook.

"Is everything okay with Steven?"

"Yes."

"Has he told you about Victoria?"

"No, he hasn't mentioned her," I replied sitting down beside him.

Tristian lay in his lap, falling asleep. He quietly said, "She's super skinny and acting strange. I think she may be…"

"Doing drugs?"

"Rumor is…it's meth," he whispered as though the baby would know what that meant.

"What about Blake?"

"He seems to be okay, normal."

"And the baby?"

"She stays with Victoria's parents a lot."

"Why can't I remember her name?" I asked, puzzled by my absent mindedness.

"Are you asking about the baby?"

"Yes, what's her name?"

"I think it's Caroline, isn't it?" He answered, getting up to lay Tristian down on the love seat.

"That's right, Caroline. Such a pretty name."

"She is a beautiful baby. Almost as beautiful as this little baby," he said in a sing-sing voice as he covered Tristian with a blanket.

Dad walked to the kitchen and I followed right on his heels. I sat down at the table, peering out the window as he opened a cabinet to get some glasses. He poured us a glass of tea then came over and sat down across from me. It was weird how not much had changed around here, it was still home but it felt so different to be here.

"Do you want me to watch the baby while you go over to see Steven's mom?"

"No. I don't see any point in that."

"Why not?"

"She never liked me, Dad. You know that."

"It's not about whether she liked you or not, Tiffany. She's part of your family and she's dying."

"After what she said to me on my wedding day I really don't want to see her; or Amber."

"Listen, Amber is nothing more than a hired hand. You've got to let go of the past, sweetheart and realize you and Steven are married. Whatever his mother said was probably just because she was tired. That was a long trip to Italy. Regardless, that's his mother lying over there across town dying. I think you need to be there."

"You're probably right," I said, not wanting to believe it.

"I am right. So why don't you go upstairs and get freshened up. You can take my car and surprise him."

After standing up a thought occurred to me that stopped me dead in my tracks. My eyes drifted toward the window and I stared outside. Then my thoughts returned to what Dad had told me and I looked up at the stairs.

"What is it?" He asked, looking past me at Tristian.

"What if he doesn't want me there?"

"That's nonsense. Of course he wants you there. You're his wife, baby," he reassured me.

Reluctantly, I got ready to go, quietly left the house so as not to wake the baby. It was weird how after all these years of knowing Steven I still felt like I was an intruder when I came to his childhood home. Maybe it was more of an outsider feeling. Maybe it was just plain unwanted but whatever it was it felt horrible. Right before I was about to turn around and leave, I noticed a face peeping out the window, staring at me. It was Amber. Of course, who else would it be?

It was then that I did what any good southern girl would do. I put that fake smile on my face and slid out from under the wheel and marched up to the door. It was only after knocking that I remembered I wasn't a good southern girl. I was a California girl and I was praying under my breath that I could be good today.

Amber opened the door without hardly looking at me, barely said hello and walked back toward the kitchen. After letting myself in, I closed the door and sat my purse down on the entry way table. My heels announced my arrival against the hardwood floors as I walked toward the living room. The old house was quiet except for the sound of my shoes tapping against the wood.

When I found the room empty, I stopped and searched for any sounds of life. Someone was in the sunroom, though I couldn't make out whose voice it was. I decided to walk out there and Amber was walking in the living room.

"She's out in the sun room. They're all out there," she said, in a somber tone.

"Thanks," I said, noticing for the first time that she was wearing scrubs. The girl I remembered as pretty and sassy had faded or maybe she was tired. It could have been from dealing with death but something had certainly changed about her since the last time we crossed paths.

"No problem," she replied, leaving me alone again.

When I walked into the room it was as though all of the oxygen had been sucked out. Steven stood up, rushed to my side and kissed my cheek. It felt like he was almost embarrassed or like he was a young boy who was ashamed of doing something wrong. His dad cleared his throat and looked out the window basically ignoring the fact that I had walked into the room. His mother let out a sigh and closed her eyes which made me feel like the sight of me had made her weak.

A moment later, Blake walked in from the back door and was the only one who acted genuinely happy to see me. He hugged me close, complimented my dress and asked if I would like to have a seat. After we talked about Caroline and Tristian he encouraged his Mom and Dad to say hello. For the first time, I saw a part of Blake that reminded me of Steven and I was thankful he was my brother-in-law.

It was a short visit, without a single word from Steven's mother. We said our goodbyes to Blake at the front door with promises of getting the kids together to play before Steven and I left. Steven followed me to Dad's house where we had dinner. It wasn't long after dinner we went back to Steven's house. Not once had we considered Tristian might be staying in this house or that we might need a baby bed. Our only choice was to sleep in the bed together so we put the baby in the middle and after such a long day fell fast asleep.

About three o'clock in the morning, the phone rang. Tristian woke up but he was not crying. I could hear who it was and immediately sat up. Steven answered yes, then he hung up the phone.

"Why in the world was Amber calling you at three in the morning?"

"She's gone."

"What do you mean? She's quitting?"

"No, it's Mom. She's gone."

"I'm sorry, Steven," I said, taking Tristian in my arms to move beside him.

He patted my knee, saying, "I'm going over there. You and the baby try to get back to sleep."

"Do you want me to go with you?"

"No. That's okay, go back to sleep."

"I could get Dad…"

"Tiffany, there's nothing you can do now. When its morning, and you and Tristian are ready, you can come then. Alright?"

"Alright."

We lay back down, listening to Steven get ready to go. It was only a few minutes and he was dressed and walking out the door. He didn't kiss us goodbye or say another word. Then the sound of his truck backing out of the driveway left empty silence. It was too quiet so we got up and I turned on the television and sat down on the couch with Tristian.

Mrs. Cross's funeral was held at the Baptist Church she and her family had been attending over the last hundred years or so. To my amazement and shock over a thousand people crowded into the sanctuary, leaving standing room only. Who would have ever thought she knew this many people much less had touched this many lives? Steven and I sat on the front pew, in the center of the church along with his Dad and brother and Victoria. Then the distant members of her family, an aunt, a few cousins and a niece sat behind us.

After the ceremony, before we went to the graveside service, Victoria pulled me away from Steven. It was true, she was as skinny as I had ever seen her but that didn't mean she had a drug problem. Once we were inside the bathroom, with the door locked, her voice told another story.

"This place sucks. I can't wait to get the hell out of here."

"Are you going with us, to the grave?"

"Not if I can get out of it," she said, hovering over the toilet while reaching for the toilet paper.

I walked toward the sink, turned the water on to wash my hands, asking, "Why don't you tell Blake you don't want to go?"

"Cause Blake thinks he's got to have me under his thumb twenty-four seven. It's only cause I'm skinny. You know...all the boys love skinny bitches," she said, flushing the toilet.

"You have lost some weight."

"Hey, why don't we run away? We'll go party together...just like when we were young," she said, draping her hand over my shoulder, looking in the mirror at our reflection.

"Really I can't, Victoria. But thanks for asking."

It was an uneasy feeling as we walked out of the bathroom. She was high and I knew it and she knew I knew it. Maybe I should have said something. It was obvious she needed help. But this was the wrong place and the wrong time to deal with Victoria's problems. That conversation would have to wait.

My stomach churned as I looked at Caroline, so beautiful, held safely in her daddy's arms. Victoria walked over to her and told him in a voice that was a little too loud that she needed her diaper changed. When she tried to take the child from Blake, the baby refused to go and started to cry. He walked away, which only made Victoria mad. When she came over to complain, all I could do was shake my head, thinking what a shame it is that she got messed up before Mrs. Cross's funeral.

The next few days were full of casseroles, smiling faces and flowers with tiny cards. It was the most time I had ever spent around Steven's Dad and it actually made me feel better to get to know him. Even though Amber and I avoided contact, her son Myles was something else and he and Tristian were becoming fast friends despite their age difference.

Blake was there too but usually without Victoria and almost always with Caroline. She and Tristian were so cute to watch together, that most of the time they were the center of attention. Steven's dad seemed to watch them a lot which kept his mind off the fact that he just lost his wife.

When I found the right moment, I asked Blake about Victoria. At first he beat around the bush, not wanting to tell me. But before the conversation ended I knew exactly what was going on and how it happened.

He explained that she had done a little meth a few years ago when they were dating. In fact, they had both tried it but she liked it a lot more than he did. She said it made her feel alive, full of energy and she loved the fact that she didn't have to eat. But when she found out she was pregnant, she stopped.

However, when I asked her to spy on Steven and he gave Victoria that wad of cash, she couldn't stop herself. As soon as she had given birth to Caroline and was released from the hospital, she was high again. Actually, he now wondered if she had even waited until she had the baby. Nevertheless, he wasn't ready to give up on her and he wasn't going to let Caroline suffer because of Victoria's problem.

With all of this fresh on my mind, I held my husband's hand and tried to pretend I was upset. Part of me felt responsible for what happened and another part was afraid of what this news would do to Steven. It was only after I thought back over the past few months, then back over the last few years that I realized that he may already know about Victoria's problem.

As we drove to his house I wondered if things between us would ever be the same again. Something had died. Was it the passion? Plenty of couples survive without a lot of passion. Was it trust? Trust can be rebuilt over time. Was it our love? If our love had died, then in my mind there was only one thing left to do. We could truly say we gave it a try and cut our losses and move on.

Once we had rounded the curve, Steven pulled the truck into the driveway and turn off the ignition. Tristian was fast asleep, looking angelic with his head laying to one side. Steven took my hand just as I was about to open the door. When I turned to look at him, I saw something in his face I hadn't seen in quite some time.

"I don't know what I would do if I ever lost you."

"Steven, don't think that way. You know what you would do. Exactly what everyone else does."

"What's that?"

"You go on. You go on living. That's what people do."

He put his elbows on the steering wheel, put his head in his hands, whispering, "I wouldn't want to."

"You wouldn't have a choice. Just like your Dad doesn't have a choice."

"We always have a choice," he said, turning to look at me, under his hand.

"I guess you're right. I didn't think about it like that."

"Do you love me?" He asked, bringing his hands down into his lap.

"Yes, I do. Why do you ask?"

"Something's different. I don't know what, maybe it's just Mom's death that's got me looking, searching…."

"No, you're right. Something is different."

"What is it, Tiffany?"

"I think we just need to get out of Mississippi, Steven. It's time to go home."

"You mean L.A.?" He asked, not sounding so sure.

"It would do us good. Walk on the beach; make love to the sound of the ocean waves crashing on shore."

"When do you want to leave?"

"Tomorrow or the next day. Whatever you think."

"I think I want to make you happy."

"I know you do," I said softly, reaching out to touch his hand.

He picked mine up and kissed the back of it, pressing his lips hard on my skin. Suddenly I sensed an urgency, a need that I had mistaken for anger or mourning. He needed me, in every way and instead of beating myself up for being clueless I surrendered to him completely.

So much chaos and turmoil had filled our days and nights that sometimes we forgot which way was up and which way was down. The unrest had created havoc on our emotions and had consumed our lives with confusion and mayhem. Had we forgotten what we had been through in the past to get to this point in our lives? If we had, I could sense we were about to build a bridge over the flames that threatened to destroy what we had accomplished. It would be a bridge of flesh. Arms, legs, lips and eyes ready to touch, feel and see the passion we both had for each other buried so deep, deep inside our souls.

At the same exact moment, we stopped touching and looked back at Tristian. He was fast asleep and without a word we both knew what the other was thinking. If we woke him up, the chance to fulfill our desires would be over. My mind raced with options but the decision would not be left to me because someone else was in control. Steven put his finger over my lip, indicating for me to be quiet. He opened the door without a sound and I did the same. We stood outside the truck, looking at each other and ever so gently closed the doors. We both gave Tristian one last look before we met at the hood of the truck.

Our lips hit so hard that it hurt which caused both of us to laugh although the laughter only lasted for a moment. Each second made the heat between us feel hotter and hotter until we both knew we had to find a place beyond the neighbors' view. Steven looked back at the house, while I looked at the baby. He stepped back, pulling me with him then he sidestepped and wrapped his arms back around me putting his lips on my earlobe. We stood for another minute or two, desperately wanting to undress right then and there but refraining.

He looked around wildly, like we were naughty children looking for a place to hide from our mother who was yelling out our names. Then he took my hand, looking over his shoulder one last time at Tristian and pulled me toward his toolshed. I had never been inside and at first thought what in the world is this man thinking. The door crept open with a squeaky sound and Steven franticly searched for the string in the pitch dark which turned on the light. As the light bathed the little room, I was surprised that it was very clean and organized. There were tools of all shapes and sizes, hanging neatly from hooks and nails on the wall. In the back corner sat the larger tools that could not be hung. Right beside the door was a work table that looked well used with markings, oil and grease staining its surface. It smelled like fresh cut grass mixed with a little oil and a hint of gas but it was close to Tristian and if I stood on my tippy-toes I could see him.

"Is this okay?" Steven asked, breaking the silence.

"I think so. We can see him and if he wakes up we'll know."

He reached out, unbuttoning my dress and said, "It'll be okay."

I looked into his hazel eyes, and shook my head and let go of my fears. Closing my eyes, I surrendered to his touch and I could feel my body begin to tremble with anticipation. He stepped forward, kissing my neck as he finished the last button. It was then that he pulled the top back, exposing my chest. His lips pressed along the edge of my black bra making me wish it was not on my body. I let my head fall back with my eyes still closed and let out a moan to let him know how he was making me feel.

Steven stopped for a moment, stepping around me to look at Tristian and I turned to look too. He was still fast asleep, looking so peaceful. Before I turned back, Steven had taken his shirt off and put it on his work table. While he made sure it was sitting just right, I reached inside my dress and unhooked my bra pulling the straps out of my arm holes while Steven watched. I handed the black lace garment to him, which he hung from a hook near the work table.

"Are you ready?" He asked, with a shy grin on his face.

With a nod I reached forward and grazed my hand down his chest stopping at the top of his pants. His eyes met mine as I pulled gently on the button that held so much pleasure that I was ready to receive. His hand covered mine as my fingers slowly dipped past the border of his waistline, touching the flesh inside. His other hand had found its way inside the top of my dress, caressing the sensitive part of my breasts.

"I need you," he whispered, waiting for a response.

"I want you."

Steven picked me up and I wrapped my legs around his waist, kissing him deeply. He sat me down on the work table and kissed me for a long time. Then he stepped back pushing a stool over so my left foot could sit on it. With a little pushing, pulling and cooperation we managed to get my little black undies off which he hung from a hook beside my bra.

"I have fantasized about putting you on this table ever since I bought this house."

"Really?"

"Really."

"Now your fantasy has come true, Mr. Cross. What comes next?"

"This," he said, pushing my legs open, then pulling my dress up.

At that moment, his fantasy became my reality. There was something so magical about his fantasy coming true that made the air around us tingle with energy. If I had ever had any control over what was happening, all of it had been lost the second his hand pushed along the inside of my upper thigh. It was a tug-of-war. Begging him to stop before he took me too far and wanting him to finish what he had begun. In the end, it was his choice because I gave him the power to do as he wished. Besides, it was his fantasy.

After my body subsided with waves of satisfaction, Steven took me to new heights and peaks of gratification that I never knew existed. He pulled me to the edge of the table, pressing his chest against mine. My right leg wrapped around his back while my left leg used the stool for leverage. We were rocking to a rhythm and holding a pace that let us indulge ourselves and our senses.

When the sounds of our lovemaking were reaching a peak, Steven reached over and closed the door. He could tell by the look in my eyes, my thoughts had turned to the baby in the seat of the truck. He pushed it back open and peered out and with a wink and a smile he closed the door shut. I pressed my body hard against his as we exchanged sweat. Then I dug my nails in his back and ran them down the length to his waist and into his hips. We pushed and pulled, moaned and groaned until we both peaked at the same moment. With heavy breathing we kissed one last long kiss before letting go.

It only took less than a minute and we were dressed and ready to walk out of the little tool shed. Steven gave me a smile when he saw I had left my bra and panties hanging on the hooks. He reached up for the light string and I leaned back to give him a little kiss before he pulled it. The door swung open and we stepped out.

We were not the same as when we had stepped in just a few minutes ago. Now we were happily married and still in love. Now we both knew everything was going to be okay and we still had each other, heart, soul and body.

With one look through the window of the truck our fears were relieved. There in his car seat lay our greatest accomplishment in life. That little boy represented our love for each other in a way nothing else on earth could do. We looked at each other and this time it was different. So much pride, so much happiness filled my heart and I could feel Steven beaming with joy too.

Today had been an ending for Steven. A tragic ending of one of the greatest relationships any person can have in life. The bond between mother and child had been broken. Only the passage of time could heal this wound her departure from this world had given to my husband. He would never be the same again and we both knew it.

Neither one of us had been sheltered from loss in this life. We had both experienced our share of trials and triumphs that had ultimately changed the very core of our personalities. Within myself, I vowed to be there for him through the ups and downs he was sure to encounter during the days to come.

The only regret I had, standing outside the truck, looking at our beautiful baby was not getting to know his mother better. Certainly, a woman who had raised such a good boy, who had turned into one of the great men in the world, had to be a special kind of mother. Why she never let me in her world, I will never know. The only glimpse she ever gave me was guarded, as if I were a thief that she needed to lock out of her life. Now our chance to learn from each other was over. The minute they lowered her casket in the ground, a new chapter had begun in our lives. It was a chapter without her in it; except for the memory of her love for Steven and the memory of her hatred for me.

Chapter 19

The beach had a way of soothing the soul like no other place on earth. Weeks flew by as Steven, Tristian and I spent day after day together exploring the coast line. We rarely discussed how much time was passing or the tears that sometimes filled Steven's eyes. Instead, we walked the shoreline discussing our future, making plans and teaching Tristian about the world. There was something about teaching a child new things that helped ease the pain. So we ignored the demands of work for a while and immersed our family in the here and now. Yes, some may have said we were hiding but to us we were healing. And everyone knows without healing, there are no tomorrows to live life to its fullest, with the ones you love.

If the pressure for my return to the big screen could have been lessened by even a smidge, we might have spent the next six months in each other's arms every day. If I had lost, if I had not won my first Oscar then certainly there would have been more time to comfort the grieving. However you sliced it, the offers were getting bigger and the tension of choosing my next role had a lot of important people in Hollywood sitting on the edge of their seats.

Steven offered little help with his mind consumed with the affairs of our only son. Whenever I would mention the diversity of roles being offered he paid little attention. His thoughts would always drift back to what we might do tomorrow or what were we having for dinner. I never complained. He needed life to be simple and for right now it could be that way, at least for him.

Slowly, I pulled myself back, a few hours each day, leaving Tristian and Steven to spend time together. It was hard but it had to be done. There was a force driving me to make the next film. Maybe it was the movers and shakers that are the spokes in the wheels of the studios. Maybe it was the fire that burned so deep in my soul for fame and recognition that fueled my desire. Whatever it was, the time had come for me to move forward and show them why I had won an Oscar.

It didn't take long to get back in the grove of things once I sunk my teeth in. My new role as Rhonda Bright would give my fans what they had been anticipating for a long time. She was an undercover cop in Chicago that exposes the biggest crime boss in the city. The only problem, she falls in love with him and is torn between a life of truth and honor or a life of love and money. Think Twice was destined to be a stellar hit and if I played my cards right, this film might help me get a star in the walk of fame.

With so much buzz about my next film making the rounds in the Hollywood Hills, Michael McFarland's name was bound to come up. It wasn't always easy to play nice but around the majority of people, I had to. However, when it came to being in the company of those who truly mattered, I let my feelings be known. I didn't wear kid gloves when the guys who run the film industry wanted to know what I wanted to happen. I wanted Michael gone. No more films, no more talk shows, no more magazine articles…nothing. With vigor, I made my desire known to some of the most powerful men in Hollywood. He was to be flushed out of Los Angeles and out of the memory of every person that enjoyed watching movies in the world. Then I wanted him to run back home to New York, with his tail between his legs, thankful that he still had a tail to tuck. But I didn't want it to end there. With a great deal of persuasion, I convinced these executives to blackball him in New York also. No need for him to be able to build an acting career there either. I wanted him to be finished, done and over with.

With unspoken words, these men let me know my wishes would be granted. In a way it made me feel so powerful but something else about the situation made me feel foolish. Maybe because deep inside, I knew that I had put myself in debt. It was a debt. In debt with some really scary people. But it was a debt I was willing to pay to never cross paths with Michael McFarland again.

Rumors spread like wild fire the day after my little discussion with the head honchos. First, it was Michael had left to go to rehab, then it was he left town with a girl and they had eloped in Tijuana, Mexico. A day or two later the story had changed, now he had a huge gambling debt in Vegas and was on the run because he couldn't pay up. After that, someone said they heard he was kidnapped and held for ransom but his family refused to pay the money. Through every word, through every lie I found a way to show interest and concern. I knew he would resurface somewhere in New York sooner or later but for now he was exactly where he needed to be. As far away from me and my family as I could get him.

It was down to the last few days before I would go back to work when Steven gave me a letter. This time he refused to stick around. He said it was better that I read it alone and he picked Tristian up, walking out the back door to the beach. I clutched it in my hand, almost afraid of what it might say. I thought everything between us was okay. Yes, I had been busy lately, getting ready to shoot a new film but I had tried my best to spend as much time with him as possible.

With my bedroom door shut behind me, I quickly walked to the window and looked out toward the sea. There they were, with the sunshine on their backs and the wind blowing their hair. Tristian's brown locks were bouncing and blowing wildly as Steven's strong arms carried him across the sand. My heart sank as I tore open the seal and pulled out the letter. I took a step back, sitting in the chair and unfolded the page to read it aloud.

Looking out onto the horizon; I can see no end.
Now, looking out into darkness, again, I see no end.
There was a light that shined so brightly
But you could never see...
Now that light is gone, it will never shine again for me.
The puzzle will never be solved
The piece will never be found.
It was the same, every time I lost you
My joy was stolen, my life flooded with pain.
How would I breathe without you?
How would I go on?
Don't want to spend another day without you
My heart refuses to be alone.
We are truly one for the first moment in time
And now true love has blossomed and grown ripe.
His smile is like a copy
From the only girl I've ever loved
And when I look into his eyes
It's like looking in mine.
Tell me what words would do
To keep you forever at my side?
I would say them over and over
Speaking them to you until the end of time.
Steven Cross

My fears subsided as I folded the paper back and slipped it inside the envelope. Once I had leaned back and closed my eyes the words and their meanings ran through my mind with great accuracy. He wasn't okay. Mourning the loss of his mother was still very fresh and real. It is something that takes time and I wondered if my decision to go back to work was too soon. He refused to start writing again and I had not added to the pressure that his agent was inflicting. It would be his choice and decision when he went back to work, not mine. Still, it was nice to see he had written something and especially nice to read that it was a love poem for me.

Only the knock at the door brought me out of my deep thought. I figured it was Steven, so I sat the letter down on the table and said come in. The door opened very slowly, then mom peeped her head in.

"I just wanted to make sure you were dressed," she said, coming to take a seat beside me.

"Yes, I was just sitting here thinking."

"Well, I don't want to disturb you but we really need to talk."

"What is it, Mom?"

"Honey, I've been here helping to take care of you, Steven and Tristian for a while and I think it's time for me to go."

"I know, Mom. I was going to tell you that if you were ready to go it's okay but it seems like stuff keeps happening."

"It's never going to stop, Tiffany. That's life."

"You're right. I wish it would slow down sometimes," I said, watching her eyes look at the envelope on the table.

"Can I give you a word of advice?"

"Sure."

"Let Steven go if you don't really love him. He doesn't belong here, in this crazy town. He's like a fish out of water."

"What kind of advice is that?"

"The kind that will set you free. You see, sometimes you forget that you're my little girl and I know you better than anyone else in this world."

"I don't want that kind of freedom."

"But you do. Remember, I watch everything. I see it all."

"When are you planning on going back to New York?"

"In a few days. Cheryl and Kenny will be leaving this evening. She'll be by in a little while to tell you goodbye."

"Wow," I said, standing up, picking up the envelope.

"I hope you will be nice to your sister. She's done a lot around here to help you."

"I will. Do you think ten thousand would be enough?"

Mom stood up, walking to the door and turned back, saying, "Really Tiffany, money is not what I was talking about."

"I know but…"

"You don't have to pay people to love and care about you. We just do it naturally. My God, Tiffany, where is your head?"

My head was shaking in disbelief as she walked out the door. The envelope fell to the floor as I went back over the words we had spoken to one another. Why did it seem my mom knew how to see past the walls I had built so high and call it like it is? It was true, I had not been very nice to my sister and she had done nothing but come across the country to help me when I needed it most. All Mom had asked was for me to be nice when I said goodbye and again what had I done? Talked about what was owed and how much money could I pay so I wouldn't owe a debt of kindness to anyone in this world.

After picking up the poem and putting it away in the night stand, I decided to go and find Mom and apologize. She would be leaving soon and I certainly didn't want her to leave angry. With my hand on the doorknob I breathed in deeply then exhaled slowly. The last thing I wanted was to say the wrong thing to her. But I also wanted to know why in the world she made the comment about me not loving Steven and setting him free. Those words started a fire under my feet that gave me no choice but to find out where she was and what she meant by them.

The ring coming from the phone on the nightstand stopped me in my tracks. A strange chill went down my spine as I ignored it and opened the door. On the third ring, I looked over my shoulder at the phone, cursing under my breath.

"Hello."

"Tiffany?"

"Yes, who's this?"

"It's Blake. You didn't recognize my voice?"

"Sorry Blake, I've got a lot on my mind."

"Tell me about it," he said, sounding tired.

"Did you call to talk to Steven?"

"I guess, either you or him."

"Do you want me to get him for you?"

"I just called to let ya'll know that Amber has left town and Victoria is in jail," he said, with a strange nervous laughter.

"Oh my, I'm so sorry to hear that."

"Well, Amber needed to move on. She's got that boy to raise. As far as Vicky, we all knew it was coming," he replied, with anger in his voice.

"Is there anything I can do?"

"Not really, Tiffany. But I did want to ask if Caroline and I could come out there and stay for a little while. We need to get out of Natchez."

"I'm sure Steven would love that. He's out at the beach with Tristian right now."

"Look, don't disturb him. Just let him know I called."

"I will, and hey, do you need money or anything?"

"No, thank you. Money is what got me into this mess," he replied, remorsefully.

"I'm sorry...I..."

"No need for apologies, Tiffany. We're family."

"Okay. I'll let him know you called."

"Don't be upset," he replied.

"It's not you, Blake. I seem to be saying the wrong thing to everybody today."

"There's always tomorrow," he said, giving me a forced chuckle.

"You're right, good ole' tomorrow. I'll tell Steven you called."

"Okay, talk to you later, bye."

"Bye."

After sitting the phone down, I walked around the house looking for Mom. She wasn't in the kitchen or the living room or the baby's room. I checked in the guest room where she had her things but she wasn't there either. Then I walked out the front door and noticed her car was gone. With that conversation put on hold, I went to look for Steven and Tristian.

The ocean was calm today and the wind was barely blowing. I looked toward the water's edge but didn't see either of them. Once I had walked a little farther out, I looked to the north but couldn't see anyone that looked like Steven and Tristian. So I turned south and finally spotted them. They were quite a way down and I wondered if they could see me. I lifted my hands high over my head and waved. A moment later, Steven waved back, as we started to shorten the distance between us.

"Hey," I said, out of breath.

"Momma," Tristian yelled out, surprised it was me.

I picked him up and Steven leaned over, kissing my cheek and said, "Hello, Mrs. Cross."

"Your brother called. He wants you to call him back. Victoria has screwed up and now she's in jail and guess who wants to come out for a little visit? You got it! Oh, and now my sister and her boyfriend are leaving…tonight. Mom got all over me about being nice to her. Can you believe that? If that's not enough, now my Mom is leaving too. In fact, we may never see her again. She just left without saying goodbye. Needless to say, she wasn't the least bit happy with me. Your brother said Amber has left town. So…"

"Are you okay?" He asked, sounding afraid to ask.

"Not really," I said, handing Tristian to him.

"Did you get a chance to…"

"Oh, I'm so sorry. Yes I did read it and it was beautiful. Thank you," I said, stopping in front of him.

"It's okay. So did all this happen before you read it or after?"

"After. Boom, boom, boom."

"You knew your Mom would be going back to New York soon, didn't you?"

"Yes."

"I'm surprised Cheryl and Kenny haven't."

"Me too."

"We both knew Victoria was heading for trouble. I would rather her be in jail than in the graveyard," he said, kneeling to help Tristian push sand into a mound.

"I never thought about it like that," I replied, wondering why he was so calm.

He stood up, looking into my eyes and said, "My brother, he's welcomed any time and any place that I'm at; he's welcome to stay with me."

"You mean at your house?"

"That's fine. He can stay over there if you don't want him here."

"I feel like we are finally getting Mom and Cheryl out of here and the last thing I want is someone else coming to stay."

"What is wrong with you, Tiffany?"

"What do you mean, baby?"

"These people are our family. Doesn't that mean something to you?" He asked, looking down at our little boy playing in the sand at our feet.

Before I put my foot in my mouth again, I turned and walked away. As the distance between us grew I kept waiting to feel his hand on my arm or hear him call out my name. Pride kept me from turning back but the need to be loved by him made my ears strain for the sound of his voice. When I slowed the pace of my steps, thoughts like firecrackers were exploding in my mind. Why did it feel like no one liked me anymore? Why did I feel so terrible, so unloved? And why wasn't Steven coming after me?

Once I laid down on my bed, I jumped back up and locked the door. I didn't want to say goodbye to Cheryl and I didn't want to talk to Mom. In fact, it would be okay with me if this day would end without me seeing another face or hearing another voice. The only good news

I'd heard all day was about Amber being gone. So with that thought in my mind, I turned the ringer to the phone off, turned up the television volume, put ear plugs in my ears and covered my eyes to shield them from light. As I laid there thinking about the day and all that had happened, I realized I wasn't feeling very well. Then, the more I thought about it, I hadn't been feeling well for several days.

The next morning I made a doctor's appointment before I walked out of my room to find out where Steven and Tristian were. To my surprise there were three notes sitting on the table all addressed to me. One from my sister, one from Mom and one from Steven.

Cheryl's said *thanks for everything, I'm glad we got to spend time together and I hope to see you soon.* She even signed it *love, Cheryl* which led me to believe she wasn't mad at me. Mom's wasn't quite as nice but still it was civil. It read, *be good to Steven and give Tristian a hug for me whenever I cross your mind. Remember what's truly important in life is sometimes hidden by what we want rather than what we need.* She didn't bother to sign it nor did she close the little note with love but it didn't faze me one way or another.

When I opened Steven's note, I had to sit down. It was short and to the point and scared the hell out of me. It read, *you locked me out when I needed you most, I'll come back when you need me the most.* He didn't sign his name and the words were almost unreadable. My first instinct took me to Tristian's room to see if he was laying in his bed. When I walked in, I shook my head, wondering how stupid could I be? Of course Steven would never leave the baby here with me locked in the bedroom.

Racing back to the kitchen, I picked up the note again and anger coursed through my veins. I charged into the bedroom, ripping off my clothes and ranting about the notes I had read. In no time, my hair was in a ponytail, face washed and clothes on. If the waves of nausea would have left me alone I could have been halfway to Steven's house by the time I got out of the bathroom.

When I finally felt well enough to leave the bathroom, I was exhausted and not good for anything except a chair. When I felt a little better, I decided to use the phone first and see if he was staying at his house. It was after the third try that I gave up. If he was there, they must still be asleep or maybe they were already up and outside. Tristian was not much for sleeping late and Steven was becoming more and more involved in his daily activities.

The clock didn't help much with my nerves as I realized I was not going to have enough time to drive over there before my doctor's appointment. The boys would have to wait until I was done. Besides, I wanted to know why in the world was I so tired and cranky all the time.

After an hour and twenty minutes in the doctor's office and a few tests, I knew exactly what was wrong with me. Now, I needed Steven more than ever. His note promised he would come back when I needed him most and it didn't take long for me to need him.

When I left the doctor's office, I drove straight to his house, praying him and Tristian would be there. My car had barely stopped rolling when I opened the door and ran to the front door calling out his name. At first I knocked, then I realized I had a key and unlocked it, letting myself in.

"Steven! Are you here?"

"Out here," he yelled from the patio.

"Steven, baby, I'm sorry. Please forgive me," I begged, suddenly emotional.

"Tiffany, I forgive you but...," he said, his head down, moving it from side to side.

"Look, I know why I've been so crazy lately. I just left the doctor's office."

He looked up at me, tears filling his eyes, "Please don't tell me something's wrong."

"No, nothing's wrong. Everything is right. It's so right, baby."

"Then what is it?"

"I'm pregnant."

"What am I supposed to say? I'm happy? How can I, Tiffany?"

"Yes, you could be happy."

"How can I, when it's risking your life? What did the doctor say?"

"He talked about terminating the pregnancy. I told him forget it. Not happening."

"Tiffany, you know I don't want you to do that either, but in this case you may need to consider it."

"I can't believe I'm hearing those words come out of your mouth!"

He looked hurt but stepped forward, putting his arms around me and said, "I can't believe I said it either."

"Why? Why would you say that?"

He looked into my eyes, searching for the right words and said, "I can't live without you. I spent a whole life time waiting. Waiting for my chance to be near you, to see you, to feel you. Now, all of my dreams have come true and then some. You are my wife. I am your husband. We have a beautiful baby boy who is healthy and strong. We are both successful, we are happy, and deeply in love. I'm scared of losing all that, of losing you."

"I'm going to be okay, Steven. You're not going to lose me. This baby was meant to be. I knew it from the moment I had Tristian that he was not going to be an only child. This new baby is going to make our family complete and I promise," I said, taking his chin in my hand, "I'm not going anywhere."

"You promise?" He asked, pulling me closer and looking right into my eyes.

"I promise, Mr. Cross. You are stuck with me, forever and a day."

"I can see I've lost this battle so I'll just surrender; with a celebration… of wild unrestrained happiness."

I shook my head, saying, "A little happiness would be nice."

Steven picked me up and swung me around, looking into my eyes. He sat me down and kissed my lips so lightly and gently it made chills run down my spine then he said, "I hope it's a little girl."

"Me too, baby," I said, as Tristian started to cry.

Chapter 20

Something deep inside made me want to go back. I wanted to turn back the hands of time and start over. I wanted a do-over in the worst kind of way. The thought of it plagued me with worry and doubt. Somehow, somewhere I had made the wrong decision. The path had grown crooked and dark and I needed a hero to save me from myself. It had to be changed. The future had to be brighter than the present or I needed to find a way of escape. So I began to search for a light. Everyone had always talked about a light at the end of the tunnel but try as I might I could see nothing. Nothing but endless days, full of wrestling with choices I had made and the consequences they had rendered.

Steven had proven to be the only one I could count on. He had stayed with me, even when I, myself would have walked away. 'Think Twice' had tested the limits of even the most patient with its constant setbacks and rewrites. What was supposed to be a four month obligation had taken seven months. As the baby inside of me continued to grow, shooting became more and more strategic. The doctors warned that if I didn't stop working, our little girl would never take her first breath. The studio threatened a lawsuit if I didn't see it through to the end. When we finally called it a wrap, I don't know if I had ever been happier to finish a movie.

Steven, Tristian and I retreated to his house in the hills, shutting ourselves off from the rest of the world. Christmas was close, so as I lay resting until it was time to give birth, letting the boys do all the necessary things to celebrate the big day. It was amazing to watch the two of them together. They were like two little peas in a pod. They looked alike, dressed alike and they even seemed to think alike. It was such a relief to know that soon there would be another girl in our family. That was if everything went the way I planned it in my mind.

Blake and Caroline took up the boys slack when it came to decorating and taking care of me. With Victoria spending the next two years in prison for selling drugs, Blake had decided there wasn't much reason in going back to Natchez. He and Caroline had filled the void Mom and Cheryl had made since they moved back to New York.

It was late afternoon and rather cool for Los Angeles when Blake offered to take the kids out so Steven and I could spend some time alone. We both agreed and within ten minutes, Tristian was dressed and waiting by the door for Caroline and Blake. After kissing Tristian goodbye, I went to our bedroom to take a shower and wait for Steven.

When I stepped out, dripping wet, he startled me when he wrapped a towel around my back. It was warm and soft which made me feel special and loved. I turned toward him, smiled and he gave me a wink. Then he reached out for another towel and kneeled down, drying my legs.

"You don't have to do that."

"I want to," he said, moving slowly up my left leg.

"It is getting harder to do it," I said, trying to cover my belly with the towel.

"It's okay, I love to see your baby bump. It's so sexy," he said, looking up at me.

"Oh yea, right. So sexy. Have you had your eye sight checked lately?"

"It is to me," he said seriously, moving to the right leg.

"When we were young, did you ever think we would have babies?"

"I didn't really think about it that much but I did hope we would get married and have a family. Didn't you?"

"Before you left for New York, I always thought about us getting married but then you broke my heart and I stopped thinking about it."

Steven stood up, brushed the wet hair from my eyes and said, "I didn't mean to break your heart."

"I know you didn't," I said, walking into the bedroom.

"Do you want your brush?"

"Yes, will you bring it?"

The towel dropped to the floor as I searched through my drawer for a night gown. My back was to him but I could feel his eyes watching. There was no hope in finding anything that looked good so I opted out for a white cotton gown with tiny white buttons. Steven sat down on the edge of the bed with the brush in his hand. I picked up the towel and sat it on the back of a chair and took the brush from his hand.

"God, I love your long red hair. I'm so glad you've never cut it off."

"I'm never going to cut it, ever."

"Good, it is your crowning glory."

"Steven, I need to ask you something."

"You can ask me anything."

"Well, I've been thinking."

"What have you been thinking?" He asked, patting the spot beside him on the bed.

"Is it okay if we lay down?"

"Is that what you wanted to ask?" He said, laughing a little and pushing his shoes off.

"No, I just want to be beside you," I said, moving the pillows.

"Let me help you," he replied, propping up the pillows and helping me get comfortable.

He moved to the other side, laid down beside me then I asked, "Are you ready?"

"I think so."

"I've been thinking a lot lately. I've realized we've never had a home. I mean you have two houses and I have the beach house but we have never had a home together. Don't you think it's about time we have one?"

"If that's what you want."

"I've been thinking that Los Angeles isn't your kind of town. You haven't written anything in a long, long time. I know you need to."

"The only thing I really need is you, Tristian and our baby," he replied, touching my growing belly.

"Seriously, I think maybe it's time to get out of here. We could sell your little house in Mississippi and this house and buy something nice in Natchez or maybe buy a big piece of land and build a house there."

"What about the beach house?"

"I thought we could keep it. Just because we move doesn't mean I want to give up my career."

"Oh, of course not. I understand."

"I think it would give us a chance to raise our kids out of the lime-light. We could try and give them some sort of normal childhood and we could be near your dad and mine."

"It would be nice to get back to a slower pace," he said, resting his head on a pillow, looking up to the ceiling.

"So, what do you think?"

"I think I love the idea of moving back to the south," he said, leaning up on one elbow, asking, "When do you want to go?"

"As soon as possible," I said, taking his other hand and placing it on my belly.

"She's going to be a fighter, just like you."

"She kicks harder than Tristian did."

"I pray she looks like you, Love."

"I pray she has a poet's heart, just like yours."

He leaned forward, kissing my lips carefully. There was an unspoken way he moved and touched me that spoke volumes of how delicate he feels I am in this condition. Almost every day, I would catch him on his knees praying with his eyes closed and his hands clasped together. I never asked, but I knew he was praying for me and our baby. So far, we were both healthy and there had not been one problem. But Steven and I both knew that it had been no different with Tristian. It was only during the delivery that so many problems had threatened our future.

With his hand still resting on my belly, I rolled over onto my side and Steven snuggled up behind me. It felt so right to lay beside him, listening to his breath as the sun slipped lower and lower in the western sky. Then the urge to feel him, to make love to him rushed through my body causing me to feel nervous.

He slowly moved his hand down to my thigh and slid it up under my gown until it rested on my naked hip. I pulled a pillow out from under my head and pushed it under my belly. Before I laid my head back down, Steven put his arm under my neck and moved his body closer to mine. He kissed the back of my neck while he unbuttoned his pants. Then I could feel what I had been missing pressed against my back, making me want him even more.

"Do you think its okay?" He asked, kissing my earlobe.

"Of course it is."

"I don't want to hurt you," he replied, pulling my gown up farther.

"It will hurt me more if you stop," I said, helping to guide him.

It was the first time we had made love in a long time. Somehow, work, family and time had kept us from being intimate with each other. It wasn't like we were strangers, but it was strange, my body had changed so dramatically. It was if we had unknowingly built an imaginary wall between us. As each of the bricks came crashing down I felt closer and more connected with him than I had in months.

His touch was strong yet tender. His concern was about me and how he was making me feel. His patience paid off as I yielded to his lingering attention, full of energy and enjoyment. My mind was empty, there were no thoughts of the past or the future. Steven had me in the palm of his hand, fully focused on the here and now. With enthusiasm, he brought so many of my imagined desires into fulfilling reality.

For the moments we spent laying peacefully in each other's arms before sleep overtook us, I was happy. Steven never said what he was feeling but I assumed he was happy too. We had made a big decision to completely change our lives and the lives of our children. Then we had sealed the decision with love in the most intimate way a husband and wife can.

As the sun rose on a new day, Steven broke the news to Blake about our plans for the future. Without hesitation or asking me what I thought, he sent Blake and Caroline back to Mississippi to pack up his house and put it up for sale. Tristian and I barely got use to the idea before they were gone and we were left to spend Christmas without them.

A few days after Blake and Caroline got home, Steven received a phone call from Blake which made me wonder what in the world was going on. When I questioned him, he told me not to worry, he had everything under control. It was only after I pushed harder for some answers that he finally admitted that he had had his eye on some land north of Natchez for a long time. Blake had contacted the family that owned it but it was still way overpriced. But in Steven's mind it was perfect for us. Sixty acres of woods and pasture with a clear running stream flowing right through the middle. He explained, through dreamy eyes, that there was an old farmhouse on the land that we could stay in until we built our dream house. The way he saw it we could be in our log house in less than a years' time.

After three deep breaths, I interrupted his Boy Scout dream to remind him who he was married to. Sixty acres of woods and pasture, I could understand. An old farmhouse was not happening. I was not living in some old rundown farmhouse full of dust and mice. Why Steven Cross would ever think I would agree to building a log cabin is beyond me. Only if it was a log mansion, painted pink with floors made out of marble, would I even consider it.

Steven looked at me like I had woke him up during the best dream of his life. His eyes were big and round and scared, like the dream had ended without him finding out what happened. He hurried out of the living room, into the office and quickly returned with a large brown envelope. Sitting down beside me, searching through the papers, he handed me a picture.

It was a house, and yes it was made of logs but it was beautiful. It had to be thirty or forty feet high in the front with huge windows jetting out to a point in the front. The house was huge with large decks on either side of the enormous windows. Then he showed me blueprints of the inside. It was seven bedrooms with eight and a half bathrooms. The kitchen looked like it was as big as half of the house we were in now and the master bedroom and bath was certainly almost as big as his house in Natchez. He said it would be somewhere around fifteen thousand square feet when it was finished.

As my mind began to change and I was reconsidering his dream of a cabin in the woods, he handed me a few real pictures of the finished product. There was one of a kitchen, not as large as he wanted but so different and beautiful with the huge windows letting in the sunlight. Another one of a living room with a huge fireplace in the center and the enormous windows and extremely tall ceilings made me change my mind all together.

Part of me wanted to resist a little so before I let him off the hook, I made him promise that he would build a swimming pool fit for a queen in the back yard. After he promised, I let him know that if he wanted to build a log mansion that I would be happy with that. He gathered up his plans and stuffed them back in the envelope and went back to his office with a smile. I laid down on the couch for a cat nap.

"Steven! Steven!"

"Tiffany, what's wrong?" He asked, running into the room.

"I don't know."

"Don't move, I'm calling for an ambulance."

"Don't do that, come here."

"There's blood, baby. Please don't try to move. I'll be right back."

"Momma's baby okay?" Tristian asked, holding my hand.

"The baby's okay. Momma is okay." I said, pulling the cover over my legs.

"I want baby."

"I want the baby too," I added, trying not to let my feelings of pain show.

"Wanna hold baby," Tristian said, rubbing my belly.

"Come here son," Steven said, picking him up. "They will be here soon, Love. Is there anything I can do or get for you?"

"Just stay here with me. I'm scared."

"I'm scared too, Tiffany," he said, kneeling down to sit on the floor in front of me, holding Tristian, his eyes full of tears.

I grabbed his hand and squeezed it tight, "It hurts so bad."

"I wish I could take your place. I would do it in a heartbeat."

"Steven, I know we never talked about this but you know if something happens, you have to go on. Do you understand that?"

"Don't talk like that. Stop it!"

"Listen to me. You are young. Tristian needs a mother. Don't you dare give up! You have to keep going for his sake."

"Why are you saying this? Nothing is going to happen to you."

"I know nothing is going to happen to me. But just in case, you have to know that I wouldn't want you to waste the rest of your life being sad over me. Be sad, get over it and get back to living. Oh, God, this hurts so bad," I cried, squeezing his hand harder.

"Momma hurts?" Tristian asked, touching my cheek.

"Yes, Tristian, momma hurts. Can you be a big boy and open the front door for daddy, then come right back here?"

"Yes," he answered, running out of the living room.

Steven got up on his knees, leaning over to kiss my lips and looked into my eyes, saying, "Don't you dare leave me here alone. I have fought all of my life to love you and I am not going to lose you now. Do you hear me?"

"I'll do my best, Mr. Cross but no promises," I mustered through a broken voice muddled with pain and teardrops.

The knocking on the door brought Steven to his feet. In a flash, the EMT's had me on the gurney and into the ambulance. They wouldn't allow Steven to ride with me because of Tristian, so I was alone. Alone, except for my thoughts of how things were supposed to be right now and how everything could change so suddenly.

By the time Steven got to the hospital they were preparing me for an emergency C-section. He barely made it into the room before they were wheeling me down the hallway. In the blur, he kissed my cheek and took my hand, walking beside me.

"Where's the baby?"

"He's with Diane."

"That's good," I said, closing my eyes.

"I'll be right here waiting for you," he said, squeezing my hand before letting go.

It was the feeling of Steven's hand letting go of mine that made me open my eyes. Then the sound of doors opening and closing that separated his heart and mine. It made me want to scream, stop, but the words were stuck in my head. The next thing I remember is counting backwards then darkness. Pitch black.

"Did I make it?" I asked, before opening my eyes.

"Yes." Steven's voice answered. "You both made it."

"Where is she?" I asked, struggling to sit up.

"Right here," he answered, getting up to stand beside my bed.

I looked at the little face peeping out of a snuggly wrapped blanket, saying, "She has red hair."

"Just like yours," he said, leaning forward so I could see her better.

"Is she okay?"

"Perfectly fine."

"Am I okay?"

"Yes. Thanks for keeping your promise," he said, choking on his words.

"It wasn't easy," I said, reaching out to touch his hand.

"Do you want to hold her?"

"I do."

He moved to the other side of the bed and let down the bed guard. After he laid her beside me, in my left arm he stood staring at us and said, "You two are the most beautiful girls I have ever seen in my life."

"This little girl is going to need a name. What do you think?" I asked, staring up into his eyes.

"Stormie Calista Cross," Steven said, looking down at her.

"I love it... and I love you."

"I love you more. Always have and always will," he said with authority, as if there was no need to ever argue the point.

So I let him win, without even a word of resistance. Besides, he certainly had proven his love for me over and over again throughout the years. But as the energy left my body again, as my heavy eyes closed, I wondered if he had ever thought about my love for him and what it had endured to survive to this point? Would he ever consider that the love I have for him is enough to last for the rest of our lives? Maybe one day, he would finally realize that I had been the one who had always loved him a little more than he could ever know or understand.

21
Chapter

Words had brought us together. They were the glue that had meshed our lives since we were teenagers and they were the reason we shared a last name. Like a magnet drawn by the invisible force of steel, Steven's words bound me to continue searching for the significant meaning behind his poetry. Sometimes it was clear, like the stream that flowed so peacefully across our land. At other times, they were like the muddy waters of the mighty Mississippi that flowed strongly not too far away.

Stormie was different. She was as different from Tristian as night is from day. Her tantrums were from the fairy tales of princesses that demanded too much. Her beauty could not be compared to normal babies, she outshined them all. Her soul did not align with her age, she had a poise well beyond her years. But regardless of her unique nature, she was completely one hundred percent the apple of my eye.

It was the celebration of her first birthday before the log mansion was complete and ready for us to move in. Nothing except the grandest party would do for our beautiful little red-headed girl. Now, with the old farmhouse renovated and the new house ready for guests, we made sure everyone who wanted to be there was coming.

Steven had spared no expense on giving us all exactly what we wanted. The house was enormous with its towering entryway and a great room full of majestic floor to ceiling windows. The kitchen was better than some I had seen in Hollywood mansions and was equipped with a live-in chef.

Our bedroom was larger than the little house Steven had owned before we married. It was the most romantic room I had ever seen in my life. Even more so than the honeymoon suite we had shared those first few days in Italy. He never asked what I wanted, instead he had kept it a complete secret. The floors were hardwood and covered by expensive rugs from India. The bed was a masterpiece he had hand carved and shipped from Italy. The canopy made of silk and dyed the color of a good red wine was draped over the sides. They partially hid a rich bedspread in burgundy and gold that covered the massive bed. There was a sitting area near the window completely furnished with a hidden television and wet bar.

If that wasn't enough he made sure to fulfill any girl's dream with the bathroom and closet. They were both the size of most master bedrooms in normal houses. The closet had enough space for me to shop for the next year before it would be filled. It smelled of cedar and gave you the feeling that there was shopping to be done. But the bathroom topped them all. The tub was big enough to fit at least four people comfortably with room to spare. The shower had several shower heads and seats made of granite to sit down and relax under the warm water. Double sinks lined one wall while the other wall was nothing but windows. The view of the country side reminded us of where we were because other than that, it felt like we were in a private spa.

The children's room had been designed and decorated to suit their taste. Tristian's was full of all things outdoors with his bed suspended from the ceiling like a glorified hammock. There were life-sized stuffed animals of every kind and jungle scenes painted on the walls. His bathroom resembled a rain forest and Steven even piped the sounds of the rainforest to play any time Tristian walked in.

Stormie's room barely resembled a little girl's room other than her small bed. It was almost completely white with only small accents of pale yellow and pink. Her dolls were lined up on shelves that were just her size yet she rarely played with them. In fact, about the only thing she enjoyed were her books. Steven had used one whole wall and had built in bookshelves placed across the bottom so Stormie could reach them. Then he bought hundreds of books on every subject that could be imagined.

The guest rooms were no different. Each had been carefully designed and decorated with the people he loved in mind. One room had everything a young family would need to be comfortable, including a child's bed that adjoined the room with a cave-like appearance. Another was very feminine and flowery and pretty, perfect for a mother-in-law or aunts. The other two felt more masculine with sturdy furniture and neutral colors.

The house was grand, everything Steven had ever envisioned and more. The landscaping was fit for a castle and designed for a king. There were plants and shrubs of every shape and size in a mosaic type of pattern around every square foot of the house. Pathways of rock and stone led you from one section of the yard to another but all of them ultimately led to the backyard.

A huge deck extended from the back of the house that was partially covered from the sun. This was our outdoor living space complete with dining table, multiple grills, refrigerator and wet bar. There was an oversized sectional couch and several large chairs that could easily accommodate twenty people or more. Then there were the lounge chairs and tables on the other side for those who wanted to lay in the sun. But the jewel of the entire place was the swimming pool. Slides and waterfalls and hidden coves with two hot tubs made this the best part of our new home. Steven had kept his word, he had gone above and beyond my hopes and expectations and no one could have been happier than me.

The old farmhouse wasn't so old looking anymore. There were plenty of upgrades with a lot of remodeling that had brought it into the future. With four bedrooms and two and a half baths there was always extra room for family, friends or staff if needed. Besides that, it was only a short walk across the pasture between the two houses. There never seemed to be a shortage of four wheelers to jump on and ride if you didn't care to walk the distance.

Stormie's party was thrown together at the last minute but no one seemed to mind. In fact, it kind of morphed into a birthday slash Christmas slash house warming party. Both of our Dads were already here and helping to get everything ready for the rest of our guest. Today, Mom was flying in from New York and Diane and her man, George were coming in from L.A. in the morning. Cheryl had declined our invitation with the excuse of being too busy. I had my suspicions that she was still mad about what had happened in Los Angeles between me and Mom. But regardless, I had to go on with my life and not dwell on the past or it would only bring me down.

Caroline and Blake would be here also because they had become permanent fixtures in our lives. With Victoria still paying her debt to society we had grown closer over time, raising Caroline right beside Tristian and Stormie. They had moved into the farmhouse and we paid Blake to take care of the day to day chores of taking care of our estate. He seemed happy to do it and Caroline was growing up happy, healthy and strong so it was working out good for all concerned.

As soon as Mom walked through the door, Tristian ran and jumped in her arms and hugged her tight then refused to let go. We sat down on the nearest couch and Tristian laid in her arms like a little baby looking up and listening to every word she said. Occasionally, she would lean down and kiss his forehead or cheek and he would snuggle closer, hugging her again. Tristian wouldn't budge. Even when his sister cried, begging him to come, he wouldn't let go of his Me-Me.

Sitting there watching them interact with each other was the first time I realized they had bonded as mother and child when I lay dying in the ICU. It wasn't my son's fault and it wasn't mother's either. It was what it was and nothing I could ever do or say could change it. Still, my heart ached, seeing the bond the two of them had with each other. It was a bond I wish he and I shared.

When everyone had gone their separate ways to prepare for the big birthday party tomorrow, Tristian, Mom and I were still sitting on the couch. Tristian was drifting off to sleep and she had kicked off her shoes propping her feet on the coffee table. I stood up, excused myself and Mom waved me back into my seat.

"I feel like I need to tell you something. I don't know if it matters or not."

"What is it, Mom? Is something wrong?"

"Well, sorta. I guess."

"Tell me what it is."

"It's your sister," she said, looking around to see if anyone was near.

"What has she done?"

"She broke off her engagement to Kenny."

"Why did she do that?"

"One of your 'old friends' started pursuing her like she was the Queen of Sheba."

"Who?"

"Michael. Michael McFarland," she said, with distaste.

"O h-m y-g o d, you've got to be kidding me?"

"What did you do to him, Tiffany?"

"What do you mean?"

She looked around the room again to make sure we were alone, saying, "There were all those rumors about you and him. Even rumors about him being Tristian's, you know…"

"Not true."

"I know that but why is he after your sister like she is the only woman in the city of New York. Don't you think that's a little odd?"

"Of course I do. So…are they dating?"

"She's living with him."

I stood up, feeling like a fist had punched my stomach, saying, "I can't believe that."

"Well, believe it, honey. He's got your sister wrapped around his finger or wrapped around something. She doesn't even act the same and she looks like hell warmed over."

"Oh, no," I said, grabbing my gut, feeling like I had been stabbed.

"I'm going to ask you one more time, Tiffany and I expect the truth. What did you do to this man?"

"I asked for him to go back to New York."

"Asked who? You asked him to go back?" She asked, moving Tristian to the couch so she could stand up.

I walked across the room to the fireplace, trying to think of what to say before opening my mouth. Then I turned back but she was right behind me and I said, "No. I asked the big-wigs in Hollywood to make him disappear. He was trying to ruin my life."

"Now he's ruining your sister's life. Does that even matter to you?"

"Of course it does," I said, looking her in the eye.

"Now I get it. I understand why he pursued her this way. Look, she needs our help. And she needs it now before it's too late."

"What can I do?" I asked, listening to the footsteps coming toward us.

"Make a phone call…talk to somebody, anybody," she replied, with desperation in her voice.

"I'll take care of it. Don't worry."

"Are ya'll still in here?" Steven asked, loudly, before realizing Tristian was asleep.

All three of us looked at Tristian, who barely moved at the sound of his dad's voice. Then I said, "Mom was telling me about Cheryl."

"How is she? Why isn't she here?" He asked, in a low voice.

"She's alright. She wanted to come but it was bad timing," Mom replied.

"I wish she could have made it," he answered, putting his arm around my waist.

"We both wish she was here," I said, looking up at his face.

"This house is so beautiful, Steven. You've really outdone yourself," Mom said, admiring the expansive room.

"Please, let me give you the grand tour," Steven offered, extending his arm.

Mom took his arm and they walked toward the kitchen with him chattering about the house and how it was built. I stood near the fireplace and looked at my little boy curled up, sleeping so soundly. The love I felt for him was overwhelming and I realized that Cheryl was to my Mom what Tristian was to me. Her first born. A dream come true and a huge part of her world.

Michael McFarland was playing dirty. In fact, he was playing dirtier than I thought he was capable of playing. But he met his match the day he met me. This battle was his to claim but the war was still raging on. As I looked at my child, my flesh and blood, I knew that there was no way I could lose. After all, Cheryl was my sister and I could not let her fall prey to the wolves in this world that threatened to eat her alive.

The next day came with the rising of the sun on our majestic cabin deep in the woods of Natchez, Mississippi. With everyone here and the house buzzing with party plans and voices, not a dull moment would be experienced. When Diane and George arrived, our guest list was complete and we all gradually retreated to the outdoor living space.

When the birthday cake arrived, the food began to flow from the kitchen to the tables outside. The presents were set on a large table, near the birthday girl's seat. Stormie didn't seem too interested in the other children that wanted to tear open her gifts. She gravitated toward Diane and George, opting to sit in Diane's lap at the big people's table rather than her seat of honor at the children's table.

Diane didn't seem to mind so we sat the huge white cake with little pink roses in front of her. The photographer snapped photo after photo as they blew out the candle while we sang our best rendition of Happy Birthday. Stormie reached out, taking a handful of icing from the side of the cake but immediately wanted it off her hand. Diane cleaned her up, then she helped her open presents.

When Stormie opened a box from my Dad that was full of new books, the party was over for her. Nothing would do except having Diane hold her on the big couch while they looked at every picture in her books. The rest of us kept ourselves entertained with the latest news, gossip and talk of the future. We had never been together at the same time under the same roof. After taking it all in, I realized this was exactly why Steven had wanted to build this house. It was the place we could finally call home and have our whole family together.

Then my thoughts turned to my sister and Michael. It was obvious what he was doing and there was no way I was going to stand for it. After excusing myself, I went to the office and locked the door behind me. With just a few phone calls to the right people, I felt like I had this little situation under control. The only thing left to do was let mom know everything was going to be alright. All we needed was to have some patience and once and for all Michael would be out of our lives for good.

As the days passed, the big house began to feel emptier and emptier. First to go was Diane and George followed by Mom and Dad. Then Steven's Dad left with the promise to come back the following weekend for a night or two. After he left, Blake and Caroline went back to the farmhouse and we rarely saw them except when we happened to be riding the four-wheelers around the property. It felt so sad to see the house, once alive with voices and laughter fall so silent and cold.

With Christmas presents unwrapped and put away and the New Year's Eve fireworks display fully enjoyed we fell into a dull routine. Every morning, it was breakfast at eight followed by riding in the woods on four wheelers with the children. After lunch we all settled down for a nap. When nap time was over the kids played out on the back porch by the pool or out on the lawn if the weather was nice. Then it was dinner at six, bath time and we retired to the great room for a little T.V. time which usually consisted of cartoons. After a good night's sleep we started all over again. That was until Hollywood started calling.

The promise of a starring role had me packing my bags and trying to stifle my excitement. Steven had the promise of a new book that he kept putting off, hanging over his head. We decided that it was time to hire a nanny. Since I would be gone for a while, he would have to hire one without my help.

Until he chose the right nanny to help with the children, my Dad and his Dad committed to taking turns with helping out. It felt like everything was falling into place, exactly liked we had planned it. I would fly out to L.A., secure my next role and Steven would revive his writing career with his next best-selling novel. There was only one little hitch that neither one of us could ignore. It was the fact that we had grown accustomed to being together every day and now we would be apart for who knows how long.

With my Dad moved into one of the guest rooms and the children fully aware that I would be gone for a little while, I double checked my list to make sure everything was ready. Steven had been sitting on the couch in our room, watching T.V. and I was running around grabbing my last minute stuff. When I noticed how his eyes followed me, I stopped and sat down beside him.

"Are you sure you're okay with this?"

"Not really, but I know it's something you have to do," he said, looking down at his hands.

"Steven, let's be realistic. We both knew this was the way it was going to be," I said, reaching over for his hand.

"I know. But I didn't factor in how hard it would be," he said, pulling my hand up to his chest.

"It won't be for long, and hopefully you'll find somebody to help out with the kids soon."

"How long?" He asked, searching my eyes.

"I don't know. Look, somebody's got to work and make some money. You haven't written a book in a long time. We have to have money to live on."

"Tiffany, we have more money than we need for two lifetimes."

"I know you think that Steven, but it takes a lot to maintain what we have."

"I thought the whole idea of building this house was to live in it and raise our children."

"Our children are going to need things too."

"They need us. They need us together."

"I can't believe you are doing this to me."

He put my hand on my leg and drew his back clasping them on his lap, before saying, "I'm sorry. You're right. I'll miss you."

"I'll miss you too, baby," I said, smiling. "I'll be back before you know it."

Steven was right though. The lure of the city and the beauty of the beach kept me in Los Angeles longer than I had expected. One week passed, two weeks passed and before I knew it three weeks were gone. But I was so busy I barely noticed the passage of time, until the day I received a letter in the mail.

My beloved,

Twenty-one days without your smile. Weeks without your kiss. Please make the sand in the hour glass stop flowing, for my heart can't stand to miss you like this.

Where can I go to see you? Why is it only in my dreams? Tell me, Love, do you even miss me? And why is being away from you harder than it would seem?

My pen stands ready to glide across the page. It's my heart that feels so heavy. It's like a door of lead. There's no one here to open it. The only one with the key has fled. She's gone too far to free me. When will she return? Please say it will be tomorrow and I could subdue the heart that eternally burns…with one word; Tiffany.

Love forever,
Steven

For the first time since I left Natchez, I truly missed Steven and the children. It was crazy how wrapped up in my career I had become. Where had my natural instinct to return to my family gone? Was my ambition smothering it? Was revenge against Michael McFarland distorting my emotions? Or was it the bright city lights and the lure of excitement that had stolen my attention? Whatever the cause, it was time for me to get my head straight and tie up the loose ends around here.

In less than a week, I was on a plane, headed back to Mississippi. There were at least five extra suitcases coming back with me, full of presents for everyone and of course, a few extra outfits to help fill up my enormous closet. Steven had told me he was coming to pick me up. There was no way he was sending a car. No, that would not do in his book. He seemed so excited saying he couldn't hardly wait another minute. So as I entered the airport I expected to see him running down the corridor toward me. Instead, he stood patiently waiting with flowers in his hand.

My shoulders instinctively pulled back when I saw him. At first, my pace quickened but then I did my best to relax. It had been less than a month since we had seen one another. I thought it was best not to get over zealous about our reunion. Especially since it would probably not be a very long one.

"I'm so glad to see you," I said, reaching for the flowers and hugging him briefly.

"You look so beautiful," he said, stepping back looking me up and down.

"You look even more countrified than when I left," I said, checking out his cowboy boots.

"Well if that was a compliment, thank you."

"Where are the kids?" I asked, as we walked toward baggage claim.

"They are with Terri," he said, taking my hand.

"Who's Terri?"

He stopped, looking over at me saying, "Terri is the nanny. Don't you remember?"

"No. You never told me you found one."

"Tiffany, I told you about her. She's been living in our house for nearly a month."

"You didn't tell me that."

"Yes, I did," he said, sounding upset and letting go of my hand.

"No you didn't," I responded, walking toward the baggage area.

"You may not remember but I did tell you."

After we pulled my luggage from the conveyer we rented a cart to carry it out. It felt like things were already going wrong. First, the mix up about the nanny and then with us trying to get all my luggage out the door. Why Steven had to be so stubborn and not hire a driver to come and get me was beyond my comprehension. He always thought he could do everything himself and save his manhood but it always felt like his thoughtfulness amounted to a lot of hassle.

Steven opened the truck door, waiting for me to get in before shutting it. As he loaded the suitcases in the bed of the truck, I dug through my purse for lip-gloss. When he got in and started the truck I opened my purse, putting the gloss away.

"Have I told you how beautiful you look?"

"Yes, you did."

"Something about you and being in California agrees. Or is it being back in Mississippi that makes you look so good?"

"I think it's a little bit of both of them."

"So," he said, patting the seat beside him, "do you want to go home?"

"Yes, I can't wait to see the kids."

"I thought you might want to go to the park first. Maybe sit under our favorite oak tree...or take a walk in the woods," he said, reaching over to put his hand on my knee.

"As tempting as that sounds, Steven, I really am tired from my trip and I want to get home and see my babies."

His eyes fixed on the road in front of us as his hand moved back to the steering wheel. Then he said very solemnly, "It was just a thought."

Terri Woodall stood in the great room with Stormie on her hip and Tristian holding on to her right leg. She was the picture-perfect country girl, with jeans and braids in her hair. Her accent matched her outfit as she pretended not to be star-struck.

"Well, Ms. Tiffany Starr, I was wondering if I was ever gonna meet you," she said, flashing a mouthful of big white teeth.

"Of course, Terri. How in the world could we not meet? You are here to take care of my babies," I said, reaching out to take Stormie.

"Momma," Tristian yelled, letting go of Terri, grabbing onto my leg.

"Hey there, stranger," Blake said, carrying in two suitcases.

"Hello, Blake. Did you miss me?" I asked, trying to walk with Tristian clinging to my leg.

"Here, I'll take him," Terri said, trying to pick Tristian up.

Blake saw the look on my face and said, "That's okay Terri. Why don't you go and help Steven."

"Will do," she replied, walking toward the door.

"It's good to have you home," Blake said, hugging me.

"Good to be home. Where is my niece?"

"She was right behind me. There she comes."

"Aunt Tiff," the little black headed beauty called out, running toward me.

I knelt down, giving her a hug and asked, "Where have you been?"

"At the farmhouse."

"My goodness. I'm gone for a few weeks and the three of you have grown up on me."

"We're getting big, momma," Tristian said.

"Momma," Stormie said, touching my face.

With Stormie still in my arms I sat down on the floor with the children. Caroline took my sunglasses off and put them on. Tristian climbed onto the other side of my lap and moved as close as he could get to me. Stormie pulled at my necklace and laughed when it made my head move.

Steven and Terri walked in with suitcases and passed Blake on his way back outside. She giggled and brushed his arm as he walked by. Steven turned to look at me and the kids on the floor and winked, making me smile. There was something about him that still made me giddy. Some raw, rough manliness that started a spark on the inside of me that I couldn't deny. It almost made me wish I had taken him up on that walk in the woods by the park. But it was too late for that now and besides, we had plenty of time to make up for lost time right here at home.

Caroline and Blake joined us for dinner and Dad surprised me by joining us too. I could tell he felt right at home, with the children, Steven and Blake and even with Terri. It made me grateful to have a home in Mississippi again so Dad could see his grandchildren and be a part of their lives. But somewhere beyond the noise of the dinner table, my mind was on California and all that had transpired while I was there.

"Did you hear me, Tiffany?" Dad asked.

"No, sir. Sorry, what did you say?"

"I asked if you had decided on your next project."

"Well, since you asked, yes, I did. We signed the paperwork the day before I left."

"This is the first time I'm hearing about this," Steven said, sounding a little upset.

"I was going to tell you tonight," I replied, in defense.

"The husbands are the last to know," Blake offered, laughing to ease the tension.

"It's called Runner's Luck. It's about a place where only the fastest runners are able to collect food for their families. Each year there is a race where only one person out of each family can compete. It's under the guise of only the strong survive."

"So you'll have to run in this movie?" Dad asked.

"No, I'll be playing the mother of one of the fastest runners in history. But he gets injured shortly before the race."

"Where will it be this time?" Steven asked.

"In Las Vegas. Out in the dessert, actually," I replied, looking at him.

"How long?" Steven asked.

"About three or four months."

"Well at least it's not half way around the globe," Dad said, picking up his glass. "Here's to...what did you say the name of it was?"

"Runner's Luck."

"Here's to Tiffany and Runner's Luck. I hope it wins you your next Oscar," He said, tapping his glass on mine.

"To Tiffany," Blake added.

"To my Oscar winning wife," Steven said, tapping his glass against mine.

It was only after dinner was over and Dad, Blake and Caroline had left that Terri came back to the great room to get the children. It was time for them to go to bed and I kissed them goodnight. Steven asked if she needed help which I thought was strange but she refused in her southern way and sashayed out of the room with my children in her arms.

Finally, it was just the two of us and I reclined beside my husband, laying my head on his shoulder. He put his arm around me and pulled me closer with a soft moan. Then I rested my hand on his upper thigh after giving it a gentle squeeze.

"What do you say we mosey on out to one of those nice little hot tubs in the backyard and relax for a while?"

"Sounds good to me, cowboy."

"What's this cowboy stuff?"

"Well, you show up wearing boots today and now you are talking about moseying. What else am I supposed to think?"

"I guess you're right. So that means I can call you my Hollywood cowgirl?"

"Your Hollywood superstar is more like it, country boy."

"Now, I'm a country boy?"

"You've always been a country boy, Steven."

"I guess you're right about that too. That's what makes you love me so much, right?"

"No, it isn't."

"Then tell me what it is?" He asked, suddenly serious.

"It's your words," I answered, playfully.

"My words," he replied, sounding puzzled.

"The poetry. Hey, why are you asking me all this? I thought we were going to get in the hot tub."

"I'll beat you there," he said, jumping up.

"I don't think so," I said, jumping up and running.

Steven chased me through the house, right on my heels. He teased me about running faster, to get food for my starving family. Then he darted around me opening the backdoor seconds before I ran through.

In moments we were at the water's edge, racing to see who could get undressed first and in the hot tub. He must have planned ahead, as he was so good at doing, and had everything ready for our relaxing soak at our fingertips. I stepped into the hot water first and almost stepped back out. It took a minute to get use to but slowly I sat down before he got his feet wet.

"I beat you," I teased pulling him into the water.

"I just wanted to know if I could see through your bra and panties when they got wet," he laughed, sitting down beside me.

"You are so full of it today. What the heck has gotten into you?"

"You have gotten into me. Damn, Tiffany. I haven't seen you in ages," he said, leaning in, kissing hard.

With sweet surrender and passionate kisses we reunited our bodies, minds and souls. His fingers knowingly addressed my desires and controlled my need for relief. Teasing and tauntingly, he quickened the pace and slowed it down. His touch made me nervous, excited and begging for liberation from the pain of anticipation.

"Do you feel what I feel?" He questioned, turning me around.

"Yes...I do."

He pulled me backwards with my back pressed against his chest, kissed my neck eagerly and said, "I feel so close to you right now."

"You should. I'm sitting in your lap."

The water made me buoyant which made it easy for Steven to lift me up. His hands held my waist then pushed me down. With one movement we were no longer on the brink, suspended by our disconnection. We became unified, finally merging into a solitary state that only lovers can achieve.

All thought left my mind, even my senses began to feel deprived except for my sense of touch. It was as if my nerve endings had developed superhuman powers or I had been given a powerful drug that heightened the nerve endings of every inch of my skin. I leaned back, taking his waist in my hands as he continued to move me easily in the warm bubbling water.

"Hold on, Love, let's make this last," he whispered, kissing the top of my back over and over again.

Digging my nails into his sides, I moaned, "Yes, yes, yes, yes…."

"Take it slow," he demanded, moving his body to reach my ear.

I looked back, reading his face and kissed him for a long time then asked, "Do you want to stop?"

"Never," he replied, picking me up.

Steven carried me until my hands grasped the other side of the tub. He was an expert when it came to making love. Somehow, even after all of these years, he found new ways to make it feel brand new. With my eyes closed, I let him have all of me. I didn't hold back one single thing. He took it all but I didn't feel like anything had been given. Instead, it felt like he had given me a present, wrapped in the prettiest box with a big expensive bow perfectly secured on top.

"Let go," he said, "I've got you."

"Yes you do."

"And you have me," he added, picking me up to sit back down.

"You make me feel soooo good," I purred, snuggling up to him in his lap.

"It's because I'm madly in love with you," he replied, looking into my eyes before kissing me passionately.

We shared a glass of wine and retired to our big inviting bed. Still damp and naked we clung to each other like we had been apart for years though it had only been a few weeks. It wasn't long before sleep took over our bodies and replaced our words of love with sweet dreams.

Before the sun hit the horizon, Steven was pulling the covers back urging me to get up. When I looked at the clock, I started to yell at him to leave me alone but he covered my mouth with his hand. He kissed my forehead while tickling my side which made me wake up very fast.

"Don't wake the children," he said slowly, in a very low voice, taking his hand from my mouth.

"Why are you waking me up before the sun?"

"Because, I want to watch it rise with you."

"That is so sweet," I said, yawning and stretching.

He took the opportunity to tickle me under both arms, saying, "Get up, sleepy head."

"The roosters haven't even crowed yet," I said, pulling him down to my face.

"Morning breath, Love," he replied, pulling away, walking toward the bathroom.

As I watched him walk, I was glad he was my husband. His body was strong, his career had made him rich and he had a sense of adventure that was alluring. The last thing I wanted to do was leave my warm bed when it was still dark outside but something inside me did exactly what my man wanted me to do.

We snuck out the back door and walked out the side gate into the pasture. Steven cranked a four wheeler and we got on, riding out toward the faintest light in the night sky. With my hands securely holding on to his waist, I looked around the landscape at the grass, plants and trees. Even though the sun had not risen the world was still beginning to receive some of its light.

Within a few minutes we had reached a rather steep hill which made Steven slow down. It also caused me to clench his waist a little harder. He took one hand and placed it on mine, patting it to tell me it was okay. Still, it felt like gravity was pulling us a little too hard so I drew myself even closer to his body.

The four-wheeler slowed to a stop on the top of the hill. As I got off, I could see we had made it just in time. The sun was climbing fast and soon we would be able to see it on the horizon. Even though I should have been surprised, I wasn't. There to the left of us were two lounge chairs and a large plastic chest and small table.

He held out his arm for me, smiling and said, "This way, madam."

I slipped my hand under his arm and strolled over, sitting down and asked, "All this for little ole me?"

"Who else?" He asked, opening the plastic chest.

He took a pillow and blanket out for each of us and made sure I was comfortable. The he pulled two glasses, orange juice, and a plate with donuts out and put them on the table. After checking to see if the sun had made its way into our day, he quickly picked up a vase with one red rose, napkins, and two small plates from the chest, putting them on the table too.

"Breakfast of champions."

"Juice and sugar. My kind of breakfast," I said, with a little giggle.

"Before that first bite, my lady," he said, leaning down to kiss me.

Steven sat down beside me and poured us a glass of juice. We tasted the sweetness of the donuts as the sky became lighter and lighter. The view was perfect, with miles and miles of tree tops before us. With a sip of juice to wash down the sugary breakfast we wiped our hands and mouth just in time for the show in the sky.

The sun broke free from the darkness in all its glory. Colors filled the sky in shades of pink, orange, yellow and many hues of blue. Steven reached out for my hand and squeezed it tight, looking over to give me a wink.

"Thank you."

"Anything for you, Love."

"You have an undeniable persuasion over me, Mr. Cross."

"Yes, I do, Mrs. Cross," he replied, handing me a pair of sunglasses.

"You think of everything," I said, putting them on.

"I try," he said moving the little table out of the way and moving his chair closer to mine before sitting down.

The sun was in complete view before he let go of my hand. He walked around to my side and sat down on the edge of the chair, pushing my hair back. Then he rested his sun glasses on top of his head and searched my face.

"What is it, baby."

"Even as beautiful as that sunrise was, it doesn't come close in comparison to the beauty I see in you."

"Why are you so good to me?"

"Because you're my girl," he said standing up, reaching his hand out to help me up.

We rode down the hill much faster than we had come up. Steven weaved through the trees and shrubs as we entered the forest and the darkness again. He knew exactly where we were going, where he was taking me. It played through my mind what he had planned next but it was fruitless thinking. My best bet was to let my thoughts go, just live in the moment and that was exactly what I did.

It was a little structure in the distance that got my attention. It looked like a few pieces of wood with a one sided roof on it. Really nothing except maybe a place to get out of the rain for a couple of people. As we got closer, I realized it had just been built and I wondered what in the world it could be. We crossed through the stream which splashed cold water on my shoes and legs. I hit Steven's arm which made him laugh and slow down the four-wheeler.

He stopped just feet from the strange little building and helped me get down. We took a moment, adjusting our glasses and walked over to a bench to sit. Steven wrapped his arm around me and sighed.

"So why are we here?"

"This is the reason I wanted this piece of land," he said, pointing to the little hut.

"What is it?"

"Come see," he said, getting up.

When we were closer, I said, "Oh. This is where the spring starts."

"Yes. It's an underground spring. The water is fresh and pure. Just like you before I took you to the peach orchard when we were kids," he said, with a laugh.

"Hey, you better watch it! You're going to get yourself in trouble, country boy."

"Now, now. If I can't pick on you who can?"

"Nobody. Nobody can pick on me," I said, pulling his face closer to mine.

"You know where kisses lead to, don't you?"

"Hugs?"

"And hugs lead to?"

"Touching?"

"That's right. And where does touching lead to?"

"Squeezing," I said, as Steven pulled me close to him.

"You know, we are alone. Just you and me. All alone, out in the woods."

"I bet the kids are up by now," I said, unbuttoning his shirt.

"That's what Terri is there for," he said, untucking my shirt.

"Then what are we waiting for?"

"I'm done waiting," he replied, pulling my shirt over my head.

A fire had been ignited between us that could not be contained or put out easily. Maybe it started with the rising of the sun into the painted sky. Or it could have been lingering from last night's escapade in the hot tub. Of course spending almost a month apart had given both of us extra fuel for our passions too.

"I wish we had a blanket," I said, unbuttoning his jeans.

"Wait a second," he said, walking back to the four wheeler. He raised the seat and pulled out a small package, saying, "Maybe this will do."

"Doesn't look like a blanket."

"It's a rain poncho. Here let me spread it out."

While he worked on our makeshift blanket, I undressed myself. It was still slightly cool, so as soon as he finished, we were on the ground in a strong embrace. I wasted no time, helping him to undress and giving him reason to be excited. We had found another place to call our own and a new way to make another memory.

The rubber under my back did little to protect me from the leaves, sticks and dirt that lay beneath it. But I barely noticed when Steven put his body on top of mine. We kissed our way together as the day grew brighter with the sun streaming down in rays through the trees.

"You feel so good," he whispered, pulling his chest away from mine, looking down into my eyes.

"Don't stop."

"Are you okay?"

"Wait," I said, lifting my legs.

He got up on his knees, putting his hands on my knees and looked down at me, asking, "Is this better?"

"Yes."

Our bodies moved in sync to the blowing of the wind in the trees and to the sound of birds singing. It had been a long time since we had gotten back to nature and it felt so natural to be here in the woods with him. We had found our place in the country. It was a perfect fit for Steven and me. Exactly like the way our bodies fit so perfectly together.

We lay side by side on the plastic poncho, looking up into the sky. His arm supported my head while his other hand lay under his head. If it wasn't for the cool chill of the morning air, we might have laid there for a long time.

With half of our clothes back on, Steven stopped, asking, "Do you hear that?"

"What?"

"Listen."

"What is it?"

"Sounds like a four-wheeler. Hurry," he said, throwing me my shirt.

"They're coming this way."

"I know," he replied, trying to get his boots on.

Just as I finished tucking in my shirt, I turned and said, "It's your brother."

"Wonder what he wants," Steven said, pulling his shirt sleeve up his right arm.

"Good morning," Blake said, after he turned off the engine.

"Good morning," Steven said, buttoning his shirt.

"Morning," I added, walking to sit on the bench to put my shoes on.

"I was wondering what happened to ya'll."

"Is anything wrong?" Steven asked, tucking in his shirt.

"Nope."

"Well, why are you here?" Steven asked, sounding irritated, picking up the poncho.

"Just come to check on you and to let you know the kids want their momma."

"Okay. We'll be heading back soon," Steven replied, folding up the makeshift blanket and putting it away.

Blake got off the four-wheeler and came to sit down beside me. Then he asked, "Did Steven tell you about Victoria?"

"What about her?"

"She'll be home in two weeks."

"That's great, Blake."

"Yea, I can't wait to be with her again."

"Is she coming here?"

"Where else would she go, Tiffany?" Steven asked.

"I didn't know," I replied, thinking about what it would be like to have her living on our property.

"Did you know that Caroline and I have been going to visit her?" Blake asked.

"Yes, I do," I replied, thinking about how quickly time passes.

"Almost two years," Blake said, seeming to read my mind and nodding his head. "I've done everything I can to help her. You know, I think she has really turned over a new leaf. I think everything is going to be better this time."

"So where are you going to stay?" I asked, looking over at Steven who had sat down on the four-wheeler.

"They're going to stay in the farmhouse," Steven answered.

"I just thought they would be going back to their house," I said, looking at Blake.

"No, I sold it," Blake said.

"Oh, I didn't know," I replied, with thoughts of Victoria living in the house next door coursing through my mind.

"Do you remember the night you and Victoria came down to the bog? It was right after you moved to Natchez." Blake said, looking into my eyes.

"Yes, I remember. It was the first time Steven and I..."

"Kissed," he finished my sentence, then added, "and it was the night I fell for Victoria. She was dancing with Brad... and I couldn't take my eyes off her. She had me hook, line, and sinker and she hardly even noticed I was there."

"That's one of Blake's most famous tall tales," Steven interjected, *"the night two brothers fell in love at the same time in the same place."*

"At least we didn't fall in love with the same girl," Blake said, standing up.

"Victoria is lucky to have you," I said, standing up too.

"No, I'm the lucky one. She's really a great girl. I know everyone thinks she's wild and crazy but deep down inside she is something else. She's so wonderful. So special," he said, sincerely.

"Look, we better be getting back," Steven said, looking at his watch.

"Those little people can't wait to see you again," Blake said, putting his hand out, indicating for me to go first.

"Beat ya there," Steven said, starting his four-wheeler.

"That race will have to wait for another time, brother. When you're not carrying precious cargo." Blake said loudly over the roar of the engine.

We rode back to the house with Blake following close behind. Terri had the children playing out on the back deck and they barely lifted their heads when we walked in the side gate. She made sure they all said hello then offered to take them inside if we wanted to be alone. It was Steven that told her to leave the children with us and told her she could have the afternoon off.

When Terri had walked inside and Blake had gone out to check on the pool, Steven turned his attention back to me. He apologized for his brother interrupting us in the woods. He also promised that it would never happen again. Then he changed the subject to making plans. Plans for the afternoon, the next day and next week.

As the days passed by quickly, I found myself feeling more and more restless. Steven was content with spending our days together. It didn't matter to him if it was just he and I or the entire family as long as we were together. So I did what any good actress would do. With a smile painted on my face, I shared myself with him and whoever else happened to be at our house. There always seemed to be someone coming or going.

All too quickly, my time at home ended with a phone call from Los Angeles. It came to my relief but to Steven's sorrow. He moped around, trying to hide it but unable to contain his feelings. Even Terri and the children tried to cheer him up with plans for when I was gone but nothing seemed to help. Maybe it was a little selfish but I was ready to get back to Hollywood. I missed my house on the beach and I missed the fast pace of the city. Oddly enough, I even missed the strange people that filled the city with excitement and wonder.

Steven said he didn't have the heart to take me to the airport so he called someone to pick me up. It felt like it had been years since I had been inside a limo though it had only been a few weeks. Tristian and Stormie sat in my lap as the long black car pulled up to the house. Then Caroline and Blake came in announcing it was time for me to go. I knelt down to give the three little ones lots of hugs and kisses, promising to see them soon and to bring them presents when I came back. After sharing a few kisses with Steven, I sat down in the back seat of that long black car. With one final wave goodbye, I picked up my black sunglasses, shielding my eyes from the warm Mississippi sun and my thoughts turned to California.

22
Chapter

The big silver bird carried me across the country with ease, leaving cares and concerns of home behind. As I walked out into the California sun, I felt the hustle and bustle of life in the fast lane. It made something deep within me bubble up with energy and enthusiasm. I felt like somebody important whenever I stepped out onto a curb and they took my picture or wanted an autograph. It was wrong to let this attention make me feel that way and I knew it, still it always made me feel the same; glamorous and adored. As I stood there posing, I couldn't remember this happening in Mississippi, not even one time.

Soon, I was in the same old grind, like I hadn't missed a beat or a step. Phone calls, meetings, lunches and party invitations came in by the dozens. It felt like everyone wanted to see me or talk to me because I was out of the loop. They all had to catch me up on the what, who and how of Hollywood.

Two weeks flew by with barely any time to think about what had been going on in Mississippi. Steven called every night to let me know how the kids were doing and kept me informed of what was going on at home. Each night, Tristian and Stormie would tell me they loved and missed me, in their sweet little voices. It pulled at my heart strings, making me want to quit Hollywood for good but that feeling never lasted. I still had so much left to prove, not only to all of the naysayers in this town but to myself.

With only a little more than a week left before we started shooting in Las Vegas, I packed my bags and went to the airport. This time, it was Blake that picked me up. He explained that Steven had been working on a project and couldn't pull his self away long enough to come. After we were in the truck, all Blake could talk about was Victoria. She had only been there a few days and he was happy to have her home. He said Caroline was even happier because now her mom was around to do girl things. He told me Victoria and Terri were becoming fast friends but not to worry about it, Victoria still couldn't wait to see me.

With night falling, we pulled down the long driveway, past the farm house and up to the elaborate log cabin. There were lots of lights on and then I noticed a few cars parked in front. I looked at Blake and he shrugged his shoulders and smiled.

After I opened the front door I heard everyone shout, "Surprise!"

My eyes searched the room until I saw Steven. He was standing near the fireplace with a drink in his hand holding it up like he was making a toast. Tristian ran over hugging my leg while Victoria reached out for a hug. Terri stood near Steven with Stormie on her hip and both our Dads stood up from where they had been sitting.

"You did surprise me. What's all this for?"

"To welcome you home, sweetheart," Dad said, walking over to hug.

"Thank you. I'm surprised to see you here."

"Wouldn't have missed it for the world. How was your flight?"

"It was good, Dad."

Steven walked over, taking my hand, saying, "Let me look at you."

For a moment, everyone in the room melted away as his eyes searched me from head to toe. Steven lifted my hand in the air and I turned slowly, trying not to lose eye contact with him. My heart skipped a beat as he lowered my hand and pulled me to him with force. He touched his forehead to mine then quickly took a step back.

"Well, do I pass?"

"Yes, you do, Mrs. Cross."

"Good. I hope you don't mind if I excuse myself."

"Not at all," he said, taking another step back.

"I'll be back," I said, walking away.

When I changed into something more comfortable, I went back into the great room to find everyone sitting and talking. There was plenty of questions to answer. What had I been doing in Los Angeles? Who had I seen? Where had I gone? But the most important question that everyone wanted answered was how long would I be at home? One week was not the answer most of them wanted to hear.

In one week we spent more family time together than most people do in a month or two. Not one day did we begin or end it without the children right by our sides. We rode four-wheelers, horses, and even went on a boat ride on the Mississippi River. There was shopping and a trip to the movies and a rainy afternoon at the arcade. Then we played board games, with some of the children's toys, and did some fairytale reading. The only time Terri had to work was when Steven and I would sneak off to our bedroom to make love.

Those seven days of time went by like a flash of light in the darkness. My babies clung to my body as the last piece of luggage was loaded in the trunk of the white limo. Terri pried Stormie from my arms and went back into the house with her screaming and crying. Tristian went more quietly but not without his share of tears. Dad took him by the hand and after giving me a kiss on the cheek, they walked back inside.

The excitement of starting a new film made me giddy and even though I would miss the kids, I looked forward to getting back to work.

Steven opened the car door and looked me up and down as if he was taking a mental picture. I reached out, touched his cheek and smiled.

"How long this time, Ms. Starr?"

"You never call me that."

"How long, Tiffany?"

"Just a few weeks. Then I'll be back."

"Promise?"

"I'll do my best."

"Then I'll do my best to finish the book I started."

"You didn't tell me you started one."

"We never talk about me," he said, lowering his head.

"I don't have time for this right now."

"No, I didn't think you did," he said, stepping back and putting his hand on the door.

"I'll call you tonight. To let you know I made it."

"Okay."

"I love you, Steven," I said, sitting back in the seat.

"I love you more," he said, shutting the door.

On the way to the airport my mind debated whether or not I was doing the right thing. On the one hand, I was a married woman with two small children. Maybe I should be at home. Whatever home means. I wasn't even sure if that meant California or Mississippi anymore. Then on the other hand, I was an actress. A damn successful one at that. I worked hard to get to the top and I had to continue working to stay there. Steven must have known, even when I agreed to build a house in Mississippi that I wouldn't be staying there all the time. Somebody in our family has to work and make a living and that somebody was me right now.

With that last thought in mind, I boarded the plane that would take me to Las Vegas. It was only after we reached thirty-thousand feet that doubt began to fill my thoughts. The memory of Steven's face haunted me. He looked like a child whose double scoop of ice cream fell off the cone and hit the ground. It was a look of what now? How am I going to pick this mess up and put it back together? Even a child at a young age has the wisdom to know there's no way it can be fixed. It's too late.

Still, I signed a contract, made a commitment and I would honor it. Steven would have to grow up and face reality. His wife, the one he pursued and married, was a movie star. It was too late in life for me to change and I didn't want to. Besides, why couldn't we have it all? There are plenty of other people who travel for work, staying gone for days, weeks and sometimes months. Certainly, our love was strong enough to stand the test of time.

Shooting began right on schedule as I settled into my new environment. Nights were spent at one of the finest hotels in Vegas while days were spent on the set. This time I didn't hang out with other crew members except when we were working. I didn't want to give the gossip magazines anything to write about so I steered clear of controversy. Whenever I wasn't on the set, I stayed in my trailer and kept myself busy. Each night Steven and I would talk on the phone about our day and make plans for the future.

When a month had passed, our conversations were getting shorter and shorter. All Steven wanted to know was when I was coming home. Each day I hoped to tell him I would be getting on a plane soon but I couldn't. The director was growing tired of me asking when I could have a few days off and I was growing tired of asking. I also knew that it wasn't good for my career. I didn't want to be labeled a diva which would make it harder to get good roles in the future.

After a few more weeks there was finally a break for me to fly south. When I told Steven I'd be leaving in the morning, he grew silent. It was certainly not the reaction I was expecting so I asked if he wanted me to come. I could tell from his voice that he was upset when he told me there was nothing in the world he wanted more than to see my face. So without another negative thought, I packed my bags and left Las Vegas for Natchez.

There were no family members waiting at the gate this time. Only a tall man in a dark suit and a small sign with and my name on it. For a moment, I was puzzled. How could Steven miss me so much and not be here? Then the memory of my own words came to remembrance. I told him it would be so much easier if he would send a driver to get me and my luggage so he and I wouldn't have to deal with it. He was only doing what I had asked. Although, this time it didn't make me feel better that he listened to me.

When the limo pulled up to the marvelous log house, I expected to see the door fly open and the children run outside with Steven on their heels. So I took my time getting out of the car but there was no one coming. Slowly, I walked up the walkway to the front door expecting it to open but it didn't. After a deep sigh, I grasped the doorknob and turned it, wondering if I would be having another welcoming party but no one was in the living room when I entered. The driver unloaded my luggage and I tipped him. I stood in the entry way with my bags at my feet and wondered why no one was here to see me.

"Hello! Is anybody home?"

"Mrs. Cross, welcome home," the cook said, wiping his hands on a towel that hung off the front of his apron.

"Thank you."

"Everyone is in the back, by the pool. I am preparing a special meal to welcome you home."

"That sounds good. I'm hungry," I said, walking past him.

I paused when I reached the door that opened onto the deck. It looked like everyone was here. Our dads, Victoria and Blake, the children and the nanny but I couldn't see Steven. Everyone was dressed in bathing suits or shorts. I glanced down at my dress, but before I could turn to go and change clothes, Tristian caught my eye.

"Momma, momma! It's my momma!"

I opened the door, yelling out, "Tristian!" I bent down and scooped him up, smothering him with kisses. Then Stormie and Caroline followed close behind so I sat down on the floor so I could give all three children my attention.

"You're finally home," Dad said, over the chatter of the kids.

"Yes, thank God. I was beginning to wonder if I would ever make it back."

"Me and you both, sweetheart," he said, leaning down to kiss my forehead.

"So, how is my favorite sister-in-law?" Blake asked, giving me a hand and pulling me up to my feet.

"Tired and hungry," I said, looking around for Steven.

"It won't be long till we eat," Terri said, looking up from her magazine.

"Hey, girl," Victoria said, hugging me. "You look so pretty."

"Thank you. You look, tan," I said, admiring her swimsuit.

"About all we do around here is swim and lay in the sun," she replied, looking toward the pool.

"Hello daughter," Steven's Dad said, giving me a distant hug.

"I'm glad to see you," I said, feeling strange about him calling me daughter.

"Where's Steven?"

"Here I am," he answered, walking toward us from the pool.

The urge to run to him was overwhelming. The moment our eyes locked, I could feel his love. No one else in the world looked at me that way and I longed to be near him. The distance between us was only a few feet but the miles that had separated us for nearly two months kept me standing still.

"Hello stranger," he said, stopping just a few feet away.

"Hello, Mr. Cross," I replied softly, stepping forward to embrace him then stepping back to study his face.

"Just like a scene from a movie," Blake said loudly, moving his head back and forth.

"This is not a movie, it's my life," Steven replied, never losing our stare.

"And what a good life it is," I added, gazing up into his hazel eyes.

"Only when you're here," Steven said, finally giving me a tiny grin.

Dinner was served on the deck with everyone talking, laughing and enjoying themselves. Steven sat at the head of the table and I sat at the other end. It felt like more distance had come between us than either one of us would have liked. But he would look at me and I would smile and then he would give me the wink. It was the same one he had been giving me all these years and it still melted my heart every time.

After dinner, it was time for a dip in the pool or a soak in the hot tub. Everyone was dressed for the occasion except for me so I excused myself to go inside. As I walked down the hallway past the living room I realized my luggage was still sitting by the door. I stopped, scratched my head and tried to remember the last time this had happened. When had I ever come home from a trip and my belongings had been left by the doorway? The answer was never. Suddenly, I felt a rush of anger that turned me around and pushed me out the back door.

"Steven!"

"He's out yonder in the pool with the young-ins," Terri said.

"What did you say?"

"He's out yonder," she said louder, like I was hard of hearing.

"Did you take English in high school? Wait. Let me rephrase that question. Did you go to High School?"

"Sure did. Went to the same one you went to," she replied, with a little more attitude.

"Steven!"

"I'll get him. What you need anyway?" She asked, hand on her hip.

"My bags are still sitting by the door."

"Well, good-god-a-mighty. Is that what's got your panties in a wad?"

"What is it, Tiffany?" Steven asked, walking towards us, soaking wet from the waist down and dripping water.

"Ya'll forgot to put her stuff upstairs," Terri answered.

"Why is this…this….g i r l, taking care of our children? She can't even speak proper English!"

"That's enough," Steven said, taking me by the arm.

"You're not my Daddy. I don't need you to tell me what to do."

"No, I'm your husband and you are out of line right now. Terri, will you please go to the pool and watch the children. My wife and I need a minute alone."

"Sure thing, Steven," Terri replied, picking up a towel, walking away.

"I want her gone! Do you hear me? Tomorrow, I want her out of my house."

"Terri is not going anywhere, Tiffany. She's a good person. She takes care of our kids. They love her," Steven said, letting go of my arm.

"I know but..."

"But, you're jealous and you don't have to be. I'm in love with you. Totally, completely, madly in love with you," he said, taking me by the waist, pulling me close.

"Then why are my bags still sitting by the door?"

"That doesn't mean I don't love you," he said, putting his arms around me.

"Well, that's the way it feels," I said, pushing him back.

"I think you need some rest," Steven said, opening the door. "I'll take your suitcases to our room."

I walked toward the living room, saying, "Maybe you're right. I think I'll just go to bed, instead of swimming."

He picked up two heavy bags which strained his muscles and said, "I think that's a good idea. Then you can start fresh in the morning."

"Will you stay with me?"

"You go ahead and get ready for bed and I'll let everyone know you said goodnight. I'll be back in a few," he said, sitting my bags down, giving me a kiss.

As Steven walked away the anger quickly left and remorse set in. Terri was obviously a good nanny or he would'nt have her around. It was easy to see that she adored the children and got along well with everyone else. Maybe my husband was right and I was jealous. As my mind searched for a reason I would be jealous of this stupid, ordinary, hick girl, it couldn't find one. She had nothing I wanted. She had nothing to covet or admire as far as I was concerned. In fact the only thing she had that I didn't was time. She had time with my children that I didn't have to give. I reminded myself that it was her job and I had a job of my own. No matter what, I was their mother and no one could replace me. Especially a redneck, slang talking, ass-backwards, country girl from Mississippi.

With my dress in the hamper and my make-up washed off, I laid down in our king-sized bed, waiting. There would be nothing between me and Steven's hands except a sheer nightie made of red lace. Every little noise made me think it was him right outside the door. But as the yawns were coming harder and more frequently, I wondered how much longer he would be.

When the light poured through the curtains and filled the room, my eyes slowly opened. For a moment, I wasn't sure where I was. Only Steven's hand on my back reminded me I was in Natchez and not Las Vegas. Then the memory of waiting for him last night entered my mind.

"Where were you last night?"

"What?" He asked yawning and stretching.

I sat up straight, pushed him on the shoulder, saying, "I waited and waited. You said you'd be right back."

"You were tired so I let you rest," he replied, rolling over.

"I wasn't that tired. Do you see what I bought for you?"

"What?"

"I'm wearing it," I answered, getting out of bed.

"That is hot, you sexy thing," he said, smiling. "Now, get back in bed."

Our bed was warm and cozy for the next few days. Steven and I did not fall asleep without being right beside each other. Terri and I avoided each other which suited me just fine. Everybody else thought she was an angel but I knew she was the devil in disguise. For now I would keep my peace about the evil little nanny everyone loved so much. Besides, there would be time to take care of her and I didn't want to cause any problems for Steven. Especially since it was time for me to get back to Vegas and he certainly didn't need the responsibility of the children without any help.

This time Victoria drove me to the airport in her little red sports car. It felt like old times sitting in the passenger seat beside her. She was as funny as always and had me laughing and cutting up like we did when we were teenagers.

She suddenly got serious, asking, "What's your problem with Terri?"

"I don't trust her," I replied, reminding myself how close she and Victoria had become.

"She is a little flirty with our men, isn't she?"

"Well…"

"I really don't think she means any harm. It's just her personality. She gets along better with men then woman," Victoria said.

"All I want her to do is take good care of my children, nothing else," I said, looking in my purse.

"She is good with them and they love her. But I know it must be hard to trust her and for that matter to trust me. You're hardly ever at home."

"Why wouldn't I trust you," I asked, watching her expression.

"I spent nearly two years of my life behind bars," she explained, glancing over at me.

"What happened?"

"You talking about the Meth?"

"Yes, why would you risk it all for a drug?"

"Have you ever done it?"

"Never," I replied, appalled she even asked.

"Man, it made me feel so alive, so full of energy. And girlfriend, you talk about staying skinny. You never have to eat when you do that stuff."

"But what about Caroline?"

"It's weird," she said, slowly, "I love her so much but I still want to get high. I'm not. Don't get me wrong. I know I have to keep it together but I still want it."

"That is crazy, Victoria."

"I never said I wasn't crazy," she replied, pulling up to the airport.

Victoria helped me get my luggage to the check in and gave me a long hug goodbye. She promised to keep an eye on the kids and make sure Terri kept her distance from Steven. Then she whispered in my ear not to worry about her, she was staying clean, for Caroline's sake.

Even though I had only been gone for a week it felt like it had been a month. Everybody needed me or my opinion somewhere on the set. It was like every step I took someone else demanded my attention. At the end of the first day it felt like I had been back for a week.

Once I retreated to my hotel suite, deep in the heart of Las Vegas, I finally felt relaxed. After a long bath and a good dinner, I laid down on the sofa to watch television. My eyes felt heavy and my mind at ease when sleep overtook my body.

A ringing phone woke me up from a hard sleep with its relentless noise. I grabbed the receiver and listened for a voice. To my surprise it was Steven's voice.

"Hey, what time is it?"

"It's eight o'clock where you are," he answered.

"Eight o'clock in the morning?"

"Yes."

"Damn, I'm going to be late," I said, sitting up on the edge of the couch.

"You didn't call me last night."

"I forgot. I'm so sorry."

"I barely slept last night."

"I had a long day yesterday," I replied, looking in the mirror.

"Tell me about it."

"I don't have time. I'm already late for work," I said, walking into the bathroom.

"I'll let you go," he said, hanging up.

It was the first time he hadn't said goodbye before he hung up the phone since we'd met. I wanted to call him back and try to make things right but I didn't have time. I figured if he wanted to be mad because I fell asleep he would have to get over it. Besides, I didn't want to make myself any later than I already was today.

Soon, I was back in the grove of shooting Runner's Luck as the days all blended together. The schedule we were keeping was grueling but I was thankful to be working. Word was getting out that this movie was poised to be a smash hit and I knew that was exactly what I needed. Having babies takes time and time means missed opportunities in my line of business. If I wanted to maintain my place on the ladder in Hollywood, I knew I had to work at it, especially now.

Before I knew it, a month had flown by and it was time for me to fly back to Natchez. The visit would have to be very short, only three days. Steven said he didn't care, even if it was only three hours he would take it. Which I'm sure was very easy for him to say. He wasn't the one who had to pack his suitcases, move out of a hotel room and fly across the country just to unpack again. Then before I can even catch my breath, I would be packing up again and flying back. In reality, I should have been excited but the only thing this trip home was making me feel was tired.

It was certainly a good thing I was an actress because I needed every one of my skills to handle being in the same house with Terri. Of course, I think the feeling was mutual but sometimes this girl was hard to read. Other than dealing with her, my reception was exactly the same as it had been over the past few months. The kids clung to me and didn't want to let go. Victoria, Blake and the Dads were as happy as they could be that I was back in Natchez. Steven gave me the same feeling he had always given me. It was the feeling that he wanted to take me somewhere, anywhere, that we could be alone.

After we had dinner and the kids were safe and sound in their beds, Steven and I walked to our bedroom. The long hours at work, the huge dinner in my belly and plain old jet lag had me dragging. As he closed the door, I walked over to the bed and fell forward, face first.

He crawled beside me, whispering in my ear, "I thought we'd never be alone."

"You thought wrong," I replied with my face still pressing into the bed.

"Please tell me you're only taking a cat nap," he said, rubbing my back.

"I'm only taking a cat nap," I said, pretending to snore loudly.

Steven pulled me toward him making me lay on my side and said, "I'm almost finished with the book."

"That's great, baby. What's the title?"

"Wasted Dreams," he said, moving to lay on his back.

"Wasted Dreams; sounds sad."

"It's a love story. Well, it has a little bit of everything in it. You know, life."

"I'm sure it's very good and I can't wait to read it. Now, will you turn out the light?"

"Yes," he answered, getting up.

Within the darkness, my mind settled down. His arms wrapped around my body. I was safe. Nothing could happen, nothing could hurt me as long as I was here, where I belonged. He wanted me. He wanted to make love to me and I could feel it. But he did nothing. He held me until I was falling asleep, wishing me sweet dreams.

Seventy-two hours, give or take a few was all we had. Three tiny days to reaffirm we were a family. So we made the most of it, squeezing out every bit of fun we could. We went on a picnic to the park, walking on the roots of the old oak tree like Steven and I had done when we were kids. We took the kids into the woods so they could see the falls for the first time, though we kept the scary story for when they were older. We even took them to the 'bog' and built a fire but it didn't look or feel the same so we didn't stay very long.

When it was time for me to go, Tristian and Stormie didn't seem as upset this time. I wasn't sure if they were getting use to me leaving or if they were ready to spend time with Terri. Whatever the reason, it wasn't making me feel good at all. I expected them to act differently but maybe I expected too much.

Steven, on the other hand was acting like a child. He was sullen as well as gloomy and there was little I could do to change his demeanor. Down in the dumps or not, he still loaded my suitcases in the bed of the truck and opened the door for me. It was depressing to see how glum and miserable he felt. Instead of trying to make him feel better, I chose to keep my mouth shut and enjoy the scenery.

"Are you mad because I'm melancholy?"

"No. I just wish you weren't so pessimistic," I said, still staring out the passenger window.

"How long will it be this time?"

"We're wrapping it up. It shouldn't be any more than three to four weeks."

"Another month?" He asked, discontentment in his voice.

"I'm not like you, Steven. I can't sit at home behind a keyboard and live my life."

"And I can't live mine without you."

"This is not working, is it?" I asked, turning to face him as we pulled onto the road that led to the airport.

"Don't say that. I'm a little sad because you're leaving that's all," he said, reaching over to hold my hand.

"Look, I'm an actress. I make movies. That's what I do. I'm not going to quit. Please stop making me feel bad about it," I said, pulling my hand away.

"I'm not upset because of what you do for a living, Tiffany. I'm upset because you wanted to move to Mississippi. We built this big house and you are hardly ever here. Damn, I miss you. Don't you get that?"

"All I know is every time I leave to go to work you make me feel like crap."

"Can we just end this conversation, right now?" He asked, parking the truck.

"That's exactly like you…story-book Steven Cross."

"What the hell does that mean?"

"You're only thinking about yourself and how you feel. What about me? What about Tristian and Stormie? Do we even matter to you?"

"Why would you even ask me that?"

"Because sometimes, Mr. Cross, you can be the most selfish, self-centered, egotistical man on the face of the earth," I replied, getting out of the truck and slamming the door.

He opened the driver's door, jumping out to say, "If I am such a self-centered asshole than why did you marry me?"

"Right now, I have no idea in the world why I married you," I yelled, turning to walk toward the airport.

Then I could hear Steven getting my suitcases and talking but it was fuzzy. It was one of my deepest fears come to life right before my eyes. Here we were, the author and the actress fighting in the parking lot like two white trash low-lifes. And there, maybe forty to fifty feet away was a photographer documenting every expression and possibly every word we were saying.

Steven was not looking at me when I turned around giving him a look that would have shut his mouth. As I walked toward him I could see the headlines now. When he finally looked up, his eyes shifted to the photographer behind me. He dropped the bags and started to run after the man but I grabbed him, begging him to stop. In an instant the situation had gone from bad to worse and all I wanted was to get on that plane and leave as quickly as possible.

When the plane lifted off the ground, I felt so much better. Soon I would land in a different place and I would be in a different environment. There was nothing I could do to change what had happened. What Steven had done, the words he had used would forever be there, haunting us for the rest of our lives. Regardless of how much he missed me, he needed to remember who he married and respect the fact that I worked very hard to get where I am. It was not easy to become Tiffany Starr and it wasn't easy being Tiffany Starr. He would have to learn that and accept it and stop thinking about himself all the time. If he didn't, I wasn't sure what our future might hold.

Back on the set with work keeping my mind busy, I barely thought about what happened between us at the airport. It was only after seeing the pictures and reading about our fight that I began to have questions. Whenever I would try to talk to him about it he always seemed defensive. The only thing I couldn't understand was what did he have to defend? If I was his world, like he had told me and I meant everything to him why was he so angry?

Without any answers and very little free time, I stopped wondering why Steven was acting so strange. He still called every night. We talked about the same things and then he would say good night and tell me he loved me. When I knew that he loved me it gave me strength to go on. It gave me what I needed to finish this film so I could finally get back home to be with my family.

It had been twenty four days since I sat in the seat of an airplane. This time I was ready to fly south. This time I would unpack my bags completely and stay awhile. Sure, there would be phone calls, letters and faxes but no more plane rides for a while for me.

There would be four-wheeler rides, boat rides, and maybe even horse riding but I would not be flying anywhere for a long time. With Runner's Luck behind me and nothing concrete coming up, I had let my agent know that I would be staying in Mississippi for the next few months. It was time to make memories with my family and give myself the opportunity to enjoy my new home.

Steven was standing there waiting for me with flowers in his hand. It was a short distance and I was in his arms. He squeezed me tightly, not letting go and I held on to him too.

"I apologize, I shouldn't have talked to you..."

"It's okay, it's behind us," I said, trying to leave his embrace.

"I don't want to let you go."

"I'm here to stay, baby," I whispered in his ear.

He leaned back, looked into my eyes and said, "I have never seen blue that was more beautiful than the blue in your eyes."

"That makes me think of a song."

"Which one?" He asked, taking a step back.

"Peter Gabriel, In Your Eyes,"

"The light, the heat," he sang.

"In your eyes, I am complete," I sang back.

"Love that song," he said, taking my hand to walk down the corridor.

"And I love you," I said, pressing my fingers into the back of his hand. "I'm so glad to finally be home.

"To stay?"

"Yes."

Steven stopped and stood in front of me. For a moment he studied my face and eyes, like he was searching for something to reaffirm what I had said. Then he took the flowers out of my hand and pulled me into his body with his other hand. With dozens of people nearby he leaned down and kissed me. It was inappropriate. It was way too big of a kiss for a public place. But not for one second was I backing up or backing down. If we could fight in public then we could kiss in public. Where were the photographers when everything was going right?

Weeks of the gossip magazines piled up high on the night stand and not one picture of Steven and me kissing. If it hadn't been for fear of boredom, I probably would have thrown them all away. But it felt like we had done it all. Steven, the kids, and me had went the rounds with things to do in Natchez. Sure, it had all been done before, nevertheless, we did it again.

Days of picnics, pool parties, movies and shopping were behind us. Then there were four-wheeler rides and walking in the woods with Steven and me stealing away every chance we could. It was the good life. Every day was full of sunshine, laughter, good food, family and friends. There were no time schedules, and obligations to keep and other than the nanny and Victoria there really wasn't any drama in our lives.

Tristian and Stormie had grown accustomed to me being here and began to gravitate more and more toward me instead of Terri. We spent hours cuddling, hugging and holding each other to Terri's surprise. When she would seem upset like she was being left out, Steven would tell her to take some time for herself. This usually sent her off, stomping like a little child who had gotten in trouble.

It was one phone call that changed our happy home into the old tug-of-war I had found myself in so many times before. After I hung up the phone with Mom, I knew I would have to break my promise to Steven and hop on the next plane to New York. The only problem was I couldn't tell the truth. If he knew what was going on between Cheryl and Michael, he would never let me go alone. But now it was obvious, if something was going to be done I would have to do it myself. So I made the decision to confront Michael once and for all and end the war between us.

"Hey, Love. What are you doing?" Steven asked, walking into our room.

"I'm packing," I answered, not looking up.

"We're all sitting downstairs waiting for you to get off the phone. Remember? We're going horseback riding today."

"You'll have to go without me. I have to leave for New York."

"What are you talking about, Tiffany. We have been planning this since last week."

"Something's come up."

"Why do you have to go to New York?"

"Business," I said, folding a shirt and shoving it into the suitcase.

"What kind of business?"

"Movie stuff," I said, zipping up the suitcase.

"How long until you leave?"

"About two hours," I replied, looking at the clock.

"Can I go with you?"

"No. I need you to stay here."

"Have it your way. I'll go tell Blake and Victoria to take the kids without us."

"Will you call and have a limo pick me up?"

"Yes," he said, gripping his hands into fists.

The water was warm and inviting as I sank into its depth. It was refreshing to clean my body and begin to work out the words in my mind. Cheryl would listen to me, I would tell her the truth about what happened between me and Michael. I would do whatever it took for her to hear what I had to say. It was clear she was on a one way street to destruction. Her life was spiraling out of control and there appeared to be only one end she was about to meet. But it wouldn't be before I had a chance to change her mind and thus change the course of her life.

Steven was angry. I didn't blame him. I am certain my short answers to his questions didn't help any. I had lied. He was smart enough to know it but I hoped he rationalized it into truth. But under these circumstances, I had to do what I had to do. If the shoe was on the other foot, I believe he would do the same for his brother, Blake.

When I was dressed and ready to go, I called out for Steven. He didn't answer so I walked down the hallway, calling out his name. The house was eerily silent with the only sound being my footsteps. I walked into the great room and there on the coffee table was a present. The card beside the dark red ribbon had my name on it, in Steven's hand writing. I opened the card and the only thing it said was open this alone, outside.

I knew I didn't have much time but I stepped out the front door with the present. The limo was sitting out front and just the sight of it upset me. Steven knew I didn't like white limos, I preferred black and I wondered why he didn't tell the driver that. When the man stepped out of the car, I told him to go inside and get my luggage. Then I told him I would be back in a few minutes.

With the box in hand, I walked down the trial that led to a small garden on the west side of the house. I was careful to step on the stones so I wouldn't twist an ankle in the red high heel shoes I was wearing. My black dressed with red embroidery was long. With one hand I balanced the box on my palm and with the other I held up the hem of my dress. When I reached the grassy opening I let go of my dress and pulled my heels off, leaving them on a stone. Then I tip-toed over to the bench and sat down.

Steven had always surprised me with special gifts and letters or poems. Why he wanted me to open this one outside was a mystery. The only reason I figured he wanted me out here was so he could jump out from behind a bush and startle me. As that scenario played out in my mind, I could picture him giving me big hugs and kisses before I left for my flight.

The box opened to reveal a silver looking plate that kind of resembled a bowl. It was old looking, not shiny and new and had me wondering what in the world Steven was thinking. He had never given me anything used before but I could tell there was something else. It was a box of matches so I sat them in the plate and dug deeper to see what else I could find.

As I pulled out the envelope I knew he had written something. It was a letter or maybe a poem but that still didn't answer why he had given me an old plate with matches. I ripped open the envelope, taking a deep breath. Then I heard something. It was behind me, a strange crunching sound which made me turn my head.

"Steven? Is that you?"

Without an answer, I returned my attention to what was in my hands. Time was running out for me to make it to the airport and I had to read this fast. My heart raced as I unfolded the page but I didn't know why.

Tiffany,

Never blame yourself. All fault lies with me. From the first moment I met you until the day you said, 'I do', I built you up in my mind. The pedestal I placed you on was so high, Love. Where else was there for you to go? You couldn't get any higher. There was nothing you could do or say that could make you better in my mind. You were perfection to me. So where did that leave you? I set you up for failure, not even realizing what was happening. There was no way in heaven or hell you could live up to what you had be-

come to me. No matter what you did or how good you were, it was never as good as I thought it should be.

Not to say I am disappointed. We have had our share of happiness and love. But for the first time in my life, I'm realizing something you always tried to show me. You are much too lady-like to tell me. Besides that, I am as stubborn as a mule when it came to my love for you. You, in your wisdom, showed me love; but it was always tied to the past, to our childhood. I was a fool to not let you go and live your life. I held on to you mentally, spiritually, and physically every chance I got. Now I see the errors of my ways.

It's not too late for you, Tiffany. If there's anything I know, I know you are not happy in Mississippi. Leaving for New York proves once and for all that we made a mistake. And I will not stand in your way, not now, not ever again. From this moment on…you are free.

If you will do me one favor, it will be the last thing I ask of you. Take the matches and the old plate and Burn The Letter you hold in your hands. I never want you to read it again and I do not want our children or grand-children to read it. I want no record of how deeply you have hurt me or how much I love you.

Steven

My hands trembled as they held the piece of paper and match. As the flame caught up, I dropped the letter into the plate watching it burn. Another rustle in the leaves caught my attention and when I looked back down at the plate all that was left were ashes. For a moment, I sat there staring into the white ashes then a gentle breeze came, whipping some up into the wind to land on my black dress. With the brush of my hand they smeared into the fabric causing little white streaks. Two tears drifted slowly down my cheeks as I slipped my heels onto my feet.

Carefully, I walked down the pathway to the front of the house. The driver stood by my door and nodded hello before opening it. Without looking back, I slid over into the center of the seat as he shut the door behind me. As we pulled away, I looked toward the front door expecting to see Steven standing there but there was nothing and no one to see. So I looked at the road that lay before me and focused my thoughts on New York and remembered the urgency in my mother's voice.

TO BE CONTINUED...

About the Author

Charna Ainsworth is an award-winning poet and the author of *The Letter*, *Mountain of God*, and *Unlikely Christian Poetry Collection*. She lives in a small southern town in Mississippi with her daughter.

Website: www.charnaainsworth.com

Follow: www.twitter.com/charnaainsworth

Friend: www.facebook.com/charnaainsworth

Watch: www.youtube.com/user/charnaainsworth